Assault and Pepper

**Other Pennsylvania Dutch Mysteries
by Tamar Myers**

Assault and Pepper

A PENNSYLVANIA DUTCH MYSTERY
WITH RECIPES

Tamar Myers

 NEW AMERICAN LIBRARY

New American Library
Published by New American Library, a division of
Penguin Group (USA) Inc., 375 Hudson Street,
New York, New York 10014, USA
Penguin Group (Canada), 10 Alcorn Avenue, Toronto,
Ontario M4V 3B2, Canada (a division of Pearson Penguin Canada Inc.)
Penguin Books Ltd., 80 Strand, London WC2R 0RL, England
Penguin Ireland, 25 St. Stephen's Green, Dublin 2,
Ireland (a division of Penguin Books Ltd.)
Penguin Group (Australia), 250 Camberwell Road, Camberwell, Victoria 3124,
Australia (a division of Pearson Australia Group Pty. Ltd.)
Penguin Books India Pvt. Ltd., 11 Community Centre, Panchsheel Park,
New Delhi - 110 017, India
Penguin Group (NZ), cnr Airborne and Rosedale Roads, Albany,
Auckland 1310, New Zealand (a division of Pearson New Zealand Ltd.)
Penguin Books (South Africa) (Pty.) Ltd., 24 Sturdee Avenue,
Rosebank, Johannesburg 2196, South Africa

Penguin Books Ltd., Registered Offices:
80 Strand, London WC2R 0RL, England

First published by New American Library,
a division of Penguin Group (USA) Inc.

First Printing, February 2005
10 9 8 7 6 5 4 3 2 1

NEW AMERICAN LIBRARY and logo are trademarks of Penguin Group (USA) Inc.

LIBRARY OF CONGRESS CATALOGING-IN-PUBLICATION DATA:

Myers, Tamar.
   Assault and pepper / Tamar Myers.
      p. cm.
   ISBN 0-451-21394-7 (trade hardcover : alk. paper)
   1. Yoder, Magdalena (Fictitious character)—Fiction. 2. Women detectives—
Pennsylvania—Fiction. 3. Pennsylvania Dutch Country (Pa.)—Fiction. 4. Church
dinners—Fiction. 5. Hotelkeepers—Fiction. 6. Pennsylvania—Fiction. 7. Mennonites—
Fiction. 8. Cookery—Pennsylvania. I. Title.
   PS3563.Y475A94 2005
   813'.54—dc22   2004021110

Set in Palatino
Printed in the United States of America

For Martha Bushko

Acknowledgments

First, I would like to acknowledge my mother-in-law, Vonnie Root, for her creative suggestion for the title. For the rest of you, though, please don't start sending me more title suggestions. I appreciate the thought, but frankly, most of the suggestions I get are not really very good.

A special thanks goes to the International Chili Society (ICS) for most of the chili recipes in the book. They are available on their Web site, www.chilicookoff.com, along with a bunch of other wonderful chili recipes. Another thanks goes to my friend Sharon Wilkerson for her contribution in chapter 30.

1

"Bless this food to the nourishment of our bodies," Reverend Schrock said, seconds before toppling, face forward, into a pot of chili. That's the gist of it. I'll spare you the grisly details, but those seconds seemed like lifetimes, and all the while we, the congregation of Beechy Grove Mennonite Church, were powerless to do anything.

By the time the rescue squad arrived, our pastor was as dead as last summer's daisies, and getting ready to push up fresh ones of his own come spring. Although there was nothing we could do to help the reverend, there was quite a bit we could do to assist his wife. The trouble is that Lodema Schrock has the personality of a flea-bitten badger. A few folks, less charitable than myself, have suggested that she even looks like a badger. At any rate, it was soon clear that everyone present at our annual chili supper cook-off wanted to pawn the pastor's widow off on someone else.

Not that any of us was rude about it. We didn't draw straws, or do anything obvious like that, but we rolled our eyes among ourselves and grunted our excuses. Apparently I didn't roll hard enough, or grunt loud enough, because I found myself driving the distraught woman home.

Normally the woman can't go two minutes without insulting me, but that evening she sat in the passenger seat of my car, just as silent as Lot's wife *after* she'd been turned into salt. It wasn't until we were in the driveway of the parsonage that she spoke.

"Peanut butter," she said.

"I beg your pardon?"

"Magdalena, are you deaf now, as well as stupid?"

I prayed for patience. "I thought you said 'peanut butter.' "

"I did. That's what killed Arnold." For the record, that was the first time I had ever heard Lodema say her husband's Christian name. It had always been "the reverend" this, "the reverend" that, as if we laypeople were unworthy of hearing anything more intimate. Once she even referred to herself as "the reverendess," and I'm pretty sure she wasn't joking.

"I'm afraid I still don't understand."

"Arnold was allergic to peanuts. You know that, Magdalena. Everyone in Hernia knows that. My husband was murdered."

"But Lodema, dear, he hadn't even eaten anything. Besides, there weren't any sandwiches at the cook-off—just chili."

"You're talking like a dunce again, Magdalena. How hard is it to stir some creamy peanut butter into a pot of chili? Who knows, it might even taste good. I'm sure it would have improved that horrible-looking stuff you brought."

"Freni made that, not me." Freni Hostetler is my cook at the PennDutch Inn. She's an Amish woman in her mid-seventies. If it was meant to be cooked, Freni can make it taste delicious. Of course delicious does not necessarily equate with healthy. To Freni, there are three food groups: starch, sugar, and fat.

Lodema grabbed my right arm with nails as sharp as badger claws. "Arnold did a lot for you, Magdalena."

"Reverend Schrock was a good friend."

"He was very fond of you."

"And I of him—of course only in a platonic sort of way."

The claws searched for my ulna. "Promise me you won't let him down."

"I promise—I mean, what can I do for him now? Write a eulogy?"

"Don't be so dense. I want you to find his killer."

"But we don't even know for sure if he was murdered. And I'm not a policewoman. You know that!"

"You might as well be. You solve all the important cases around here, not your cousin."

"Melvin Stoltzfus is only a distant cousin. Otherwise he couldn't have married my sister. And I only solve these cases because— okay, so maybe I am a smidgen smarter than he is, and maybe I am a bit on the nosy side. . . ." I waited in vain for her to contradict my last statement. "All right, I'll make sure Melvin looks into all the possibilities."

She let go of my arm. "You know what, Magdalena? You're not so bad after all."

"Thanks—I think. Shall we go in now?"

She threw open the door. "*In?* Who said you're coming in?"

"Don't you want me to? Lodema, I'd be happy to spend the night, if you need the company, that is." By the way, the Lord doesn't mind lies that are told for the purpose of sparing some-one's feelings. I read that somewhere, in some kind of religious book, so I know it has to be true.

The not-so-merry widow glared at me. "You're nuts if you think I need a babysitter. What I need is to be left alone."

I nodded. I wasn't agreeing with the "nuts" part, but I under-stood about the need for privacy. When my pooky bear abandoned me, I wanted nothing more than to burrow under my covers with a flashlight, a good book, and two pounds of dark chocolate. I needed to lick my wounds, and maybe the chocolate as well. Un-fortunately the world impinged on my grieving process before I'd gotten even halfway through the chocolate, much less the book, and even though I am in a healthy relationship now, I will always feel somewhat cheated.

"Well, call me if you need anything," I said, hoping that she wouldn't.

Lodema slammed the car door and stalked up the walk to her house without so much as a thank-you. Suddenly all the negative feelings I'd ever had for the woman, and which I'd managed to suppress ever since my peppy pastor plotzed in the peppery pot, came rushing to the forefront. If it weren't for the fact that her hus-band had indeed been a good friend, I might have chased after Lodema, tackled her, and, by twisting one arm behind her back, forced the woman to cry uncle. Or at least acknowledge how grateful she was.

Instead, I backed sedately out of her driveway and drove home in a rage. That is how the first week of November got off to a really bad start.

2

Home is the PennDutch Inn, located just north of the bucolic town of Hernia in the mountains of south-central Pennsylvania. We are primarily a Mennonite and Amish farming community, but not to be confused with the high-profile folks over in Lancaster County. We're a mite too far from major metropolitan centers to attract day-trippers, and although we get tourists, I'm just about the only one who profits from them.

My name is Magdalena Portulaca Yoder. Portulaca is a variety of flower, and Mama got the name from the back of a seed packet. As for Magdalena—the twisted limbs of my family tree contain five ancestors who bore that moniker. Of course Papa got the name Yoder from his papa, and there have been Yoders in Pennsylvania since the early 1700s.

The immigrant Yoders were Amish, as were the rest of my people, but I was born and raised Mennonite. I am often asked about the differences between Amish and Mennonites. Unfortunately, when I try to answer that question, most often the listener's eyes will glaze over. But since you asked so politely, I will endeavor to answer it one more time.

Mennonites are the followers of Menno Simons, a sixteenth-century Dutch theologian, who was formerly a Catholic priest. He rejected the practice of infant baptism, espousing the baptism of believers only, and adhered firmly to the doctrine of nonviolence. The Amish, on the other hand, are the followers of Jacob Amman, a seventeenth-century Swiss Mennonite who believed that the Mennonite Church had become too lax in some of its practices. In a nutshell, Amish are more conservative than Mennonites. They are also likely to be more identifiable by their dress. Amish people who cannot live up to their faith's rigid requirements often become Mennonites, as was the case in my family. There is, however, very little movement in the other direction.

Now that you are an expert on that matter, let's return to the subject of me. I am a godly woman in my mid-to-late forties (my exact age is none of your business). I have a younger sister, Susannah, who left the faith of our fathers altogether when she married a Presbyterian. She has since been divorced, and is now remarried to Melvin Stoltzfus, our town's Chief of Police. I have never been married—not from a legal point of view, at any rate. I once thought I was hitched, to a hunk named Aaron Miller, but he turned out to be a bigamist, making me an inadvertent adulteress. Aaron and his legal wife have a daughter, Alison, whom they cannot control. Since my womb will forever be as barren as the Gobi Desert, I have graciously assented to be this child's guardian.

It was Alison who met me at the kitchen door that night. "Hey, Mom, can I have a raise in my allowance? Donna Wylie gets five dollars more a week, and she's almost a year younger."

I tried to smile. "Can we talk about this some other time, dear? Something tragic happened tonight and—"

"Yeah, I know all about that."

"You do?"

"Auntie Susannah was just here. Said the reverend drowned in his chili bowl. Did that really happen?"

"Yes—well, sort of. It wasn't his bowl, but someone's pot, and I don't think he drowned. It's more likely he had a heart attack."

For a moment her eyes clouded over, and I thought she might cry. I could recall several occasion on which she'd expressed how much she liked our pastor, who, although childless himself, always seemed to get along well with the youth.

"Bummer," she said softly.

"He was a fine man, Alison. It's going to be hard getting used to not having him around."

"Yeah. So, can I have that raise or not?"

Needless to say, I was shocked by her callousness. "Not!"

"Aw, Mom, ya don't have to get sore about it."

"I thought you liked Reverend Schrock."

"I do—I mean, I did. But he's dead, ain't he? That ain't gonna change if you keep my allowance the same."

She had a point. But she also needed to learn a lesson about priorities. I was just the person to teach her this lesson, and was about to begin with some basics, but the dining room door flew open and in flapped Freni, my cook.

"Ach, Magdalena," the stubby woman squawked, "the English are crazy!"

"Like, I'm outta here." Alison darted through the still-swinging door.

"Freni, dear," I said to my Amish cook, "maybe you haven't heard about Reverend Schrock."

"Yah, I hear." She stared at me through glasses as thick and blurry as ice cubes.

"So don't you have anything to say about that before launching into your litany of complaints about the English?" The Amish, by the way, use the word "English" when referring to anyone not of their faith. An Amish man from London (although there aren't any to my knowledge) would not be English, whereas a Buddhist from Japan would most certainly be English.

Freni continued to stare.

"You could at least express your condolences, dear."

"Yah, the reverend has my dolences, but that woman—she gives you so much trouble."

"That may be, but her husband is dead. Anyway, we can be sad about the reverend's passing, without letting our feelings for Lodema get in the way."

Freni hung her head in shame. At least she attempted to do so. Unfortunately the woman has very little neck, so her penitent gesture did little more than tilt her face just enough so that her beady eyes gazed over the top of her glasses. She looked ominous, rather than sad, and it was all I could do to keep from laughing.

I did manage to maintain a straight face long enough to force Freni to give up her charade. "So," she said, her gaze once again impenetrable, "I can tell you now why the English are crazy?"

"I doubt you can tell me *why* they are crazy, but I'll settle for a list of what they've done to make you think they are."

"The couple from California want only vegetables to eat, but the couple from New York say they want only meat and cheese. The Fat-Kids Diet, I think they call it." She shook her head. "So I make chicken and dumplings with carrots and potatoes, and the couple from New York eats the chicken, but no one eats the dumplings, or the carrots and potatoes."

"Freni, you've cooked for vegetarians before. You know they won't eat anything that's been cooked with meat. What about our fifth guest, the redhead from Dallas?" Thank heavens I'd had two last-minute cancellations for that week, and there were no more guests to inquire after.

"Yah, the redhead, but she also has a complaint. Why is the toilet paper not folded to make a point? she asks. Magdalena, I do not understand such a question."

"It's something hotels and motels do nowadays. Only the Good Lord knows why. Who wants to use paper that's been handled that much?"

Freni pursed her lips in a way that accused me of being nuts even for knowing about this strange custom. Then she took off her working apron, folded it neatly, and placed it on the kitchen table.

"I quit," she said.

I couldn't help but smile. This was the ninetieth time she'd quit in the last six years. When she reached a hundred, I was going to give her a plaque. Perhaps I deserved one too, for giving her so many chances.

She took two steps toward the back door and stopped. "This time I mean it."

"I'm sure you do."

"Ach! I mean I *really* mean it."

"That's nice, dear."

She took three more steps, baby steps all, then stopped and turned. "You'll be sorry, Magdalena."

"Yes, I suppose I will. Just not half as sorry as you."

"Yah?"

"I saw your dear, sweet daughter-in-law, Barbara, at Yoder's Corner Market this morning. She shared that she is suffering from a severe case of PMS."

"Ach!" Freni clapped her hands over her ears.

"Not premenstrual syndrome," I said loud enough to wake the dead three counties over. "She's got pre-Mennonite syndrome. She said she thinks the Amish here are too strict. Said she and Jonathan are seriously considering joining the Mennonite Church."

Freni's usually florid face turned cake flour white. Barbara is the bane of her existence. If you ask me, it's not just because the big gal—she stands six feet in her patched woolen stockings—hails from a more liberal Amish community in Iowa. The crux of the problem is that Freni refuses to cut the apron strings that tie her to her son and only child.

The fact that Jonathan and Barbara, along with their triplets, live with Freni and Mose makes any kind of separation virtually impossible. Put two alpha females into the same pack, and you can beta there will be trouble. But all this talk about the younger generation becoming Mennonites is, in my opinion, just a way for Barbara to seek her independence. While it is true that if the young couple did become Mennonites, Amish Church law would force them to move from his parents' home and, in fact, have no further contact with them, I don't believe that is their intention. I believe that they would prefer to move out voluntarily and stay within the Amish fold. I am convinced that Barbara would be happy to remain Amish—just not under her mother-in-law's roof.

"She needs more space, Freni."

"But she has her own house."

"Yes, but it's attached to yours, and you feel free to come and go as you please."

"But I own it."

"Barbara needs to feel like she is the mistress of her own house. Tell me, do you let her cook for Jonathan and the children?"

Freni's lips twisted into a pale pink pretzel. "Even the pigs do not like what she cooks."

"It doesn't matter. She needs to take care of her own family."

"Yah? So what am I supposed to do?"

"For starters, you can unquit. Believe me, dear, I need you more than Barbara does. In fact, Lodema Schrock has asked me to look into the reverend's death, and if it turns out to be murder—well, you know how time-consuming those cases can be. So here's what I'm proposing. How about if I move in with Alison upstairs, and you and Mose take my room down here? Think of it as a vacation away from you-know-who."

"But I will still work here, yah?" Her tone made it clear that the mere thought of doing nothing was at least frightening, if not downright sinful. After all, idle hands are the Devil's playground, and even plump little hands like Freni's can get into a peck of trouble if not kept busy.

"You'll run the whole show, Freni. You'll be the grand pooh-bah, the queen."

"What is this pooh-bah?"

"Lord-High-Everything-Else. It's from the opera *Mikado*. It means someone with an extremely important position." Believe me, the only reason I know this word is because I keep a dictionary in the powder room for those days on which nature prefers to work slowly. Dictionaries, unlike magazines, can last for years without going out-of-date.

Despite the thickness of her lenses, I could see Freni's eyes glitter. We Mennonites and Amish have humility bred into our DNA. I, for one, am very proud of my humility. But we all have our thresholds, past which temptation becomes too strong to resist. My stumbling block was a sinfully red BMW. Now I am proud to say that I saw the error of my ways and traded it for a more humble vehicle. At any rate, I had no doubt but that Freni could manage her own ego. And anyway, she wasn't my sister. But even if she was, I was certainly not her keeper.

She took a few minutes to deliberate. "So maybe not the grand pooh-bah," she finally said, "but the queen, yah?"

"Then you'll do it?"

"Yah, I do it. But that means you must listen to me too, yah?"

"Whatever," I said, borrowing Alison's favorite word.

I fled to move my things before she had a chance to change her mind.

Despite the late hour, I managed to collect Mose from the farm and ensconce the couple into my downstairs suite. Then I struggled up my impossibly steep stairs one last time to throw myself into a bed—quite frankly a pretty awful bed. I know I certainly wouldn't pay the huge amount of money I charge for its use. At any rate, it seemed like no sooner did I hit the hay than I heard a loud rap on the door.

"I'm not here!" I hollered.

"Yoder, you're an idiot, you know that?"

It was my nemesis, Melvin Stoltzfus. He had a lot of nerve calling me an idiot. The man couldn't pour water out of a boot if the instructions were printed on the heel. The only reason Hernia keeps him on as Chief of Police is that no one else wants the job.

"Melvin, do you know what time it is?"

"It's almost nine o'clock, Yoder. And you're the one who's always telling me it's a sin to sleep in so late."

"Yes, but nine in the evening, and nine in the morning—" I caught a glimpse of the cheap bedside clock. Heavens to Murgatroyd! It was 8:50 in the *morning*. Only Satan and unrepentant sinners slept that late. Well, at least according to Mama.

My knucklehead brother-in-law rapped again. "Yoder, open up, or I'm going to break the door down."

Melvin is built like a praying mantis: huge knobby head, skinny neck, swollen torso, and arms and legs so spindly one must conclude they're reinforced with rebar. He barely had the strength to open a door, much less break one down. Still, I knew from experience that he wasn't going to leave until he'd gotten what he'd come for.

I threw a heavy flannel robe on over my thick cotton pajamas, which in turn covered my sturdy Christian underwear. Then I crammed my size eleven tootsies into shaggy slippers shaped like bunnies. If eye candy was what he was after, he was going to leave hungrier than ever.

"Yes?" I snapped as I flung the door open.

Melvin recoiled. No doubt he was surprised at how quickly I'd made myself decent.

"Yoder," he said, catching his breath, "you look hideous."

"Thank you. I try my best. Now what is it that's so important you have to disturb my beauty rest?"

"It's about Reverend Schrock. Aren't you at least going to invite me in?"

I stepped aside. There wasn't anyplace for him to sit except the bed. I don't believe in coddling my guests with luxuries like chairs. Better to get them downstairs in the dining room, I say, where I have a quilting loom all set up for their bored fingers. A surprising number of them are deft with a needle, and I am usually able to sell their handiwork for a tidy sum. Every now and then some novice will make stitches that resemble the footprints of a drunken chicken, but I sneak in at night and replace them with tight little stitches of my own.

Melvin surveyed my rumpled bed with one eye, while his other seemed to be ogling the bunny on my right tootsy. "What's the thread count, Yoder?"

"Say what?"

"Susannah and I sleep on four-hundred-thread-count sheets. These look more like burlap bags."

"Cut to the chase, Melvin, or else march your bony carapace back to your car and drive yourself home to those four-hundred-count sheets, pick a nice strong one, and then hang yourself with it." I know—those words should never have come out of the mouth of a Christian. But I had awakened on the sinful side of the morning, and there is only so much Stoltzfus one can take on an empty stomach. For the record, I immediately whispered a prayer asking for forgiveness.

Melvin sat on the corner of the bed nearest the door. "Touchy this morning, are we?"

"Spill it."

"I thought you might like to know that the lab called already with a preliminary report on the cause of death. I'd asked them to do a rush on it, you see. Fellow there by the name of Neubrander owed me a favor, on account of back in junior college, I held his head out of the toilet for him when he puked—"

"Peanut butter."

"No, beer, stupid. Whoever heard of drinking peanut butter?"

"I meant in the chili. Reverend Schrock died from an allergic reaction, didn't he?"

In a rare moment of coordination, Melvin managed to get both eyes to focus on me. "How did you know that?"

"Lodema told me about his allergy."

Surely Melvin holds the world record for staring, at least with one of his eyes. I was beginning to believe in the heresy of teleportation—perhaps the real Melvin was happily munching aphids on a rosebush somewhere—when he finally responded.

"Yoder, I want you to be the first to hear the news."

"What news?" Could my sister possibly be pregnant? If so, would her baby be human, or insect, maybe even a hybrid, thereby violating the laws of nature and incurring the wrath of God? *Or*— and this really gave me chills—what if the big news was that he was planning to divorce her? As much as I dislike the man, I have no doubt that Susannah loves him dearly.

"Yoder, I quit."

"Quit what?" For all his annoying habits, Melvin neither smokes nor drinks. And he certainly isn't overweight.

"My job, that's what."

I couldn't believe my ears. "As Chief of Police?"

"No, idiot, as a male stripper over in Bedford."

Melvin loves the power that comes with his job. It's what gives him confidence, as undeserved as it may be. His pigeon chest was a sparrow chest until he pinned on that badge. This could only mean that he was telling the truth about being a stripper, because he would never quit the force.

"Does your mama know?"

"Don't be ridiculous—of course she does. It's always been a source of pride for her. She especially loves to see me work."

I tried to imagine Elvina Stoltzfus at the Bigger Chigger, or wherever it is male insects strut their stuff. I am happy to report that even my imagination doesn't stretch that far.

"Do you at least wear a G-string?"

"Yoder, you're a fool. Why would I wear a G-string under my uniform?"

The sudden rush of blood to my cheeks made me top-heavy and I needed to sit down, but I sure wasn't going to share my bed with Melvin, not after having made such an embarrassing boo-boo. The twit might think this nitwit was coming on to him.

"You're resigning as Chief of Police?"

"Are we talking in circles, Yoder?"

"No, and you can't quit! And besides, you have to give notice."

"That's why I'm here. I told the mayor first thing this morning, and now I'm telling you, seeing as how you're on the town council—although how that ever happened, I'll never know."

That was only a minor insult, by Stoltzfus standards, so I let it pass. "If you think for one minute that I'm going to support you and my sister, well, think again."

"Don't need your money, Yoder. I already got me a new job. I start in two weeks."

"Doing what?"

"Making staples, that's what."

I must confess that making staples is one profession I'd never given much thought to. But someone has to make them, and why not Melvin? Just as long as he didn't get bored doing it and go bonkers. I could see the headlines already: HERNIA MAN GOES BERSERK, TERRORIZES COWORKERS WITH STAPLE GUN.

"Melvin, dear," I said, ever the practical one, "who's going to investigate Reverend Schrock's death?"

"That's why I'm here, Yoder."

"Oh no, you don't. You're not dumping this into my lap. I'd be happy to help, but I'm not flying solo on this one."

"You gotta, Yoder, because I'm going fishing."

"Say what?"

"I got me two weeks of vacation time saved up, and I mean to use it."

"But you can't!"

"What are you and the mayor going to do, fire me?" He moved his mandibles silently, but I knew he was chuckling inside.

If it were not for the three hundred years of pacifist inbreeding that was my heritage, I would have smacked the smirk off Stoltzfus's face. Instead, I only pretended to swing at him. Unfortunately, my arms are long and gangly, and my hands the size of Delaware at low tide. Those factors, along with my still engorged cheeks, caused me not only to lurch forward onto the bed, but to somehow become tangled up with Melvin. I guess it should have come as no surprise that the demented mantis should take that as an advance on my part.

At any rate, that's when the second uninvited visitor appeared at my door.

3

"Ach!" Freni squawked.

"It isn't what you think!" I wailed.

"A sin, Magdalena, that's what it is."

I struggled to free myself from my brother-in-law's bony embrace. "I lost my balance, that's all."

"Yah, that is what they all say. Sarah Burkholder lost her balance thirteen times, and now she and Enoch have more mouths than they can feed. Ach, it is such a shame."

"That's not what Melvin and I were doing! Tell her, Melvin."

"Okay, if you insist. You see, Freni, I was just sitting here, on the edge of the bed, minding my own business, when Magdalena—"

"Forgot to give you your monthly stipend," I growled.

Melvin's limbs immediately found their own space. If it weren't for the allowance I dole out on a regular basis, my sister and her husband would be living under a bridge, pretending to be trolls and charging folks for safe passage. They both know which side their brand-name bread is buttered on, and whose hand it is that does the spreading.

"We were just talking," Melvin said quickly. "Police business."

Freni grunted, which meant she wasn't committing herself to believing, but neither would she disbelieve. "So now you go back to police work, and leave us alone, yah? I need to speak to Magdalena."

Melvin skedaddled without another word. Freni and his mother were as close as two plaits in a bun. It has been rumored that Elvina still spanks her forty-year-old son, and if this is true, I have no doubt Freni would gladly fill in for her.

"What do you want to talk about?" I asked nervously. It has been years since Freni's spanked me, but the last time she did, it made quite an impression on yours truly.

"Magdalena, you said I was in charge of the inn this week, yah?"

"Yah—I mean, yes."

"So then I can fry scrapple for breakfast, yah?"

"Yes. But you have to make something different for the vegetarians."

Her glasses were caked with grease and cornmeal, so I couldn't see her eyes, but her silence spoke volumes.

"Well, did you?"

"But the scrapple has corn in it, yah? And corn is a vegetable."

"Freni, you expect others to respect your beliefs, so in turn you need to respect theirs."

"But some of the English are so strict."

"That would be the pot calling the kettle black, dear."

"Ach," she squawked again, and fled before reason had a chance to contaminate her thinking.

I started my investigation with the most obvious suspect: our church's treasurer. Little Samson was given his name at birth, but nonetheless has managed to live up to it. Although just five feet five, he is built like an ox. His father, Big Samson, was six feet five, and his mother, Delilah (I kid you not), at least six feet. Throw in the fact that Little Samson is a redhead, and both his parents were brunet, and one might figure in a milkman somewhere.

Little Samson's last name is Livengood, but folks invariably use his nickname. He is Hernia's only farrier, and because so many Amish live in the area, Little Samson is always busy. Still, he finds time to attend every PTA meeting, and since his election to the school board, his attendance has been perfect.

There were three buggies in the parking lot of Little Samson's smithy, their owners waiting patiently to have their horses shod. The men were not surprised to see me.

"Ach," said Jonas Speicher, "the Mennonite preacher's murder."

The other two men, whom I didn't know, nodded. Apparently my reputation as a pseudosleuth preceded me, as did rumors of a murder that had yet to be confirmed.

"*Gut marriye*," I said, and breezed past them.

The inside of the smithy smelled like burned fingernails—not an odor to which I am accustomed, mind you. Little Samson had his back turned to me, a horse's hoof propped against a muscular thigh. I waited until he was through driving in the nail before I spoke. To his credit, he turned slowly and regarded me calmly.

"I've been expecting you, Magdalena."

"You have?"

"Well, I'm the most logical place to start, aren't I? That's what I would do if I was in your shoes."

"You'd step right out of my shoes, dear." I wasn't being unkind, merely stating a fact.

"So I would. Speaking of shoes, Magdalena, I don't mean to be rude, but I have two more shoes to go on this one, and eight hooves waiting for me outside. Do you mind if we get started?"

"Perhaps you'd like to ask the questions yourself."

He didn't even spare a second to smile at my audacity. "Certainly. I'm the treasurer at Beechy Grove Mennonite Church. Your hypothesis is that I stole from the congregation, that the reverend got wise to it, and that I murdered him at the chili supper to cover my tracks. Am I correct?"

For the record, Little Samson got a perfect score on his SATs. Since only God is supposed to be perfect, showing off like this smacks of arrogance, if you ask me. I might have gotten a much higher score if I'd tried harder. Now what was I about to say? Oh yes, a lot of Amish, and to a lesser extent Mennonites, have brilliant minds that they hide under bushels, to use a biblical metaphor. Little Samson is a Mennonite, and could have gotten a scholarship to an Ivy League school. Instead, he chose to follow in his father's footsteps, insuring that our horses' footsteps rang out loud and clear on our county's highways and byways.

"Yes, you are correct, but—"

"I have seven children, Magdalena. Do you think I would risk prison for twenty thousand dollars?"

"Twenty thousand dollars? Is that how much is missing?"

"That was just an example. I didn't say anything was missing."

"Don't scare me like that, Little Samson. You'll turn my hair white, and I much prefer the mousy brown shade the Good Lord gave me. And just the same, you should check the books—to make sure nothing is missing."

"Do you have other suspects on your list, Magdalena?"

"Of course."

"Then I suggest you interrogate them, before the trail gets any colder."

"Well, now, that's up to me to decide, isn't it? I'm the one conducting this investigation."

"Yes, but harassing me is a waste of both your time and mine, because I have an alibi."

"You do?"

"Certainly. Do you recall seeing my seven youngsters at the supper last night?"

"Come to think of it, it was remarkably quiet. Nobody put gum in my hair. No chairs were knocked over. There wasn't any shrieking—except for when Lydia Bontrager thought she found a tooth in her chili. No, I don't remember seeing the little brats—I mean, darlings."

"That's because we were at my mother-in-law's house over in Somerset. It was her birthday. We didn't get back until almost ten o'clock. If you like, I'll give you my mother-in-law's telephone number. You can call her, see what time we left."

"That won't be necessary." Somerset was less than an hour away, and Reverend Schrock departed for his heavenly home at six thirty sharp. Little Samson was off the hook.

I thanked him for his time, given grudgingly though it was, bade a cheery farewell to the Amish men in the parking lot, and made tracks for my next victim.

Edwina Bishop is one of Hernia's most beautiful women, if viewed from the left side. After her fourth marriage (that husband ran off with a convenience store clerk) Edwina underwent a total physical makeover. The results were astonishing. Edwina's left side looked like a young Sophia Loren, while her right side resembled an old Karl Malden. Okay, so perhaps that is a slight exaggeration, but the surgeon did cut too deeply near her temple, severing a nerve that cannot be repaired, and one that controls the entire right side of her face. As a consequence, Edwina will show her face only in profile.

The reason this partial beauty held a high position on my list of suspects is because she held a grudge against the reverend. Personally, I agree with Reverend Schrock. If after four marriages, you can't get it right, stop asking for the church's blessing. "Serial monogamy" is what the good man called it, and he would not be a part of it. He even went so far as to say that he would rather officiate at the wedding of two committed homosexuals than at the temporary marriages of someone like Edwina.

Thus it was that Edwina failed to gain husband number five. Although raised a Mennonite (and a Kauffman), Edwina got so peeved with her pastor that she left the church altogether, not even stopping to join the Presbyterians along the way. Of course the nuptial-hungry Hernian could have had a civil ceremony, but her bitterness alienated bachelor number five, who, by the way, was not put off by the duality of her looks. He, so I am told, was legally blind.

Living off a generous alimony settlement, Edwina does not have to support herself, and I found her at home in the historic section of Hernia. She must have been starved for company, because she opened the door to her immaculate Victorian before I even pressed the bell.

"Magdalena! Won't you come in?"

"Don't mind if I do."

She kept her left profile to me as she guided me into the living room and offered a carved wooden chair upholstered in blue cut velvet. "Would you care for something to drink?"

"A cup of cocoa would be nice, with whipped cream and chocolate sprinkles—but not if it's any trouble." If folks ask, why not give them an honest answer?

Her left eye blinked, so I could only imagine what her right eye was doing. "I'm afraid the cocoa would be instant, and the whipped cream from a spray can."

"No problem."

While she was busy, I took stock of my surroundings. Either Edwina had a maid, or she amused herself by housecleaning. I'm sure she would have passed even Granny Yoder's white-glove test. Perhaps there was something to the rumor—spread by husband number two—that Edwina was a neat freak.

I didn't have time for an in-depth snoop before she returned with my morning snack. The cocoa may have come from a packet, but it was served in a bone china cup, on a matching saucer, which in turn was embellished by the addition of a ladyfinger—of the cake sort, not the real thing. She carried a cup for herself as well.

"To what do I owe the honor of this visit, Magdalena?"

I sipped the beverage immediately, risking a foam mustache. It's one thing to serve the Hershey's instant variety, but one should at least endeavor to get the lumps dissolved.

"I don't know if you heard, dear, but Reverend Schrock died last night."

With her head turned to the side, I could see only half a frown. "Yes, it was on the Bedford morning news."

"I know you didn't care for him, but he was a big part of this community and will be missed."

"He was a hypocrite," she said, and took her first sip.

"Aren't we all, dear?"

I was treated to a glimpse of her entire face. Frankly, it wasn't as bad as I'd remembered.

"Magdalena, I am most certainly *not* a hypocrite. Everyone knows my history. I have nothing left to hide—well, you know what I mean."

"Yes, but we all have secrets that we try to keep."

"Like the fact that you committed bigamy?"

"I didn't know Aaron was married," I wailed. Stupid me, I should have known. I was truly happy for the first time in my life, and everything was coming up roses. Only a fool wouldn't have seen the thorns coming up as well.

Having scored a point, she chuckled softly. "We have a lot in common, don't we?"

"I don't think so, dear. I made an honest mistake."

"Maybe. But that's more than I can say for Reverend Schrock. He knew full well that he was committing adultery."

"I beg your pardon?"

"Don't look so shocked, Magdalena. And it wasn't with me, if that's what you're thinking."

I set my cocoa cup down on the end table next to my chair and jumped to my feet. "I'm not going to sit here and listen to this filth. You should be ashamed of yourself, Edwina. It's one thing to bad-mouth a good man like the reverend, but to do so when he's dead and can't defend himself—why, that's inexcusable."

"I'm just stating a fact."

"You're lying." I headed for the door.

"If you don't believe me, then ask Clarisse Thompson."

I slowed, but didn't stop. "Who?"

"She's a masseuse at Happy Backs, over in Bedford."

I turned and wagged a finger at her, presidential-style. " 'Thou shalt not bear false witness against thy neighbor.' It's in the book of Exodus. Look it up."

"I know exactly where it is, just two commandments below 'Thou shalt not commit adultery.' "

Why stand when you can sit? I always say. I hoofed it back to the chair and plopped my bony butt back down. "You really hated him, didn't you?"

"With a passion. Magdalena, if he hadn't been so strict about some silly church rules, I'd be married to the only man I ever loved."

"But you've had four husbands."

She waved a well-manicured hand. "There's love, and then there's *love*. Gerald loved the real me. He didn't care one iota about my butchered face."

"It's not that bad," I said, in a random moment of kindness.

"You really think so?"

"I really do. But if Gerald loved you so much, why did he leave you when the reverend refused to officiate at your marriage?"

"His parents refused to recognize a marriage that was not per-formed in a church. Gerald is very close to his parents, his mother in particular."

"They were Mennonite?" If so, this was certainly news to me.

"Methodist. Their pastor wouldn't do it either."

"So you hate him as well?"

"No, because he's not *my* pastor."

"Are you glad he's dead? Reverend Schrock, I mean."

She started to turn her face in my direction, but caught herself. "What an awful question to ask. Of course I'm not glad. You can hate someone without wishing them dead."

Bigger is not always better. My size eleven feet aren't more tasty than tinier tootsies. It behooved me to haul my bony butt out of there before I stuck my foot in my mouth again. I stood for the final time.

"Well, if you ask me, it should be Gerald you're mad at, not Rev-erend Schrock. Gerald sounds like a mama's boy."

She followed me to the door, her face still in profile. "You should know."

"What is that supposed to mean?"

4

"Why, Magdalena, don't you dare act surprised. Everyone knows you're engaged to a mama's boy."

"I am not!"

"I hear his mother cuts his meat for him."

"Only the tough pieces."

"And that's not all I hear. The grapevine has it that she's been shacking up with old Doc Shafor. If she moves in with him altogether, who's going to cut your pretty boy's meat?"

"What he does with his meat is his own business!" I wailed. My ears were burning, and so was my heart. I was the one who fixed Doc up with Ida Rosen, but it had never occurred to me that they would do the mattress mambo without the benefit of matrimony. Okay, so Doc talks racy, but he's in his eighties, for crying out loud. I was sure a stiff upper lip was the most he could muster. And who was this grapevine anyway? For a split, sinful second, I wished that a real grapevine would materialize and choke Edwina Bishop.

The woman treated me to half a smirk. "Care for some more cocoa before you leave, Magdalena?"

"Yes, to go," I said. "If you don't have any Styrofoam cups, put it in a thermos. I promise to wash it and return it. Oh, and another ladyfinger would be nice."

"Are you being sarcastic, Magdalena?"

"Merely practical, dear. It's chilly outside, and you offered."

It took her forever, but she returned with a large disposable cup and a little plastic bag of cakes. It was my turn to smirk.

Gabriel Rosen is the second love of my life, but of course the true one. A retired doctor from New York City, he chose to live in Hernia because it is a small, quiet town in a bucolic setting. Gabe, or the Babester, as I am wont to call him, has decided to spend the second half of his life as a writer—a mystery writer to be exact. Of course he hasn't published anything, and I'm not sure he ever will. I don't think he has the tenacity it takes to succeed in what I hear is a very competitive field. Frankly, I sort of hope Gabe doesn't publish, because if he does, I'll be forced to read one of his books. In recent years I have stopped reading fiction. I mean, what's the point if it's all made up?

At any rate, the ironic thing is that the property the Babester bought used to be a working farm owned by the first love of my life, the bigamist Aaron Miller. The Miller farm, as it is still known, lies directly across the road from my own farm. Every morning I wake up to see a reminder of one of the greatest pains of my life, as well as one of the greatest blessings the Good Lord has bestowed on me.

Did I mention that Gabriel Rosen is Jewish? That shouldn't be anyone's business, but sadly, it is. Hernia is a remarkably homogeneous town with a well-defined religious pecking order. The bulk of us are Mennonites, followed by Methodists, Lutherans, Presbyterians, and then Baptists. We used to have an Episcopalian, but he was brutally murdered recently. Of course there are many Amish about, but they live on farms surrounding Hernia, and generally keep to themselves. Last, and certainly least, are the folks who belong to the church with thirty-two words in its name over by the turnpike. But Gabriel and his mother, Ida, are the only Jews, and there are folks in town who still don't know what to make of it.

After leaving Edwina Bishop's fancy Victorian home, I headed straight for the Babester's farm. As usual, I had mixed emotions as I drove up the long gravel road to the house. Today there was one more emotion added to the stew. Perhaps I can be excused then for knocking somewhat vigorously on the front door.

"Hey, hon," Gabe said, his tanned face pale with concern, "is something wrong?"

"It's your mother."

He stepped aside to usher me in. "I thought we'd settled this. She'll continue to live here after we're married, and she'll only cut my meat if it's something she's cooked, and it's really tough."

That was news to me. The last I'd heard, Ida was going to move into the PennDutch Inn with us, and Gabriel was going to sell the farm.

"Since when did we settle this?"

He bit his lip. "Well, maybe we didn't settle this, but we can now. Magdalena, you were absolutely right. Having Ma live with us is no way to start off a marriage. After all, she can be a wee bit pushy."

"Pushy? She could move a forest of rubber tree plants by herself." I clamped a hand over my big mouth.

I needn't have worried. Like all men, Gabe practiced selective hearing.

"Would you like something to eat or drink, hon?" he asked.

"No, thanks, I'm full. Gabe, we need to talk."

"Okay, let's talk."

We sat on the same butter-soft Italian leather sofa. But we sat at opposite ends. At times the chemistry between us is so strong that we find ourselves sliding together, like a pair of magnetic dogs. When this happens, we invariably get to first base, and once we got halfway to second. But I've made it quite clear that Gabe's bat will stay in the dugout until after we've exchanged vows. Hence we both agree that it is better to at least start off on opposite sides of the sofa.

"Gabe, do you know where your mother is?"

"Of course I do. She had breakfast at Doc Shafor's this morning, and then she went to Bedford to shop."

"Does she ever stay out all night?"

He recoiled slightly. "Sometimes she does. She stays with this new friend she met at Yoder's Corner Market."

"What's the friend's name?"

"Ima Dunce."

"That's a joke, right?"

He shook his handsome head. "Odd name. Is it Mennonite?"

"Most certainly not. Gabriel, dear, I don't know how else to say this, except that your mother is having an affair."

"With Ms. Dunce?"

I tried to keep a serious face. "I'm afraid you're the dunce, dear. She's shacking up with old Doc Shafor."

His normally classic features twisted through a plethora of contortions. The one he finally settled on made him look like he was about to cry.

"Are you sure?"

"That's what the grapevine says."

"Just who is this grapevine?"

I shrugged. "But Edwina Bishop is one of the twigs."

It took a few minutes for his face to resume its usual shape. "Do you have this woman's address?"

"Two thirty-five Maple. It's the yellow house with the white gingerbread trim. The one you always say reminds you of a lemon meringue pie. But Gabe, perhaps you should start with your mother, or maybe Doc. They're the only ones who know the truth. Besides, even if they're not—well, you know—doing it, they need to know that they are at least doing something that's the catalyst for these rumors."

He sighed. "Yeah, maybe you're right. I just can't believe that about Ma."

Neither could I. I certainly couldn't picture it easily. Ida Rosen was less than five feet tall and shaped like an inverted isosceles triangle. Doc, on the other hand, was wiry and hairy—I had to either stop envisioning them doing the horizontal hootchy-kootchy or poke out my mind's eye.

I slid on the buttery sofa just far enough to give the Babester a peck on the cheek. It was time to hustle my bustle to the far side of town to put the screws to suspect number three.

Noah Miller lives in the part of town that we locals shamefully refer to as Ragsdale. I know—it's a sin to judge others on their lack of material possessions, and I promise to repent for even sharing this bit of information. And not that it's a valid excuse, but the habit was ingrained in us as children.

When Susannah and I were girls (at separate times, of course), our school bus used to stop in this part of town to take on students. It was common knowledge among us children that the Ragsdale kids were a breed apart. Some of them sported tattoos, many of them smoked, and on at least three occasions Miss Proschel, our bus driver, had to confiscate knives. Like many other stereotypes in this world, Ragsdale's reputation was based on both fact and fancy.

The neighborhood remains poor, but frankly, today I feel safer walking through it than I do visiting Foxcroft, our newest subdivision. Foxcroft, by the way, is where Susannah and Melvin live, in a house that can be distinguished from its neighbors only because my sister ignores the covenants and hangs scarlet drapes at the windows. Anyway, in the last five years since its establishment, Foxcroft has seen a homicide, eight cases of nonlethal domestic violence (that have been reported), four break-ins, and a rash of mailbox bashing. During that same time period Ragsdale has been virtually crime free.

Still, I was as nervous as a hen in a fox den when I walked up the drive to Noah's house. This was no gingerbread, to be sure. The two-story structure, covered with tar paper shingles, leaned ominously toward the street. Both the roof and the front porch sagged, and one of the second-story windows had been boarded over. The frost-browned grass in the tiny lawn was ankle-deep where it wasn't weighed down by fallen leaves.

But it wasn't just the house, or even the neighborhood, that had me spooked. The thing is, I knew for a fact that the owner was an ex-con. Noah Miller had only recently been released after serving a seven-year sentence for the killing of two high school girls. He would have served two consecutive life sentences had not a zealous young law student from Philadelphia taken his appeal to the state supreme court, where he presented new DNA evidence that supposedly cleared Noah of both charges of homicide. I say supposedly, because not a soul in Hernia believed the man was innocent. It is widely assumed that Noah returned to Hernia because he now owned the family home (his parents both died while he was incarcerated) and, with the exception of prison, had never lived anywhere else. A month ago, a factory owner in Bedford gave Noah a job as a night janitor. Since then no one has seen him around town.

The doorbell was obviously out of commission, so I rapped with knockers that were the envy of woodpeckers. It wasn't until Noah appeared at the door, his eyelids barely open, that I remembered he worked at night.

"Oh, it's only you," he said, and actually closed his peepers for a second.

"Sorry about waking you, but may I come in?" I know—it would have been safer talking to him on the sagging porch, but I didn't want to be seen with him. For that reason, I'd parked three blocks from the house.

"Yeah, sure, come in," he said.

I patted my purse as I slipped past him. "I'm here on police business," I said. That was to make him think I carried a gun—although if he was thinking at all, Noah, who was raised a Mennonite, would know that I would never carry an instrument of violence.

He offered me a comfortable chair, which, to my surprise, was entirely clean. In fact, the living room was altogether clean, and as neat as an Amish hairpin.

Noah might have been sleepy, but he was no slouch. "I get my first night off next month. As soon as I catch up on my sleep, I'll get around to fixing the outside of the house, and then the yard."

"You might take the man out of the Mennonites, but you can't take Mennonite out of the man." Noah once belonged to my church. In fact I'd taught him in my Sunday school class.

"Oh yes, you can." He spoke quietly, so that I had to strain to hear. "Miss Yoder, I no longer consider myself a Mennonite."

"Then what are you? Oh no, don't tell me the Presbyterians got to you."

"I've given up on church altogether."

"Then I'm afraid your final destination—pre- or not—is going to be a very warm place."

He slumped into the nearest chair, but his eyes opened wide

enough for me to see their bright blue color. Noah Miller had been one of the most attractive young men in the church. Prison had certainly taken its toll. Now there were bags under the eyes and his shoulders slumped.

"Well, if I'm going to Hell, then I'll see Schrock there."

"Excuse me?" But I knew what was coming next; that's why I'd gone to see him.

"After what he did to me, the man deserves to burn in Hell. Seven years of my life—you can't put a price tag on that."

"Noah, you asked him to be a character witness at your trial. You should have known better than that. Everyone in Hernia knew that you were—uh—"

"A bully?"

"I was going to say hoodlum. Breaking into the church on Halloween and making doo-doo in the offering plates—you could have gotten into serious trouble for that, but he went easy on you."

"I was fourteen, and trying to find myself."

"And yes, you were a bully. There wasn't a kid in Hernia who wouldn't run for cover when they saw you coming. Killer Miller, they called you."

"I was hurting. Ma and Pa were in the middle of a nasty divorce, and I didn't know how to act out. And just so you know, I learned to deal with those issues in the lockup."

"A therapy class?"

He nodded.

"You see? You ought to be thankful that the reverend testified against you."

He swore, using words I refuse to repeat. "Now my life is ruined," he added. "I'll never be able to get a decent job—here, or anywhere. And even though I was given a full pardon, I feel like I have the mark of Cain stamped on my forehead."

I gave him what I hoped was a sympathetic look. "So you killed the reverend to get back at him. Has it helped with the pain?"

"I did *not* kill the reverend," he said through clenched teeth. "But I won't deny that I'm glad somebody else did. If I knew who it was, I'd send them a thank-you note."

Of course that made me very angry, since I'd always considered

Reverend Schrock to be a dear friend. But I had come to solve the mystery of his death, not to defend him. It behooved me to play along.

"Noah, do you have any idea who else might have wanted the reverend dead?"

"Yeah, but this information is going to cost you."

"I beg your pardon?"

"Miss Yoder, it's you that wants the information. Either you meet my price, or you get up and walk out that door."

My heart pounded. What if he wanted his way with me? Allowing him to hit a home run was certainly out of the question, but in the interest of justice, would letting him get to first base be so bad? After all, in the grand scheme of things . . .

"Get behind me, Satan," I said under my breath.

"What was that?"

"I said, what is your price?"

5

Puppy's-Breath Chili
World Champion 1993

Source: Cathy Wilkey
Submitted by: www.chilicookoff.com

Ingredients:

3 pounds tri-tip beef or sirloin tip
    cut in small pieces or coarse
    ground
2 teaspoons Wesson oil
1 small yellow onion
1 14½-ounce can beef broth
3½ tablespoons ground cumin
½ teaspoons oregano
6 cloves garlic (finely chopped)
3 tablespoons Gebhardt Chili
    Powder
1 tablespoon New Mexico mild
    chili powder

5–6 tablespoons California chili
    powder
1 8-ounce can Hunt's tomato sauce
1 dried New Mexico chili pepper,
    boiled and pureed
3 dried California chili peppers,
    boiled and pureed
1 14½-ounce can chicken broth
1 teaspoon Tabasco pepper sauce
1 teaspoon brown sugar
1 lime
Dash of MSG
Salt to taste

Instructions:

Brown meat in Wesson oil for about ½ hour over medium heat.
Add onion and enough beef broth to cover meat.
Bring to a boil and cook for 15 minutes.
Add 1 tablespoon cumin and ½ teaspoon oregano.
Reduce heat to light boil and add half of the garlic.
Add half of the chili powder and cook for 10 minutes.
Add Hunt's tomato sauce with the pulp from the dried peppers and remaining garlic.
Add any remaining beef broth and chicken broth for desired consistency.
Cook for 1 hour on medium heat, stirring occasionally.
Add remaining chili powders and cumin.
Simmer for 25 minutes on low to medium heat, stirring occasionally.
Turn up heat to light boil and add Tabasco pepper sauce, brown sugar, juice of lime, and salt to taste.
Simmer on medium heat until you are ready to serve.

6

"I want you to write a piece for the *Hernia Herald*. In it, I want you to say that you talked to me and are convinced that I never even touched those two girls. Say that you believe I was set up by the reverend."

The truth be told, I was both relieved and disappointed. But there was no way I would write that article. On the other hand, I could use all the help I could get on this case. Maybe if I stalled him, I could think of a way out of this conundrum.

"Why settle for the *Hernia Herald,* dear? It's just a weekly rag filled with grocery ads. Nobody really reads the articles. I say we shoot for one of the Bedford papers. Clear your name countywide. Better yet, how about Pittsburgh's *Post-Gazette*?"

He smiled for the first time since I'd appeared on his doorstep. "Yeah. But why not get it in all three papers? Hey, Miss Yoder, you're really cool after all."

Unfortunately, I still did not have a plan. "But if I promise to do this—look, I can't do it. Not the reverend part. But I can promise to write a nice article saying I believe you didn't kill those two girls. Because after talking with you this morning, I really believe that."

He stared at me. Any second he was going to leap out of his chair and boot my patooty to the door. Once a bully, always a bully—at least until proved otherwise.

"You really believe that?" he finally said, his voice cracking with emotion.

"Yes, I do." Bullies are invariably cowards, and a coward would have lit out of Hernia like a fox with a tare tied to its tail—unless the bully had something utterly important to prove.

"You swear?"

"Noah, you were once a Mennonite. You know I can't swear. This may come as a surprise to you, but I have been known to lie—always for a good cause, of course. Only this time I'm not lying. I really believe you are innocent."

I looked away while he rubbed an eye with the back of his hand. "Thanks, Miss Yoder. You don't know how much this means to me."

"I think I do. When Aaron Miller—my third cousin, twice removed, if I remember correctly—left me to go back to the wife he had stashed up in Minnesota, I was the town's pariah. There are still folks who call me a bigamist and an adulteress."

"Yeah, I heard about that."

"In prison?"

"There's not a lot going on in prison. Any gossip that comes in gets passed around pretty thoroughly. Even heard about the time you had a bunion removed and it looked just like Elvis Presley."

"That's wasn't me! That was Veronica Saylor."

"Must have been a nifty thing to see."

"Oh, it was. And it was a young Elvis Presley too, not him in his fat stage. Veronica charged two bucks a peep, and she had a line of folks that wrapped around the block. Hernia hasn't had such a big attraction since back in the seventies when Emma Rickenbach saw the Virgin Mary's face peering up at her through the curds in her buttermilk. Of course that didn't last long on account the buttermilk eventually went sour."

"Buttermilk goes sour? I thought it was supposed to taste that way."

It was time to go, because I was getting to like the guy. If it wasn't for his hatred of the dear departed reverend, Noah Miller and I might have become friends.

"Well, sorry to have wakened you, Noah."

"No problem. Glad to be of service. And Magdalena—may I call you that?"

"Certainly."

"That therapy really worked. I'm not a bully anymore."

"Good. I hate bullies—if I wasn't a peace-loving woman myself, I'd slap them silly." I launched myself out of the surprisingly comfortable chair.

"Just one more thing," he said just as I reached the door.

"Yes?"

"Don't you want to know who it is that I think might be guilty of the reverend's murder? I mean, if you're going to write that article."

I pivoted. "Absolutely!"

"You might try talking to Tobias Gindlesperger."

"Tobias?" I asked in disbelief. The man did not fit my mental profile of a killer. I doubt if he steps on roaches.

He nodded. "The man's been over to see me several times. Not because we're best buds or anything, but because we share something in common."

I leaped back into my chair. "Do tell," I urged. I couldn't imagine a thing the two of them had in common, except for a limited string of ancestors—something all Mennonites of Amish derivation share.

Noah smiled. "You will have to ask Tobias about that. Trust me, it will be worth your time."

"Can't you give me a hint? Is it smaller than a breadstick?"

"You mean box, don't you?"

"Whatever." Silly me. Not all boxes are created equal—come to think of it, not all breadsticks are either. Aaron Miller proved that on our honeymoon.

But I digress. In the end Noah Miller refused to tell, and I had no option but to beat it over to Tobias Gindlesperger's house.

Fortunately, I found Tobias at home. I didn't even know if he was still working, or retired. Like with Noah, it had been years since I'd last seen him, but unlike with Noah, I couldn't remember why. Always a quiet man, Tobias seemed to have dropped off my radar shortly after his wife, Agnes, died. Every now and then I would catch of a glimpse of him driving around town, spot him in another aisle at Miller's Feed Store, but we never actually spoke. I am ashamed to admit that during those years, I had thought many times of paying him a pastoral visit, so to speak, but had never managed to find the time. After all, I had my own crises to deal with.

Susannah was forever getting herself into trouble, I endured a pseudomarriage to the world's biggest liar, Alison came into my life with more hormones than a brothel full of prostitutes, and let's not forget Ida, my future mother-in-law, who hailed from the zip code where hail melts on contact. How could I be expected to keep track of every wounded soul who passed through Beechy Grove Mennonite Church? It's not like anyone ever stopped in to ask how I was doing, for crying out loud.

At any rate, it took me a few seconds to realize that it was Tobias who'd answered the door. My first impression was that I was being greeted by a giant basset hound.

"Magdalena," it said, without moving its lips.

"Tobias, is that you?"

"You're a little late, Magdalena."

Dogs rarely talk in my experience, so this is when I knew for sure it had to be Mr. Gindlesperger. I mean, everything about him drooped. Even his words seemed to sink as soon as he spoke them.

"May I come in?"

He faced me through the storm door, his breath forming rivulets of moisture. "We don't have anything to talk about."

"If you let me in, I'm sure I can find something to chat about."

"I don't chat—not since my Agnes passed away."

"That's just it. I know you said it was too late, but I'm here to see how you're doing. Losing a spouse has got to be just about the worst thing that can happen."

"You wouldn't know about that, now, would you? Aaron Miller wasn't exactly your spouse."

"Touché. But I know what it's like to feel utterly alone. When my parents died—squished as they were, between a milk tanker and a truck full of Adidas shoes in the Allegheny Tunnel—I felt abandoned. I didn't think there was a soul in the world who could understand how I felt."

The storm door opened, and I felt the delicious rush of warm air. "Come in," he said, "but I'm afraid the place is a little messy."

That was the understatement of the year. I have no doubt that the Gindlesperger house had not been cleaned since Agnes's death. There was enough dust lying about that, with only the addition of a little water with which to make mud, the Good Lord could have created a whole Agnes. Of course I had to accept a seat when offered. After all, I had invited myself in, and anyway, it would have been mean-spirited to refuse the hospitality of a grieving man.

"Would you care for something to drink, Magdalena? I don't have much in the house—well, I have water. But I'm not sure how clean the glasses are."

God expects us to be gracious, not fools. "No, thanks, I just had something to drink. Tobias, dear, how *are* you doing?"

"Do you really care?"

I nodded vigorously. I did care *then*. It's just that I hadn't cared so much in the past.

"I'm stuck," Tobias said.

"I beg your pardon?"

"Why doesn't God answer prayers?"

"He does."

"When Agnes was sick, nobody prayed harder than me. But she died anyway."

"We all prayed for Agnes, dear. But her cancer had gotten out of control."

"But God is supposed to be able to work miracles, isn't He?"

"I think God chooses to work miracles within the laws of nature. Otherwise, it wouldn't be fair, would it? I mean, why would He choose to save one person's life, and not another's?"

"In the Bible He worked real miracles—you know, like healing folks, and raising Lazarus from the dead."

"Indeed He did." I didn't know what else to say. I was taught to believe the Bible literally. The little bits of theology I read on my own merely serve to confuse me. It is so much easier to accept the Bible blindly, and not have to think. Pity the poor Episcopalians who think reason and history have to be dragged into a proper interpretation of the Scriptures.

"So you see? I'm stuck. I can't believe in God, but I can't not believe in Him, because that's how I was raised. But I *can* hate Reverend Schrock."

"*Hate* him? Why?"

"Because he told me everything would be all right. That things work out for the best if you love God, and that God never gives you more than you can handle. Well, you want to know what I have to say about that?"

I didn't, but he told me anyway. Halfway through his expletives I put my hands over my ears. At least now I knew what it was Tobias and Noah had in common.

"So there you have it," he said as he wound up his tirade. "I hope Reverend Schrock burns in Hell someday."

"He won't be there, I can assure you."

"Oh yes, he will. He gave me false hope. And let me tell you something, Magdalena. God did give me more than I can bear. My wife meant everything to me."

I had no response. Martha Gnagey's house burned to the ground the day after her husband, Eli, was killed in a car wreck. Martha's four-year-old twin sons died in the fire, and Martha burned over eighty percent of her body when she tried to rescue them. When Martha was released from the hospital three months later, the first thing she did was rent a motel room and slash her wrists. Who am I to say that Martha didn't have more than she could bear?

As much as I like to think I'm smart, there are times when my brain observes a five-second delay. Okay, maybe as a much as a minute. At any rate, didn't Tobias just say that he hoped "Reverend Schrock burns in Hell *someday*?"

"Tobias, dear, have you heard the news?"

"I don't listen to the news. Don't read it either. My Agnes and I used to eat our suppers in front of the TV. She liked to kid around and say she had this thing for Dan Rather. Anyway, I don't do anything now that I used to do with Agnes—well, I eat supper of course, but you know what I mean."

"Reverend Schrock is dead."

He looked stunned. "What?"

"It happened last night at the church chili supper."

"How did it happen?"

I sighed, raising clouds of dust from my chair's arms, as well as the end table. "Well, I was hoping you could tell me—but obviously this has come as a big surprise to you."

Tobias took his time to process what for him had to be good news. "I was one of your suspects, wasn't I?" he finally said.

"Yes—I mean, we're not even sure yet it's murder. But if it was . . ."

"But you knew I hadn't been to church in seven years."

"Has it been that long?" My, how time flies, even when you're not having fun.

"So if I wasn't at church last night, how could I have been a suspect?"

"Good point," I said, feeling like the day I ran out into Hertzler Road screaming that the sky was falling, only to discover that the blue objects drifting down from the heavens were bits of confetti, spread by a crop duster to celebrate the birth of Hiram and Iona Kauffman's baby boy (they'd previously had nine girls). Of course I was a lot younger then, having just finished junior college.

Come to think of it, neither Noah Miller nor Edwina Bishop showed their faces at the church door anymore. And Little Samson had an alibi. To prove someone guilty of murder, one most show that the suspect had motive, means, and opportunity. If none of my suspects were at church, how did they have the opportunity to slip peanut butter into some unsuspecting congregant's kettle? Unless one of them wore a disguise, entered the kitchen through the back door, and dropped off a pot of potentially poisonous pottage.

"Tobias, may I use your phone? My cell's in the car."

He nodded his assent, but no sooner had I uttered my request than I yearned to retract it. Tobias may have stopped coming to church, but he hadn't stopped using the phone. The receiver was crusty with dried grime of all descriptions. I tried to hold it with two fingers and well away from my ear.

Thank heavens my nemesis picked up on the first ring. "Stoltzfus here. You have two seconds to make this worth my time."

"Melvin! How did you know it was me?"

"I didn't. Your two seconds are over." He hung up.

I punched REDIAL with the knuckle of my pinkie. "You dunderhead," I roared before he had a chance to even draw a breath, "hang up on me again, and you can kiss your allowance goodbye."

"Yoder, is that you?"

"Who did you think I was? The Queen of Sheba?"

"She's dead, isn't she? I thought you were a telemarketer. The ID says 'blocked.'"

Silly me. Of course. I was calling from Tobias's phone. Well, there was no point in letting Melvin know that I was the dunderhead. As they say, the best defense is a good offense, and I can be quite offensive if I put my mind to it.

"Melvin, what are you doing answering the phone? You're supposed to be off on a fishing trip. What happened? Did the worms fight back?"

"Very funny, Yoder. For your information I fly-fish. And I decided I want to spend my vacation right here, watching television. They're showing reruns of *My Little Skinny Obnoxious Brother-in-law*. Did you know that guy got a million bucks for pretending to be married to a beautiful woman with big—well, you know."

"I can guess." What I couldn't guess was how my sister could marry a man who couldn't see the irony in that television show's title. "Melvin," I said patiently, "what happened to all the pots and kettles that were at church last night?"

"Zelda dusted them for prints, and took samples of their contents to the state lab over in Harrisburg. As far as I know, the pots themselves are still at church."

"Good work, Melvin."

"Yoder, you mean that?"

"Of course. Why wouldn't I?"

"Because you're always sarcastic, that's why."

"I am not always sarcastic. Just last week I had an eight-hour stretch during which I wasn't the least bit sarcastic. And back in April—"

"You see what I mean?"

I thanked Melvin for having done the right thing with the evidence, and then I hung up. Taking my leave of Tobias was a bit trickier. Even though it seemed like he had lacked the opportunity to kill Reverend Schrock, he was still on the list—along with everyone else who had hated our sweet departed pastor. But Tobias was more than just a suspect; he was someone whom the congregation in general had failed.

We live in a society geared toward couples. Believe me, I know whereof I speak. In some ways it is worse to have been part of a couple than never to have been coupled at all. Widows, widowers, and divorced persons fall off social calendars as easily as stick-up notes. At least the never-been-loveds have been forced to develop skills with which to insert themselves into situations where they are tolerated, if not welcomed.

"Tobias," I said, taking my leave, "we'll still be having services, even without the reverend. You're always welcome to sit with me."

"Unless, of course, you manage to prove that I was the one who killed him."

I chuckled politely. "I am on the prison ministry council—although I must say, we don't have a lot of Mennonites in the hoosegow."

He stiffened. "I may be confused about God, Magdalena, but I'm not confused about His so-called followers. I'd just as soon burn in Hell along with Reverend Schrock as have anything to do with you bunch of hypocrites."

If the shoe fits, wear it, they say. Fortunately there was enough hypocrisy in me alone to make a nice comfy pair of size elevens. Not that I'm proud of being a hypocrite, mind you, but Papa always said, "Whatever you do, Magdalena, make sure you do it well." At least on this count, I did not disappoint him.

I made a beeline to Beechy Grove Mennonite Church. It wasn't the pots that made me press the pedal to the metal, but the potty. I wasn't about to use the john at Tobias's house. But as one of the most influential members of my church (certainly the wealthiest), I had long since made sure that the toilet situation at my house of worship was adequate.

Perhaps it dates back to Grandpa Yoder, who built the county's only six-seater outhouse. At any rate, having long experienced the injustice perpetrated on us women by male architects, I decided to rectify this situation when we renovated the church eight years ago. When a few men dared to ask why we required more time in the restroom than they, I replied with the truth. Simply put, we have more to juggle than they have to jiggle. Let them deal with lining seats and wrestling panty hose. But I digress. The point is that the ladies' room at Beechy Grove Mennonite Church is all that one could ask for.

I was admiring the blue-and-white tiles on the floor when I heard the front door of the church close. Actually, there is a pair of oak doors, which must weigh over a hundred pounds apiece. These were my idea as well. Since they cause a major disturbance when they open and close, they have cut down on stragglers, and virtually eliminate the problem of folks ducking out early.

There was, however, no reason for the doors to be shutting now. "Who's there?" I called pleasantly. Perhaps it was the Good Lord— after all, this was His house—although I am quite sure He doesn't need to enter through a door.

But whoever it was refused to answer.

"Zelda, is that you? Are you back from Harrisburg already?"

Again, no answer. But there was definitely someone there. I could feel it in my bones.

7

I wrapped up my business and hoofed it out into the sanctuary. Yes, I know—it may have been a dangerous thing to do, but I feel very protective of Beechy Grove Mennonite Church. I also feel quite protected in the church—although why the Good Lord didn't protect His offering plates from Noah Miller is beyond my ken. But anyway, if it was a suspicious intruder, I was quite capable of hurling hymnals at him (or her) in my defense. Even conk them on the head with the cross if necessary—although that seemed a bit much, seeing as how I am supposed to be a pacifist.

Imagine my surprise when I saw an angel silhouetted in the dim blue light of a stained-glass window. All my life I'd yearned for an encounter with one of these heavenly beings. I used to pray that I would encounter one in the woods, or in the pasture behind our house, or even in the hayloft. Now when I least expected it—well, who would have thought there'd be an angel in church!

By the way, there is a lot of misinformation circulating about angels. This is because folks no longer take the time to read their Bibles. Angels are not the spirits of departed loved ones, returning to look after us like celestial babysitters; they are messengers from Heaven. For years I'd longed to hear one announce that my barren womb would bring forth a child, but now that I have a teenage foster child, that would no longer be good news. Perhaps this angel had come to reveal the identity of Reverend Schrock's killer or, better yet, inform me that Ida Rosen had decided to leave Hernia, and was planning to emigrate back to Russia.

"Welcome," I said, and then remembered that since the angel wasn't from these parts, and I didn't know a word of Hebrew, language could well be a problem. "Do you speak English?"

"Of course I speak English. What kind of silly question is that?"

"*Susannah?*"

"Mags, are you drunk again?"

"That was an accident," I wailed.

"Both times?"

My sister has no right to pick the splinter out of my eye when there's enough wood in her peepers to build a new set of church doors. Besides, I had every reason to be shocked by her presence in my church. She hadn't set foot in that building since our parents' funeral eleven years ago. After that, she married her first husband, the Presbyterian, and when that marriage fell apart, her spiritual life appeared to unravel altogether. To my knowledge, she hadn't been in a church in a decade except for weddings and funerals.

"I'm sure Reverend Schrock's funeral isn't for several days. Murder victims can't be released until the authorities are sure they've collected all the available evidence."

"I'm not here for a stupid funeral. Now, will you be a good sister and leave me alone?"

There was a catch in Susannah's voice, like she'd been crying, or was about to cry. To my knowledge, my baby sister hasn't cried since she was four and Papa spanked her for pushing Emily Gingerich off the front steps. But even then she had cried only with her mouth; not a tear was shed. When Mama and Papa departed for their heavenly home, squished flatter than pancakes, my sister remained dry-eyed—at least as far as I could tell.

Now that she sounded like she was finally on the verge of tears, leaving my sister alone was simply out of the question. Au contraire. I rushed to her and threw my arms around her spindly frame. It was a brief embrace.

"Ouch! Are you wearing your dog?"

"Mags, you know I never go anywhere without my poochie-woochie."

My sister's so-called poochie-woochie is two pounds of menacing mongrel she wears in an otherwise empty bra cup. The cur is half teeth and half sphincter muscle. It has a name—Shnookums—but lacking a brain as it does, the creature hasn't a clue, and never responds when it's called. Susannah can get away with carrying a dog with her wherever she goes, because she doesn't wear normal clothes. Fifteen feet of filmy fabric draped loosely around the body can cover a multitude of sins—a mangy mutt included.

"The beast just bit through my sturdy Christian underwear," I bellowed, forgetting for a moment we were in church.

"What's the matter, sis? Worried that now you won't be eligible for a wet-T-shirt contest?"

"Very funny. And there are no animals allowed in this building," I said, having remembered where we were. "Well, except for Augusta Nafziger's miniature Seeing Eye horse."

"That's not a horse—it's a Bernese mountain dog. Now will you leave me alone, sis, so I can pray?"

"Pray?" I braced myself against the nearest pew. At any moment our parents were going to start turning over in their graves. They do this for shocking news of any kind, by the way, not just when we upset them.

"Yes, pray."

"What about?"

Susannah burst into tears. I stared at her for a few seconds, unable to immediately process this unprecedented event. Then, fool that I am, I embraced her again. My well-meant gesture was perhaps too enthusiastic, if I judged by the yelp that escaped from her billowing costume.

"Sorry," I said, but before releasing her, I gave her another tight squeeze. Shnookums screeched like a schoolgirl.

Susannah continued to sob, and I, restricted by genetics, was at a loss as to how to comfort her. "There, there," I said, and swatted her back, as if it were covered with flies.

After a while she ran out of steam, or liquid, and when the sobs turned into a rasping cough, I pulled her down into a pew. Mama and Papa had yet to turn in their graves, but I was tired of standing.

"Okay, dear, tell me about it—but not if it's about sex."

She fought for her breath. "It's not about sex, sis. It's about my sugar booger."

"I didn't squeeze him *that* hard."

"Not that sugar booger. I'm talking about my widdle Melvy-Welvy."

"Gag me with a spoon," I said, borrowing from her vocabulary.

"Mags, you don't have to be so mean. You know I love my Melkins with all my heart."

I sighed. "Unfortunately, yes. And I know he loves you too. So what's the problem?"

"He's depressed, Mags. This whole quitting-the-department thing has gotten him so down that even I can't reach him. We haven't been able to—"

"But he wants to quit!"

"No, he doesn't. Not really. He's only doing it because he feels like such a failure. He thinks everyone in Hernia feels that way about him. Sure, he's been putting on a brave front, but Mags, I think he's about to . . ." She let her voice trail dramatically.

"Commit suicide?"

"No, he's about to listen to the Captain and Tennille. He always does that when he's really feeling blue. "Muskrat Love" is the greatest song ever written, you know." She paused. "Like I said, he thinks everyone in Hernia has him pegged for a failure."

I bit my tongue. Lying is a sin, isn't it? There was no point in saying anything.

"You could argue," she said, reading my mind.

"Well, not *everyone* thinks he's a failure." Surely the DuBoise twins didn't share that opinion—never mind that they were six months old.

"You're not very convincing, Mags." She started to boohoo again. The minimonster in her bra joined in the racket, but was several keys off.

"I'm doing my best," I wailed. "I can't create something from nothing. Maybe this depression is only a phase. I talked to him just this morning, and he seemed excited about watching one of those reality shows."

"Mags, you promise not to kill me if I tell you what he did yesterday?"

"Of course I won't kill you, dear—you know that. What did he do, sort a bag of M&M's into alphabetical order?"

"That was only the one time. You promise you won't even get mad?"

I sighed. "I'll try not to. But I'm only human, despite what my critics say. Tell me quickly before I lose my resolve."

"Melvin bought a new car."

"He *what*?"

"You promised not to be mad. And anyway, it's not like I had anything to do with this. He came home driving this thirty-thousand-dollar car and—"

"*Thirty* thousand?"

"Mags, that's barely a luxury car these days. And besides, your car cost that much."

"Yes, but I've earned the right to drive a car like that. Where did Melvin get the money?"

"You're such a goofball, Mags. You don't need money anymore. Credit is what it's all about. That, and zero percent financing. And anyway, you're missing my point."

"Which is?"

"My sweetiekins is going through a midlife crisis. I'm scared, Mags. Yesterday it was a car, but tomorrow it could be that new waitress at the Sausage Barn."

"I've never seen her. Is she cute?"

"Mags!"

"All right, I'm thinking. What if I convinced him that we still needed him as chief?"

"Would you?"

"If you'll stop crying."

"Oh, Mags, you're the best sister ever!" She threw herself into my arms, precipitating a plethora of pips from the pitiful pooch. I pushed her away as soon as possible.

"I have a job too, dear."

"Can I help?" she asked gratefully.

"I doubt it. I'm going to examine all the chili pots, kettles, and tureens to see if there are any I don't recognize, on the theory that the killer may have been able to slip into the kitchen unnoticed. Then after the murder, he, or she, was unable to retrieve his or her dish without drawing attention to him- or herself." Heaven bless the grammarian who decides that "their" and "them" are acceptable as singular pronouns.

"But Mags, what if it wasn't murder? What if someone innocently put peanut butter into their own chili? I put peanuts into just about everything I cook."

"That would be hot-fudge sundaes, dear. Besides, everyone in the congregation is acutely aware of the fact that Reverend Schrock is—was—very allergic to peanuts. There's a big notice posted in the kitchen, and it's been in the bulletin a number of times. If you were still a member, you'd know that."

I swept off to the social hall and Susannah trotted behind me. The remnants of last night's dinner were spread over a multitude of tables and into the kitchen. Now that the chili was cold and congealed, it was an unappetizing sight. I hardly knew where to start.

"That's LaVerna Koenig's pot," Susannah said, pointing to the first container we came to.

"Excuse me?"

"See how the handle is broken off on one side? It's been that way since I was a little girl."

"You may be right, but—"

"And that's Nancy Beiler's."

"That's new. You can't possibly have seen that pot before."

"No need to, Mags. Nancy Beiler is the only person I know who uses navy beans in her chili, instead of kidney. And over there is Mildred Troyer's concoction—I'd hardly call it chili. You can tell it's hers because of the inch of grease on top. And that dry-looking stuff . . ."

Between the two of us, Susannah and I were able to identify every one of the cooks who had contributed to the dinner. With only one exception (Clifford Waldron is a widower with a knack for spices), they were upstanding churchwomen. I told my sister that if any of them had tried to harm Reverend Schrock, I'd eat my hat. Thank heavens I keep one of the pillbox variety—but made of bread dough—in my freezer.

Before I left to continue my investigation elsewhere, Susannah thanked me a dozen more times. She insisted on hugging me again, which, I assure you, was not good for Shnookums's health a few of those times. And although my sister begged to accompany me to my next destination, I adamantly refused. Correctly identifying cold chili does not make her a sleuth, and besides, as with hugging, there is just so much sisterhood that a body can take.

Following up on Edwina's accusation, that Reverend Schrock had been having an affair, was the act of a desperate woman. Especially since there were no unidentifiable pots left behind at the church. But I had just recently purchased a Crown Victoria with genuine leather seats and a six-CD changer in the trunk. Driving my new acquisition was still highly pleasurable, and as long as I kept both hands on the steering wheel, surely it was not a sin. Before I started out for Bedford, I put on my favorite Russell Watson album, *The Voice*. I don't normally listen to secular music, but since most of the lyrics on this album were sung in Italian, I figured there wasn't much chance they would impact my soul.

By the time I reached Happy Backs Massage Parlor, I was uncharacteristically happy myself. So mellow was I that when a Grand Am slipped into the last available parking space, just as I reached it, I merely smiled and waved. Let that rude woman get my spot; after all, she couldn't afford to drive a car as nice as mine.

So what if I had to parallel park and walk two blocks? Walking is good exercise—just as long as one does not needlessly spend the finite number of movements allotted to one at birth. My point is that I was still quite happy when I walked into Happy Backs. The fact that my mood deteriorated rapidly was certainly not my fault.

"Hello," I said to the receptionist, who had just hung up the phone.

"Yeah, hi," she said, and turned to another girl who was filing folders behind the counter. Both girls were short, brunet, and on the chunky side. I silently dubbed them Anti-Barbie 1 and Anti-Barbie 2.

"Excuse me, dear. I'm looking for a woman named Clarisse Thompson."

Anti-Barbie 1 held up a shushing finger and turned to her coworker. "We have fifteen minutes to put our order in if we want lunch delivered by twelve. I'm getting the Monster Burger, with a side of onion rings, and an order of supersize cheese fries. Have you decided yet?"

Anti-Barbie 2 scratched her chin with the corner of a folder. "I had the Monster Burger yesterday. Do they still have the Bacon-Swiss-Cheddar-Colby-Monterey-Jack-Muenster Melt? If not, I'd like the Super Macho Meat Tacos with the jumbo cheese fries. And a diet cola, of course."

"Of course."

They both laughed.

"Excuse me, ladies, but I only need a second of your time."

Anti-Barbie 1 gave me a look that would have freeze-dried her Monster Burger. "You need to learn how to wait," she snapped.

"I've waited less time for head colds to clear," I said pleasantly, and without further ado opened a door to my right and sailed on through.

"Hey, you can't go in there without an appointment," one or the other of the Anti-Barbies yelled, but I knew that she wouldn't follow me. Not with a deadline looming on her cheese fries.

Although the Anti-Barbies had robbed me of my happy spirit in the anteroom, I found it again in what I can liken only to paradise. I'd entered a large room painted a soothing shade of green. Straight ahead, partially hidden by potted palms, was a rock waterfall that produced the most melodious sound imaginable. Scattered about were padded lounging chairs, upon which reclined somnolent people wrapped in thick terry robes. But what really got the cake was a table loaded with doughnuts and other pastries, as well as a sinful array of flavored coffees.

Before continuing my search, I poured myself a large hazelnut decaf, and helped myself to three glazed doughnuts from the pile. Ever since I was trapped in a wrecked car for several days, my philosophy of life has been to eat, and tinkle, whenever an opportunity presents itself. Just as soon as I was done with my snack, I would look for the bathroom.

I was deliberating on the wisdom of downing a fourth doughnut, when a voice from behind surprised me.

"Are you here for the Ultimate?"

I wiped the telltale flakes of sugar from my lips before turning. There was no way to hide the coffee cup.

8

"I'm here to see Clarisse Thompson."

"That's me." She was a large woman with a pleasant enough face and was dressed in green scrubs and white, nurse-style shoes.

"Do you have a minute? We need to talk."

She laughed. "Miss Englebrect, right? You're down for two hours. We'll have plenty of time to talk."

"But I—"

"And by the way, congratulations on winning the free Ultimate. When you leave here, you'll feel like a different woman—look like one too. Well, shall we get started?"

Is it a lie if someone presumes something about you, and you don't contradict them? I think not! I mean, folks are forever thinking I'm crabby, when I'm really not. And what about women who've had plastic surgery to make themselves look younger, or even those who just dye their hair? Of course they're not lying.

"By all means, dear. Let's get started," I said.

She motioned for me to follow her down a long hall, which I did, still toting the empty coffee cup. After passing several closed doors, she stopped and opened one. Inside was a long high table, over which were draped several thick, fluffy towels.

"Take everything off—there are hooks on the back of the door—

and then lay on your stomach, with the towels over you. I'll be back in a few minutes."

"I beg your pardon? Did you say *everything*?"

She smiled. "It's customary."

"Not for me, it isn't. There are parts of me even the Good Lord hasn't seen."

"Then feel free to leave your panties and bra on."

"And my slip!"

"Miss Englebrect, I assure you that—well, I have no interest in you as a woman. And if it will make you more comfortable, I won't even look at you while I'm massaging. But you see, I use a wonderful, relaxing herbal oil, and I'd hate to see your things stained."

"Will the towels stay on?"

"Absolutely. But I do put my hands under them. If you become uncomfortable, just say so, and I'll back off."

"Remind me, dear—just how much would this Ultimate have cost if I hadn't won it?"

"Five hundred. Plus tax."

"*Dollars?*"

She nodded.

"Times a-wasting!" I cried gaily.

Clarisse Thompson was right; the herbal oil was indeed relaxing. I might even have drifted off to sleep, had I not felt a need for vigilance. Idle hands may be the Devil's playground, but Clarisse's hands were the Devil's play*things*. Heaven forfend I should suddenly find myself enjoying a game of tetherball while using the other team's equipment—so to speak.

To keep myself awake, and my thoughts pure, I decided to begin my interview. "I hear that Reverend Schrock comes here sometimes, dear."

Was I imagining her fingers tensing? "Yes, he does. He's such a nice man, don't you think?"

"Salt of the earth. Does he ever get the Ultimate?"

"Oh no. Reverend Schrock has back problems. Miss Englebrect, I hope you don't mind, but I really shouldn't be discussing other clients. By the way, how do you know him?"

"He's my pastor, dear. Or was, I should say."

"Excuse me?"

"Well, him being dead—I really should stop using the present tense. But it's hard, if you know what I mean."

There followed a very long, pregnant pause. I wondered if I should say more.

"When did he die?" she finally asked, her voice barely a whisper.

"Yesterday evening."

She stopped massaging. "Was it his heart?"

"No, peanuts. A severe allergic reaction, I'm afraid."

"I see." She'd been working on my shoulders, which she now covered with a towel. My face and head were covered with a towel as well. "If you'll excuse me, Miss Englebrect, I need to check on another client who's soaking in the milk bath. Just lie here while I'm gone and let the oils soak in. Try not to move a muscle—it's better that way. Because if you do, you'll bruise the amino acids in the oils, and they won't be that effective."

"But you've barely begun on me. You still have another hemisphere to do on this side—you haven't even reached the equator. And just so you know, I'm no longer worried about the Tropic of Capricorn."

My exhortations did no good. She left the room, and I had no choice but to lie there, still as a mummy, and wait for her return. I tried to entertain myself by doing my multiplication tables but, having never had a knack for numbers, couldn't get past my sixes. I was about to resort to reciting Scripture when I heard the door open.

"I don't mean to sound critical, Miss Thompson," I said gently, "but by now that milk will have turned into cottage cheese."

Clarisse Thompson didn't answer, but I soon felt her warm hands on my legs. *Very* warm hands. But there was something else too. Something sticky.

"What's that, Miss Thompson?"

"Wax."

"I beg your pardon?"

"You have the hairiest calves I've ever seen, Miss Englebrect."

The voice was not that of Clarisse Thompson. At the risk of bruising my oils, I shrugged off the towel. It was Anti-Barbie 1!

"Where's Clarisse Thompson? And what do you think you're doing?"

"Miss Thompson had an emergency. She asked me to wax your legs."

"I don't want them waxed. The Good Lord put the hair there, so that's how he wants it."

She continued to slather my leg with molten wax. "Miss Englebrect specifically requested a leg wax."

"But I'm not Miss Englebrect! I mean—I've changed my mind."

"There's nothing to be afraid of, Miss Englebrect." She slathered my other leg while I lay pondering my dilemma.

I couldn't very well run out of there with wax on my legs—not unless I wanted to be put on display at Madame Tussaud's. Neither could I blow my cover. But wait. Even if the wax job was on my schedule, someone would have first completed the massage. There was no doubt about it; Clarisse Thompson had figured out I was an impostor, and had sent in Anti-Barbie 1 to torture me.

"Stop! I can explain everything."

"There's no need to explain anything, Miss Englebrect." She let go of my leg. "There. We just need to let that cool for a minute."

I rolled over and sat up. Somehow the towels stayed behind, causing me to scramble. Fortunately, I was more angry than embarrassed.

"You're not going to get away with this."

"Is that so? What are you going to do, tell the police you tried to cheat Miss Englebrect out of a five-hundred-dollar gift certificate?"

"But I am—"

"You're Magdalena Yoder—that's who you are."

"How do you know?"

"Connie—she's the one who does the billing—thought she recognized you. Said her mama goes to your church, and told her that you think you're really something on account of you own some kind of hotel down in Hernia. So I checked the records and gave the real Miss Englebrect a call. Seems that she had forgotten all about her appointment."

"For your information, dear, the PennDutch is a full-board inn, not a hotel. And what kind of a receptionist ignores customers while she plans her lunch? By the way, how was the Monster Burger? I can tell you already enjoyed the onion rings."

Her response was to rip off a strip of hardened wax. Words cannot adequately describe the pain. Forget about Hell having fire and brimstone. I'm now convinced that the Devil spends his days ripping wax off the bodies of hirsute sinners. Blessed are the smooth of skin, if you ask me.

Not wanting to go out into the world like I was, half woolly and half smooth, I submitted to the entire treatment. You can be sure I did not do so quietly. Having exhausted my arsenal of bad words ("ding," "dang," "dong"), I borrowed a few from Susannah.

When the ordeal was over my legs smarted so bad that I couldn't put my stockings back on. Wincing with pain, I tottered back through the lobby while Anti-Barbies 1 and 2 twittered. As the door closed behind me, I thought I heard Anti-Barbie 1 talk about ordering supper.

Someone was going to pay for the pain and indignity I had just suffered, and it might as well be Wanda Hemphopple. A liberal Mennonite, Wanda lives in Hernia, but runs and owns a restaurant out by the turnpike. The Sausage Barn has long been ahead of diet fads. "Fat's where it's at" is printed on top of every menu, and Wanda claims Dr. Atkins stopped by for breakfast years ago, when he was still a nobody.

It is no secret that Wanda and I rub each other the wrong way, although mine is the right way, I assure you. At any rate, Wanda was filling in as hostess that day, and when she saw me her beady eyes brightened.

"Well, well, look what the cat dragged in."

"I decided to risk my health yet again and get some lunch."

She grabbed a plastic-coated menu, but let it slip through her fingers. "Magdalena! You're not wearing any stockings."

I gazed down at my gams, and not without admiration, mind you. "So I'm not. What do you think?"

"Isn't going bare-legged some kind of sin in your church?"

"Maybe it is, maybe it isn't. What business is it of yours?"

"I'm only saying this as a friend, Magdalena, but aren't you afraid of being branded a hussy?"

"I'll have to take my chances, dear. And anyway, I don't plan to do this every day. I just got my legs waxed."

Wanda's peepers widened with horror. "*That* has got to be a sin in your church."

"It happened by accident," I wailed. "I'm sure the Good Lord understands."

"Hmm."

"You should try it yourself, dear. I hear they do upper lips."

"Really?"

"But I must warn you. It hurts like the dickens. It feels like being skinned alive—not that I've experienced a whole lot of that, mind you."

She shuddered, which in her case is a dangerous thing. It was Wanda who invented the beehive hairdo back when the Good Lord Himself was just a boy, and I don't think she's washed it since. Like the Tower of Babel, Wanda's do strives to reach the heavens. Should Hemphopple's tower topple, Hernia could be obliterated by an avalanche of dandruff and assorted vermin. Rumor even has it that the U.S. military has been begging Wanda to travel to various hot spots in the world and let down her hair. I did not start that particular rumor, by the way. I merely passed it on.

"So, Wanda, are you going to seat me or not?"

"Do I have a choice?"

"No."

"In that case, do you want your favorite booth back by the kitchen, or would you like to sit across from your future mother-in-law?"

"She's *here*?"

Wanda nodded, while I contemplated ducking for cover. "She and Doc Shafor are behaving shamelessly over there in booth seventeen. For a while they were playing footsies, but she's so short she slipped off the banquette. Made quite a scene."

"Across from them," I said, and grabbed my own menu from the counter.

*   *   *

Doc's smile and Ida's scowl would have canceled each other out, but I threw another scowl into the mix. "What on earth are you two doing eating here?"

Ida snorted. "Eating. Vhát else?"

"But Doc's an excellent cook, and even you—well, the food here is edible, but it's certainly not first-rate."

"I heard that!" Wanda hollered.

I rearranged my scowl into the vaguest of smiles. "Be a dear," I said to my future mother-law, "and scoot over—no, never mind. I'll just slide in next to Doc."

"Vhy, I never!"

"That's not what I hear, dear. The word is you and Doc have been doing everything imaginable, including swinging from the chandelier."

Doc laughed. "Chandeliers are overrated. Ida sprained her back and we both took a pretty bad tumble when it broke loose from the ceiling."

Of course I was scandalized, but curiosity is a God-given quality, so it is our religious duty to practice it from time to time.

"You *really* swung from a chandelier?"

Doc nodded. He didn't even have the decency to look sheepish.

"Zee rafters vere much more sturdy," Ida said before shoveling a forkful of scrambled egg into her painted maw.

"Doc, I'm shocked," I finally said. "Do you know that the entire town is talking about you two?"

He had the audacity to wink. "It could have been you and me, Magdalena."

"No, it couldn't have. And aren't you in the least bit concerned about your reputation? Or Belinda's memory?"

"My wife's been dead for twenty years. What I do now has nothing to do with her memory. As for my reputation—I'm eighty-six years old. Why should I care what these whippersnappers think?"

Ida jerked to attention, causing her considerable bosoms to spill over onto her syrup-covered plate. "Vhat? You said you vere seventy-six."

Doc reached for one of her stubby hands, but she yanked it

away. "Does it make a difference?" he asked. "The equipment still works, doesn't it? Okay, so maybe we have to wait a few minutes between—"

"T.M.I.!" I cried. I took a gulp of Doc's water. "Maybe the two of you have no shame, but Gabriel is mortified by what you two are doing. You could at least think of him."

Ida hoisted her bosoms off her plate, trailing strings of sticky syrup. "So vhat are you saying? My son doesn't vant that I should be happy?"

"I'm sure he wants you to be happy, dear. But you don't have to be happy in front of the town. Some kinds of happiness are meant to be kept private."

"Like you should know."

I am sick and tired of defending myself. I had no idea Aaron Miller was already married when I walked down the makeshift aisle in my barn. And not that it's anyone's business, but we never once swung from those rafters. Even if they were mighty sturdy. At any rate, I simply refused to respond to Ida's goad.

"Doc," I said, and laid my hand gently on his wiry arm, "isn't there anything that can be done about Edwina Bishop's face?"

He shook his head. "I'm only a vet, but from what I've read, those nerves are severed forever. Pity, isn't it? Now, there was a looker—but not as handsome as you," he added quickly for Ida's benefit.

She was pretty quick herself. "You call me handsome?"

"It's a generational thing," I said wickedly. "For men as old as Doc, 'handsome' and 'beautiful' are interchangeable. But then, given your age, you probably already know that."

"Down, girl," Doc whispered. "She may be a lot of fun, but she's no match for the likes of you."

"Vhat did you say?" She seemed to be addressing both of us.

I stepped up to bat. "He said—why, ding, dang, dong! You'll never guess who just walked in that door."

9

"Well, I'll be," Doc said. "If it isn't Noah Miller. I haven't seen him since—well, since your pastor sent him up the river."

"He wasn't just my pastor, and he didn't send him up the river."

"Oy, such riddles."

"Look," Doc said. "Wanda's refusing to seat him."

"She wouldn't dare."

But Wanda Hemphopple had indeed turned her back on the waiting man, and was tapping her foot and humming to herself. When Sam Ediger stepped up to pay his family's bill, Wanda turned around just long enough to handle the transaction. The same thing happened when the Neubranders and the Leises presented their checks.

"So vhat eez dis man, a criminal?" Ida demanded.

"Some would say," Doc said.

"That's nonsense," I said. "Noah Miller didn't kill those two girls. He was wrongly imprisoned, Doc, and you know it."

"A murderer yet!" Ida's eyes shone with what might well have been excitement. She glanced at Doc, then back at Noah, as if she couldn't make up her mind.

I'd had enough. "Hey, Noah," I called. "Get your ark over here."

So many forks dropped at once that the resultant noise was deafening. I had to jiggle a pinkie in my ear to get my hearing back. Alas, the first words I heard were Wanda's.

"That man is not allowed in my restaurant."

I slid out of the lovebirds' booth and stretched to my full, but not very intimidating, self. "Noah Miller is my guest, Wanda."

"He's a killer, and he's not welcome."

"He was found innocent. You know that. If his money isn't good here, then neither is mine."

Wanda rested her fists on hips that were ample enough for two. "That's fine with me."

I pointed at Doc. "Then neither is his."

"Doc never comes in by himself, anyway. Only when he has some tart in tow."

"Tart? Oy, another riddle, and this one about food."

I gestured in Ida's direction. "And the tart's money isn't any good either." I jumped sideways to the next booth. "Now take Dwayne Gerber here and his wife—both of whom, if I may be frank, are obviously fond of eating."

"What about them?" Wanda snapped.

"If you don't serve Noah, these fine people—and these cute tubby kids of theirs—will never darken the doorway of this establishment again."

"What?" the Gerbers cried like a Greek chorus.

I glared at Dwayne. "Remember last spring when your roof leaked? You borrowed five thousand dollars from me, and have yet to pay back a single penny."

"Serve the man," Dwayne said to Wanda.

Wanda jabbed a pencil into her teetering beehive. I knew I wasn't the only one who perceived that as a threat, because a collective gasp deprived the room of its oxygen. By the way, there is nothing like a threat to hike my hackles.

I fumbled in my bag for my cell phone. "I'm sure the board of health will be interested in that dead rat you found in the cooler."

It was Wanda's turn to gasp. "How did you know?"

The truth is I hadn't known. Not for sure. But given that the layers of grease on the walls of the kitchen betrayed its age, much like the layers of a tree trunk, it was a pretty safe assumption that rodents found their way into the kitchen on a regular basis. From the kitchen to the walk-in cooler was only the next logical step.

"I have my ways," I said quite honestly. "So what will it be, Wanda? Should I be a rat fink, or do you want to reconsider your serving policy?"

"He can stay," she grunted, "but if he kills somebody, their blood is on your hands."

I wasn't expecting applause, and indeed there was none. But neither did I expect half the patrons to either wolf down their food or leave their meals uneaten. On the bright side, Noah Miller had his choice of tables. After bidding adieu to Hernia's oldest couple, I joined the town's most hated resident for a second breakfast.

I can eat breakfast at any hour of the day, and apparently so can Noah Miller. He ordered his eggs sunny-side up, while I ordered mine poached hard. Other than that, our meals were identical. Lots of bacon fried crisp on the ends, but with a little play in the middle, whole wheat toast with butter and grape jelly, fresh squeezed orange juice from a can, and coffee with so much cream and sugar in it, the spoon could stand on end.

"So tell me," I said after licking the last of the bacon grease off my fingers, "what prompted you to come here today? Aren't you supposed to be home sleeping?"

"It's because of you," he said.

"I beg your pardon?"

"Miss Yoder, until you came by this morning, I'd pretty much given up on this burg. You might ask why I didn't just move someplace else, like maybe a big city. But you see, Hernia is all I know. And yeah, I acted like a bully when I was growing up, but I'm really kind of a shy guy. It was easier for me to stay here, go to work each night, and stick to myself during the days. Yeah, some people hate me— they honk their cars in front of my house when I'm trying to sleep— but it's not like I could keep my incarceration a secret in a big city. My record will follow me everywhere I go, even though it's expunged. I'll always have a time gap to explain. Anyway, then you came by this morning acting like Jesus, and I thought, what the heck, maybe there's more decent folks in Hernia than I was giving it credit for."

"I hardly think I was acting like Jesus. I came to interrogate you about a possible murder."

"Yeah, but you came in and sat down. That's something Jesus would have done."

That was the first time anyone had ever compared me to the Lord. I wasn't deserving of the comparison, but I knew what he meant. If Jesus had chosen to live on earth in my generation, he would no doubt be found among the homeless and those folks whom society discriminates against the most. I believe that in Pennsylvania his friends would include people of color, the obese, and of course homosexuals. Instead of whipping money changers in a temple, he'd most probably turn the whip on tel, evangelists—at least the ones I've seen on TV. And not my own TV, of course.

"How does it feel to be out in the world again?" I asked, not knowing what else to say.

"Great."

"Folks like Wanda don't bother you?"

"Yeah, of course they do. But I got to thinking after you left— which is why I'm not sleeping now—that the same folks will hate and distrust me if I'm home or out trying to enjoy myself. I may as well try and have a good time." He drained his coffee, and immediately refilled it from the thermos pitcher on our table. "Did you talk to Tobias yet?"

"Indeed I have. And I see what the two of you have in common. But it isn't healthy, Noah. Hate only hurts the hater. Look at Wanda—she looks like she's ready to explode. If she does, it could be curtains for the world as we know it."

He smiled over his cup. "When I was in high school we used to call her the Volcano. Once on a dare I tossed a hard-boiled egg into the middle of that bun. Do you think it could still be there?"

"I rather doubt it—but only because my sister's dog ended up in that crater—don't ask me how. I don't think there would have been enough room for Shnookums *and* an egg. At any rate, I took your suggestion and paid Tobias Gindlesperger a visit. Spoke to him in person."

"And?"

"He hated the reverend, all right, but he seemed genuinely shocked to hear of his death."

"Some people are good actors."

"True. But Tobias has so little energy, I'm surprised he's not covered with moss. I don't think he has it in him to sneak through the back door to the church kitchen, add peanut butter to somebody's chili, and get away undetected."

"Hmm."

"You disagree?"

"No, you're probably right. When he comes to visit me, he usually spends the night—to gather enough strength to go home."

"What do you two talk about when he visits?"

"How much we hate the reverend—and how crappy life is." He actually used a much stronger word that, as a Christian, I would never repeat.

"Noah, I can tell you're holding something back."

"What?"

"You tell me."

"How do you know?"

"I have a hunch."

"Never trust a hunch, Miss Yoder. That's one thing I've learned. I had a hunch the jury was going to find me innocent—because I was—but then look what happened."

"Yes, but a hunch from a woman is worth two facts from a man. There's something very important you're not telling me."

He took a sip of coffee and then sighed. "Your precious reverend was hooked on drugs."

"He most certainly was not!"

"Okay, have it your way."

"I don't want it my way. I want the truth."

"You're not capable of hearing the truth."

"Yes, I am!" And I was, just as long as I could get my rational side to tell my emotional side to shut up. Thanks to generations of inbreeding, I am my own cousin. All I had to do was assign my cousin the task of shushing my emotional side. It took a few minutes, but it eventually did the trick. "I'm ready now," I cried. "Trot out the truth."

Noah cleared his throat. "Like I said, he was hooked on drugs."

"You mean painkillers? Like Rush Limbaugh?"

"No, these were illegal drugs—uppers. You know, things to boost his energy level."

"But why? He had such an ideal life. We only required one sermon from him a week. Sure, he had to visit the sick and shut-ins, but it wasn't a high-pressure job by any stretch of the imagination."

"Are you forgetting his wife?"

"Lodema Schrock. How could I forget? But I would think he wanted sleeping pills, not stimulants."

"Touché. But uppers is what he asked for."

"Did you sell him any?"

Noah looked as if I'd slapped him across the face. "I don't sell drugs, Miss Yoder. That's one thing I've never done, and hope never to do."

"I'm sorry," I said. "I didn't mean to offend you. I'm just wondering why the reverend would come to you, then."

"Because I've been in prison. Those were almost his exact words. He figured that anyone who's been through the system would come out either using or dealing. I told him that he had a lot of nerve coming to me after what he did, and that if I ever saw his holier-than-thou face sniffing around my house again, I'd rearrange it for him."

I gasped. I'm not used to such rough language, and besides, this was a dear friend he was talking about.

"Noah!"

"I'm sorry, Miss Yoder. I apologize. But you have to put yourself in my shoes."

"They'd be too small, but apology accepted. Just don't do it again."

"You got it. Miss Yoder, are you seeing someone now?"

"I beg your pardon?"

"Are you dating anyone?"

I could feel my face flush. "Yes, I am. In fact, that's his mother sitting over there with Doc Shafor."

"And here I thought that was Doc's mother. Well, you certainly have my sympathy."

As a native Hernian, Noah Miller had to have known that Doc's mother had been dead so long that her halo needed polishing.

Clearly his comment about Ida had been meant to cheer me up. For that I was grateful, but there was something I needed to explain.

"First of all, the man I'm dating doesn't look anything like that. And secondly"—I waved my ring hand—"I'm engaged to be married."

"No matter what he looks like, if you get tired of him—well, you know where to reach me."

I won't deny that I was flattered. And having an ex-con for a boyfriend would not only scandalize the community but have Mama and Papa spinning in their graves so fast, the earth would be in danger of tilting off its axis. These weren't necessarily bad things, mind you. But I was deeply in love with the Babester, and if I could survive his mother, I had every intention of spending the rest of my life with the hunk from Manhattan.

Having thanked Noah for his generous offer, I paid our bill, tipped our waitress, and then slipped Wanda a fifty-dollar bill.

"What's that?"

"Just a little something for your kindness."

"But I wasn't kind," she shouted.

As everyone in the restaurant turned to stare, I skipped merrily through the door.

The parsonage is a white gingerbread Victorian on a corner lot in the historic district of Hernia, only a sugar bowl toss from Edwina Bishop's house—a fact that has got to irritate the woman of many marriages. At any rate, I parked in a pile of fallen maple leaves. Our deceased spiritual leader was not big on yard work, which means he usually waited until some bighearted parishioner stepped up to do the job. You can be sure that Lodema never touched a rake.

There was a car with Ohio tags parked in the driveway, a fancy-schmancy late-model Oldsmobile with genuine leather seats and spoke hubcaps. Frankly, I was surprised to see it. Ordinarily one might assume that a widow would be swamped with well-wishers bearing casseroles, but this was Lodema Schrock after all. "What ye sow, so shall ye reap," the Bible says, and by the looks of things, our pastor's wife had planted very little.

I rang the doorbell, prepared to dodge Lodema's lacerating lingua, so I was pleasantly surprised when it was answered by the driver of the Oldsmobile.

"Hello. My name is—"

"Flowers should be delivered at the church," she said, and started to close the door.

What better use can size eleven feet be put to than to serve as doorstops? Over the years my littlest piggy has developed calluses that protect it from all but the most severe punishment. Unsure what was preventing the door from closing, Lodema's guest opened it again to take a look. Taking advantage of her curiosity and my bony frame, I slipped past her and sailed on into the parlor.

"Like I was saying, I'm Magdalena Yoder."

She was right behind me. "And like I was saying, we're not accepting deliveries."

"I'm not here to deliver flowers, dear. I'm here to deliver sympathy."

She would have been an attractive woman had it not been for her wide-open mouth. I was tempted to dash outside, find a nice fat earthworm, and pop it into her gaping maw. Fortunately for her, she closed it before I could act on my fantasy.

"Uh—uh—are you a friend of Lodema?"

"That would be an overstatement. I'm a member of Beechy Grove Mennonite Church."

"What did you say your name was again?"

I told her.

She smiled, confirming my diagnosis of beauty. "Of course I've heard of you. Arnold used to talk about you all the time."

"Only good things, I hope."

"He said you were quite a character. But it was obvious my brother was very fond of you. The backbone of his congregation, he called you."

"Reverend Schrock was your brother?"

"My baby brother. He was six years younger. A real pain in the neck too. Our mother used to tell him that she wished that when he grew up he had twin boys just as ornery as he was. Of course he and Lodema never had children."

"Thank heavens for that—I mean, at least there are no bereaved children."

"I like you," she said, taking me quite by surprise. "Won't you please have a seat?"

"Does it come with hot chocolate?"

"If you can stand instant from a packet."

"That'll do in a pinch. But do be a dear and try and pinch some marshmallows from the cupboard. I know Lodema keeps them on hand, because they always appear on her casseroles. By the way, I didn't catch your name."

"Catherine. I'm from Cincinnati. Be right back with your cocoa."

The mug she returned with looked like it had been capped with an igloo. I knew we could be friends.

"Magdalena, it was really nice of you to drop by—considering."

I had to pluck a few marshmallows from the top just to give me room to slurp. "Considering what?"

She glanced at the stairs. "Considering," she said, starting to whisper, "that Lodema is about the least likable person on earth."

"Actually that distinction goes to Melvin Stoltzfus, our Chief of Police, but Lodema certainly runs a close second. And speaking of nice, what you're doing for her is beyond the pale."

"I'm doing it for Arnold, believe me."

"Doesn't Lodema have any relatives?" It was pitiful just how little I knew about Reverend Schrock's extended family, even though I'd considered him a friend.

"She has a rather large family, but they've elected to stay away until the day of the funeral. If I recall correctly, you're a detective or something. You wouldn't happen to know why they're not releasing the body, would you?"

Extra marshmallows, and now a compliment. Catherine and I were destined to be bosom buddies.

"I'm not really a detective—I just help out our nincompoop Chief of Police. But do you mean to say Lodema didn't tell you?"

"Well, I know it was probably the peanut butter that killed him, but she said something about it being a possible murder. Is that true?"

I shrugged my bony shoulders. "Lodema claims—and I'd have

to concur—that virtually everyone in Hernia knew your brother was allergic to peanuts. This is a small town, and clergymen are expected to attend all public events. There have been 'Peanut Free' signs at these gatherings for years. Of course, it's possible that someone forgot and slipped up."

"But what you're saying is that it is also possible that someone wanted him dead."

"Anything is possible in this fallen world of ours. But hey, as soon as I hear anything, I'll let you know."

"I'd appreciate that." She sounded on the verge of tears.

What an insensitive jerk I'd been. I hadn't given her any sympathy at all. All I'd done was to ask for a hot beverage. If it hadn't been for five hundred years of inbreeding, which had eliminated the gene for hugging, I would have thrown my bony arms around the woman and held her to my mammary-challenged breast.

"I'm so sorry," I said, better late than ever. "Your brother was a wonderful man."

She nodded. "Arnold was the best. This will sound awful, Magdalena, but he deserved far better than Lodema."

"True. But that's one of the things that made him such a good person—he took his marriage vows seriously."

"I wish I wouldn't have allowed her to keep me away so much."

"Where is she now?"

"In bed."

"Do you think it would be all right if I went up and spoke with her?"

"I think that would be very nice—but I have to warn you—"

"She might try and snap my head off?"

"There must be *something* nice about her, something Arnold saw."

"Maybe there was." That was as charitable as I could get.

She smiled thinly. "It's the second room on the right, at the top of the stairs."

I took the steps slowly, not because they were steep, but because I felt like I was about to enter a lion's den. When I peered into the open doorway of the master bedroom, I nearly dropped my teeth. And just so you know, I don't wear dentures.

10

Chili and Dumplings

Source: ICS Admin
Submitted by: www.chilicookoff.com

Ingredients:

*4 to 6 servings of your favorite
     chili*
2 cups Bisquick baking mix
⅔ cup milk

Instructions:

Heat chili in large pot to near boiling. Combine baking mix and milk until a soft dough forms. Drop by spoonfuls into hot chili. Simmer at low heat, uncovered, for 10 minutes. Cover and cook 10 minutes.

Servings: 12 dumplings

11

My pastor's widow was standing on her bed, dressed in a wedding gown. The room smelled of onions and lavender, no doubt the product of years of storage in the back of a closet. Lodema's face was fully veiled, so I couldn't make out her features. She, however, had no problem seeing me.

"Magdalena, who invited you to my wedding?"

"Excuse me?"

"You're not on the guest list. My father is paying good money for the reception, and he won't stand for any interlopers."

Clearly the woman had flipped her lid. I'd heard of grieving folks going around the bend, but up until then had no firsthand experience. Fortunately for Lodema, it hadn't been a long trip.

"Consider the source," Mama always said. For once I decided to take her advice.

"I'm not on the list, dear, because I'm not a guest. I'm your maid of honor."

"Nonsense."

I chuckled pleasantly. "You're always such a kidder, Lodema. That's what everybody likes about you."

"Really?"

"A regular barrelful of monkeys."

"So if you're my maid of honor, Magdalena, why aren't you dressed up?"

"We agreed that I would wait until the last minute, so that I could help you first. After all, you're the star of the show."

"Where are the rest of my bridesmaids?"

"They're getting dressed, just like you told them to. Okay, Lodema, you can get off the bed now. I'm finished pinning up your dress."

"Pardon me?"

"What a tease. That's why you're on the bed, silly. Your gown was dragging a little bit in the back."

She held out her hand, so I could help her off the bed. Her skin was cool and dry, like that of a snake—not that I've felt a lot of those, mind you. She hopped to the floor with a suppressed grunt, and immediately began rearranging her skirts.

"Where did you put my shoes, Magdalena?"

I didn't let go of her hand. "Well, there is a box—just a minute. Catherine," I called toward the door, "can you please come up here?"

Lodema tugged slightly, but didn't try to get away. "Who is Catherine?"

"Your sister-in-law. I mean, she's about to become that."

"Arnold's sister?"

"Brad Pitt's sister."

"Really?"

"No. Sorry. I was yanking your chain. Yes, it's Arnold's sister."

"Is she one of my bridesmaids?"

"Sort of. Catherine," I bellowed, "get your patooty up here now!"

Catherine thundered up the stairs. She stopped at the doorway with a jerk when she saw Lodema.

"Oh, my heavens!"

I forced the corners of my mouth to turn up. "Doesn't Lodema look beautiful?"

"But she's wearing—"

"Now, Catherine, we don't want to be responsible for getting her to the church late, do we? So be a dear and grab her other hand, so we can help her down the stairs. Sideways, of course."

The good woman, bless her heart, was only a few heartbeats behind. She blinked twice, and then obediently took Lodema's free hand in hers.

Although Lodema offered no resistance, she was remarkably chatty. "But what about your bridesmaid dress? Oh, and you did remember to pick up my bouquet from the florist, didn't you? I just love gardenias. I would have had just gardenias, but Father can be so cheap sometimes. 'Put lots of ferns and baby's breath in it,' he told the girl. Well, just you wait until he dies. Plastic flowers, that's what I'll order for his funeral. After all, there's no point in using live flowers for someone who's dead. How are they supposed to tell the difference? If he's in Hell—that's where I expect him to go—he'll have more important things on his mind. And if he does manage to make it into Heaven, he won't care one whit about flowers. Not real ones. They probably have golden ones up there."

I jumped in as soon as I could. "My dress is waiting for me at the church, remember?"

"So we're going to the church," Catherine said, and gave me the business with her eyebrows.

"Ix-nay on the urch-chay," I grunted without moving my lips. "E're-way oing-gay to the unny-fay arm-fay."

Lodema chortled. "I just love the sound of Pennsylvania Dutch. Speak some more, Magdalena, will you?"

I'd forgotten that Lodema was a pure Mennonite of German extraction (from Missouri to boot), and not descended through the Swiss Amish like yours truly. My grandparents spoke Pennsylvania Dutch at home, and although I grew up being able to understand it, I can speak only a few words. Clearly that was not going to be a problem.

"Ou're-yay uts-nay, ear-day."

"Oony-lay unes-tay," Catherine said, getting into the spirit of things.

We continued yapping to Lodema in pig Latin as we guided her downstairs and steered her to Catherine's car. Without the slightest bit of resistance, she allowed us to strap her into the backseat. I climbed in the front to ride shotgun.

"Ere-whay is the ental-may ospital-hay?" Catherine asked.

Having never had need of it, I hadn't the foggiest where the Bedford County facility was. Instead, I gave her directions to Hernia Hospital, which is really just a glorified private clinic run by a despotic doctor and an exceedingly nasty nurse. On the way there Lodema decided that she too spoke Pennsylvania Dutch, but nothing she said made any sense, except for *"Ich bin ein Berliner."*

When we arrived at the clinic she allowed us to help her out of the car and escort her into the waiting room, just as meekly as if she'd been Mother Teresa. She remained calm, although a bit wide-eyed behind her veil, when Nurse Ratched stormed through the pair of swinging doors that separated the common area from the inner sanctum.

Nurse Ratched's real name is Nurse Dudley. She's a behemoth of a woman, with a football player's shoulders, and it always surprises me to see that she doesn't wear a helmet with horns on it. Alas, the massive matron eschews my innards, even though I have never knowingly done anything to irritate her. When she saw me standing there, one fist closed around the bride's wrist, her eyes lit up demonically.

"What have you done now?" she roared.

"Nothing. This is Lodema Schrock."

Lodema giggled. "I'm not Mrs. Schrock yet."

"She's uts-nay," I hastened to explain. "Onkers-bay."

"Spent too much time hanging around you, I see."

I smiled patiently. "She needs to be looked at by an octor-day."

Nurse Ratched snorted. "Dr. Luther is busy."

"She needs elp-hay," I persisted.

Lodema wrenched free from my grasp and lifted her veil. "Is this the church?"

There was no purpose served by telling her the truth. "Yes, isn't it lovely?"

"It's very different from the churches in Missouri."

"We have different traditions here. Now if you'll just go with this nice lady (I tried not to choke), she'll show you where the bride's room is."

Nurse Ratched stomped a foot the size of Maine. "I will not be part of this nonsense!"

I rubbed my thumb and index finger together. "Weren't we discussing a five-hundred-dollar donation to your favorite charity?"

Nurse Ratched is her own favorite charity, and as its CEO can be remarkably pragmatic. "Make it a thousand dollars and I'll show her to the bridal *suite.*"

Of course she demanded the money right then and there. While I wrote out a check with three painful zeros, Lodema hummed the wedding march. Meanwhile Catherine, a newcomer to Hernia high jinks, stared wide-eyed at the proceedings.

"There," I said, ripping a check out of my book and dropping it onto an outstretched hand the size of Minnesota, "she's all yours."

"You mean I'm marrying *her*?" Lodema asked, sounding surprisingly pleased.

I grabbed Catherine's elbow and maneuvered her out the front door before Nurse Ratched came to her senses and demanded more money.

"What's going to happen to her now?" Catherine asked on the way back to her brother's house.

"That's Nurse Ratched—uh—Dudley's problem."

"She's my brother's widow. I can't help feeling responsible for her."

"Don't worry. Nurse Dudley and Dr. Luther will know what to do. But maybe you should call her relatives and fill them in."

"Has she ever acted like this before? Arnold never said anything about her being delusional."

"She's always acted hostile—at least to me. But no, I've never seen her quite this nutty. My guess is that losing her one true friend is what's sent her over the edge."

Catherine sighed deeply. "Poor Arnold. Imagine having to live with her all these years."

"I'd rather not. I have nightmares as it is."

"If only I'd known, I could have been a better sister."

"I take it you and your brother weren't very close."

"Actually we were. We talked on the phone all the time—it's just that I seldom came here to visit."

"Can't say that I blame you."

We drove in blessed silence for a few minutes. "Magdalena," she said, breaking my reverie, "did Arnold have any enemies?"

"Well—I—uh—I thought he was the salt of the earth, mind you. But there were a few people—and there are crackpots even in Hernia—who thought he'd either failed them or double-crossed them."

"Like Edwina Bishop?"

"Whom did you say?"

"Edwina Bishop. Arnold used to joke about how all the unmarried ladies in his congregation chased after him—except for you, of course."

"Of course." Thank heavens she couldn't read my mind. While it was true that I had never chased after my pastor, I once saw him without his shirt at a church picnic. Someone had spilled lemonade all over him and—well, never mind, that part's not important. The thing is that for several days afterward I was plagued by impure thoughts, and the only way I could rid myself of them was to volunteer at a nursing home.

"Anyway," Catherine continued, "my brother implied that Edwina Bishop made a particular nuisance of herself."

"But she's not an unmarried lady. Au contraire, she's been married almost as many times as the Samaritan woman Jesus met at the well."

"Then these episodes must have occurred between marriages. Arnold mentioned her name several times."

"Hmm."

The rest of the way back to Lodema's house, Catherine told me all about her exciting life in exotic Cincinnati, Ohio. She was a technician at a veterinary clinic, and liked to rock climb. When she wasn't busy working or climbing, she jogged up and down the city's many hills.

I also learned that in Ohio one got a driver's license at the Bureau of Motor Vehicles, not at a police barracks. Buckeyes called their shopping buggies "carts," and their gum bands "rubber bands," and not that I cared in the least, they could buy beer in their supermarkets. I'd been to eastern Ohio but never the southwestern part, and wondered if it was necessary to pack in provisions, like I do when I visit Maryland. Being raised to mind my own business, I wasn't about to ask.

We parted practically friends, and I promised again to keep her posted on the status of the case. When she waved good-bye there was something about the gesture that reminded me of Reverend Schrock. But there was no time for sadness, not when I needed to speak to Edwina face-to-half-a-face.

It wouldn't have surprised me if Edwina admitted not having moved from her post at the door since I last saw her. Even as I mounted her steps, she swung it open to greet me.

"Back for more cocoa and ladyfingers?"

"I certainly won't refuse, if they're not too much bother."

She ushered me in and then strode off for the kitchen. It was then that I noticed that on the back of her head, the half corresponding to the botched surgery was unkempt. On the beautiful side, the hair had been styled and neatly combed.

There were a number of other things that I noticed this time around. The immaculate interior of Edwina's Victorian home was decorated with what looked to me to be period furniture. Crimson velvet covered the settee and its companion chairs, which felt like they contained the original horsehair stuffing. Doilies, slightly yellowed with age, dotted the back and arms of each piece like giant snowflakes. Porcelain figures and other knickknacks, all of which were a mite too frilly for my blood, artfully cluttered the end tables, mantel, and even parts of the floor. To complete the scene, numerous potted palms arched gracefully over the ordered chaos of the room.

When Edwina returned bearing my refreshments, I complimented her on the decor.

"That's all my first husband's doing. Leonard was rather flamboyant—frankly, that was the reason our marriage didn't work."

"I see."

"But he had great taste. In fact, I like it so much, I haven't changed a thing since he moved out. All I do is dust and vacuum."

"Did your other husbands like this room?"

She smiled—at least half of her face did. "Men! Do they really care, as long as they have a TV and a good recliner? Through those pocket doors on your right is the den."

"How did Reverend Schrock like this room?"

"Excuse me?"

"Surely he paid you a pastoral visit. I mean, he was supposed to visit every member of his church family at least once a year."

"Oh, that. Well, he stopped coming, of course, after I dropped out. But when he did come, we never discussed decor."

I took a sip of my cocoa. It was good, but not the best I'd had that day.

"Reverend Schrock was a very handsome man," I said. "Don't you think so?"

"I'm sure I never noticed."

Right. The truth is that until her latest, unfortunate surgery, Edwina Bishop was famous for noticing any male on the shady side of puberty. If memory served me right, it was between husbands three and four that she caused a local uproar by noticing Michael Lapp. Although a member of the Old Order Amish community, this young man, who was as handsome as any movie star, temporarily fell for her feminine wiles. The tragic outcome of this short-lived liaison was that young Michael started taking pride in his good looks, and soon began to notice how many other women were noticing him. The last I heard he'd become a Presbyterian and moved to California, where he got a job doing beer commercials.

"Frankly, dear, even I noticed what an attractive man our pastor was." I slurped from the cup until there was no danger of spilling, and leaned forward conspiratorially. "Not that we girls ever stood a chance with him, seeing as how he only had eyes for Lodema."

Edwina recoiled, just as surely as if I'd spit on her. "For your information, Magdalena, Arnold and I were dear friends."

I feigned surprise. "But I thought you hated him."

"That was after he said no to performing my fifth marriage."

"Surely he didn't perform marriages two through four—did he?" If that was true, and anyone else had found out, the reverend would have lost his job.

"Don't be silly, Magdalena. You knew Arnold better than that."

"I thought I knew him. Now I'm not so sure."

"Like I said, I knew him very well."

"That's nice." She wasn't going to get my dander up.

"Did you know about the birthmark shaped like a Christmas tree on—"

"The small of his back?"

She treated me to a full-frontal glare.

In for a penny, in for a pound of very attractive flesh. "And what about those six-cylinder abs?"

"That's called a six-*pack*, Magdalena. And just how do you know all this?"

"Funny, I guess I knew him better than I thought." God bless two-year-old Amy Burkhart for spilling her lemonade all over Reverend Schrock at that church picnic.

Some women refuse to be outdone. "We would have had an affair as well, but I put a stop to it. I draw the line at adultery."

I waggled a ladyfinger at her. "That's unfair, and you know it. I didn't know Aaron Miller was already married, and besides, that was a onetime thing. Not like your—your—serial monogamy."

"So you're not denying that you and the reverend had an affair?"

What would have been the point in denying that assumption? She wouldn't have believed me—would possibly even have called me a liar, which would have made a liar out of her. I would have been her reason to sin, and the Bible specifically warns us not to be stumbling blocks before others. No, the Christian thing to do was to suck it up and pretend to be a harlot.

Filled with righteous resignation, I struggled to my feet. "You wouldn't happen to have a zip bag for the rest of these ladyfingers, would you?"

I suppose that having a door slam on one's patooty hurts less than having it slammed on one's proboscis. At least for those folks who have patooties plump enough to absorb some of the shock.

Being on the sparse side, I limped to my car. I limped again when I got out at my next destination. Unfortunately, I was nowhere near able to run.

12

"Zelda," I shouted, "come back!"

The woman was striding away from me, and her house. I would have followed in my car had it not been for the fact that Blinker Alley, which was built for Model A Fords and bicycles, is so narrow I can reach both sides by extending my arms. Willing myself to ignore my painful patooty, I hobbled after her.

"Zelda Root, stop!" I shrieked.

The woman ignored me, even when I was just feet behind her. Perhaps this was a case of mistaken identity. Quite possibly I'd been lured into the narrow alley by a look-alike, and foul play would ensue at any second. After all, it's no secret that I am Hernia's wealthiest citizen. Strict pacifist though I may be, upon occasion I've been tempted to mug myself.

Against my better judgment I propelled myself forward. It wasn't my intent to tackle the woman, certainly not to knock her to the ground. But, and this is putting it kindly, Hernia's only other police officer is built very much like a rooster. She's short, with enormous breasts, no hips, and matchstick ankles. The two things that distinguish Zelda most from a chicken are that chickens have essentially one breast, while Zelda has almost no feathers. She does, however, wear her bottle-red hair in spikes, which approximate a rooster's comb. Give her a few more years, and she'll develop wattles naturally.

She landed on gravel and broken glass, but miraculously did not sustain injury. The fact that I landed on the counterfeit cock is what saved my coccyx from further damage. One would think that Zelda, and it was indeed her, would be grateful that we were both unscathed, but that was far from the case. As we struggled to our feet, she let loose with a string of invectives that would have made a sailor blush.

Considering the source—Zelda is an *ex*-Mennonite—I waited until she was winded before I piped up. "Well, I was shouting at you until my throat hurt. You could have at least turned around. Frankly, Zelda, just because you're Melvin's sidekick doesn't give you the right to be rude."

She ripped off a headset I hadn't noticed, hidden as it was by the spikes. "What?"

"Never mind, dear. We need to talk."

"I was listening to Andean flute music. Would you like to hear?"

"No, thanks. Let's go back to your house, make us some nice rich hot chocolate, and have ourselves a little chat."

"No can do."

"Sure you can. And as I recall, you make the world's best peanut butter cookies."

"It's not that, Magdalena. It's that I'm busy working now."

"Undercover?"

She glanced up and down the otherwise deserted alley. "Yes."

"But I need to talk to you about your trip to Harrisburg, and the chili samples you took in to be analyzed. And speaking of chilly, it's getting downright cold this afternoon, and this alley is acting like a wind tunnel." The truth is, if you must know, that Edwina's cocoa was searching for a new home.

Because Zelda applies her makeup with a trowel, one has to observe her scalp to see when she's blushing. At the moment it was cockscomb red.

"Aha! You've got those heretics in your house right now, don't you?"

She hung her bristly head. "Not all of them—just Esther Rensberger, Mary Lehman, and Agnes Baumgartner. They're conducting a leadership meeting."

Not only does Zelda have a crush on her boss—my brother-in-law, Melvin Stoltzfus—but she worships him. Literally. As bizarre as this may sound, she maintains a shrine devoted to him, in her home. And like all zealots, she feels compelled to evangelize. At last count she had managed to convert fifteen other misguided souls—all female but one—to the movement. They meet on a weekly basis to sing odes to the menacing mantis, and to affirm their everlasting affection. One of them—Mary Lehman, I think—is hard at work on a volume of supposedly holy sayings. Very soon, I am told, they will apply to the government for tax-exempt status.

"Shame on you, Zelda. Shame, shame, shame. I'm sure your parents are rolling over in their graves. Not to mention that you are in danger of hellfire."

"*There is no Hell but separation from Melvin Stoltzfus. The Book of Melvin, chapter one, verse seven.*"

"Stop! I can't take any more of your blasphemy."

"It's not blasphemy—it's the truth. Agnes Baumgartner had a dream in which—"

So I was wrong about the scribe's identity, not that it mattered any. It was all a bunch of nonsense. Any reasonable person could see this was the case.

"You believe that?" I demanded.

"Yes, I believe it. And you would believe it too if you only opened up your heart. Besides, it says it's true in the Book of Melvin, chapter eighteen, verse nine. *Behold, these words, which I speak unto thee this day, are verily mine.*"

I'd had enough. I'm all for freedom of religion, just as long as it's mine. Okay, that position will never float in the political arena, so I'm willing to accept other faiths, on the surface at least, provided they don't espouse absurd beliefs that are sacrilegious. And by the way, as any doofus can tell you, one can't prove a text's veracity by quoting from the document in question.

"Zelda Root, if you don't stop it this minute, I'll—I'll—well, I'll think of something."

She had the gall to regard me placidly beneath lashes so thick with paint, they resembled colonies of mating bats. "It's the Devil who's preventing you from seeing the truth, Magdalena. He's hardening your heart."

The Devil was certainly present, but he wasn't in *my* heart. "Get behind me, Satan," I cried.

No sooner had those powerful words escaped me than a mighty wind roared through the alley, and a pair of disembodied hands hurled me against the door of someone's utility shed. I lay there, trembling, with my eyes closed, too frightened even to pray. If I survived this assault from Satan, the first thing I would do was see to it that Zelda was relieved of her duties as policewoman. Public servants, entrusted with the welfare of the community, had no business believing in such poppycock.

I have no idea how long I'd lain there, at the side of the alley, when I thought I heard a heavenly voice. "Magdalena, are you all right?"

"Lord, is that you?"

"Don't be silly, Magdalena. It's me."

I opened one eye. "Zelda?"

"Who else could it be?"

I opened the other eye. Yup, it was definitely Hernia's biggest heathen. She offered to help me get up, but I preferred to do it on my own.

"What happened?" I rasped.

"That car almost hit us, that's what happened. Magdalena, if it hadn't been for me pushing you out of the way, you'd be roadkill."

"Those disembodied hands were yours?"

"You're strange, Magdalena, you know that?"

"*Moi?*"

"There are folks here who've been saying you need psychological help, but I've always defended you. Now I'm not so sure."

"*Who* says that?"

"I'm not going to name names, Magdalena. Let's just say there are a lot of them."

"Are they all Melvinists?"

"That's Melvin*ites*, and no, they're not all of the faith. But that's neither here nor there. If you're not going to be grateful that I saved your life, you can at least help me identify that car. I saw the last three digits on the rear plate. Nine, three, seven. What did you see?"

There wasn't any point in telling her that I hadn't even seen a car, much less its plates. "It all happened too fast."

"I guess since I'm younger, my reflexes are better."

I swallowed my pride, along with several small pieces of gravel. "Whatever you say, dear. Can you trace it on just those three?"

"Well, it was green—and not that 'burnt' shade that's so popular lately. More like puke green, I'd say. And probably not a factory paint job. I can certainly give it a try."

"You do that. And if you catch them, give them more than just a speeding ticket. Is there an extra penalty for reckless endangerment?"

The colonies of mating bats stirred. "Magdalena, you do realize that whoever it was, was trying to kill us—don't you?"

The loose hairs on the back of my neck stood up. The hair captured by my bun tried in vain to do likewise. I'm sure Zelda could see my white prayer cap bobble.

"Did you say *kill* us?"

"This alley wasn't meant for today's cars, and everyone hereabouts knows it. So you can bet it wasn't a local just taking a shortcut. And no tourist would drive that fast through a strange town. I'm telling you, Magdalena, that maniac knew he was taking a risk, and he did it to mow us down."

"It could have been teenagers out for a joyride."

Zelda frowned so deeply her makeup began to crack. "I don't think so. Teenagers like attention, so they tend to stick to the main roads—unless they want to you-know-what."

"I'm afraid I don't."

Zelda waggled her eyebrows suggestively, sending a hundred bats into frenzied flight.

I gasped. "You mean the horizontal hootchy-kootchy?"

The woman had the nerve to laugh. "Oh, Magdalena, you're such a prude. But yes, I've often seen cars parked back here. And don't think it's anything new—I was conceived in a 1956 Studebaker."

"T.M.I.!" I cried, although frankly, I was dying to ask how she'd gotten that information. How did she know such a thing? Mama had me believing I was found under a cabbage until I took a biology course in college. Never mind that I had been born and raised on a farm.

Zelda absentmindedly patted the putty on her face back into shape. "Well, we can stand here and yap about sex, or we can get our visit to Clifford Waldron over with, so I can trace that plate."

"Clifford Waldron? Why are we visiting him?" If Zelda wanted to include me in her plans, who was I to argue? Always somewhat of a neatnik, Clifford was bound to have a clean bathroom. And perhaps if I waggled my almost nonexistent eyebrows, he could be coaxed into making some cocoa.

"You know those samples I took in to Harrisburg?"

"What about them?"

"The one that came from Clifford's pot had a minute trace of cyanide."

"You're kidding!"

"It was a minute amount, Magdalena. There wasn't enough to kill a mouse, much less a man. But until we get the full autopsy report, following up on this gives me something to do."

"Wait just a second! You said 'Clifford's pot.' How did you know that sample came from his?"

Zelda rolled her eyes so that only the whites showed. Mama repeatedly warned me that my peepers might get stuck in that position, supposedly a bad thing, but on Zelda it looked rather good.

"Magdalena, I'm a professional. Last night I called the membership from the church and made them identify their pots over the phone. Then I labeled the samples. How else could I expect to learn anything from taking the samples in for analysis?"

How else indeed? And here I thought I'd been pretty clever just in making sure all the pots belonged to upstanding church members. Dolt that I am, I would never have thought of labeling the samples.

"So what are we waiting for?" I practically shouted. Enthusiasm, I've learned, is a good way to cover up embarrassment.

Zelda's irises descended just far enough for her to roll her eyes again. Then, without another word, she resumed wobbling down the alley on her nonregulation platform shoes.

I hobbled after her.

Clifford Waldron lives in a modest 1970s ranch-style house. Nothing inside, or outside, of that somewhat humble abode has changed since his wife, Esmerelda, died almost thirty years ago. Unlike the heretic Zelda, the widower does not maintain a shrine; he simply lacks imagination. For decades he has worn the same hairdo (a part down the middle) and the same style clothes to church, and at potluck suppers told the same tired jokes. The single women of Beechy Grove Mennonite Church, yours truly included, have long since abandoned the idea of trying to snare this otherwise eligible man.

As we mounted the concrete steps leading to the kitchen door, we observed Clifford hunched over a Formica table playing solitaire. Conventional playing cards are eschewed by my branch of the Mennonite faith (we do enjoy a good game of Rook), so I was understandably shocked by what I saw. Perhaps a bit titillated as well. Clifford Waldron wasn't so boring after all.

Zelda didn't bother to look for the bell, but rapped on the storm door with knuckles that could crack walnuts. Clifford jerked to an upright position, glanced at the door, and without even a second's hesitation swept the cards to the floor. Then he hopped to his feet and greeted us with the same innocent smile I've seen on the faces of gassy babies.

"What an unexpected pleasure this is, ladies."

"Likewise," I said, "and it is bound to become even more pleasurable after I've used your facilities."

"I beg your pardon?"

"She needs to pee," Zelda said. "Can we come in?"

He held the door open. "I'm afraid the house is a mess."

As urgent as my need was, I couldn't resist having a little fun. "My, my," I said, picking up a card with the picture of a king on it, "what have we here?"

Clifford colored. "Uh—it's not what you think."

"She thinks it's none of her business," Zelda said.

I needed to go more than I needed to glare, so off I went. When I returned, the cards had disappeared and Zelda and Clifford were deep in conversation. They didn't appear to notice me at first, but in order to eavesdrop I had to clamp a hand so tightly over my mouth that my fingertips left bruises on my left cheek.

"The thing is," Zelda was saying, "we found a minute amount of cyanide in your sample."

"Cyanide? Ah, yes, of course."

"Excuse me?"

"Esmerelda's parents were missionaries to Africa—to the Belgian Congo, more specifically. She grew up very fond of a dish called *bidia*, which is made from manioc flour. Unprocessed manioc contains dangerous levels of cyanide, but I guess even the processed must contain, as you say, minute levels. Anyway, Essy found an Asian grocery in Pittsburgh that had an African section, and she cooked *bidia* often. I got to like it, and make it now for myself."

Zelda nodded. Esmerelda Waldron's missionary adventures rank among Hernia's most worn-out stories, even now, two decades after her death. When I hear these stories I just want to scream. What's the big deal about being raised surrounded by a tribe of headhunters? Who cares about army ants and goat-swallowing snakes? Try living with the likes of Lodema Schrock, or the late Elspeth Miller, or the Mishler brothers, who are blind, and therefore see nothing wrong in wandering naked about their property.

At any rate, Heaven forfend Clifford and Zelda should lapse into repeating a dead woman's tales. It was time to announce my presence.

"Clifford, dear, I hope you don't mind that I took the liberty of fixing your toilet paper roll. It should go over, not under."

You would have thought that I'd walked in as naked as a Mishler brother. Clifford's eyes widened, his jaw dropped, and he bolted for the powder room.

"Apparently Esmerelda hung it under," Zelda said, not without some satisfaction. "That's the correct way, you know."

We were still debating the issue of tissue when Clifford returned. Instead of sitting again, he appeared anxious for us to leave. In fact, he may even have said something to that effect.

"Aren't you at least going to offer us something to eat or drink, dear? Some hot chocolate would be nice. With whipped cream and marshmallows, of course. And I don't suppose you have some dipping cookies to go with. They don't have to be homemade; store-bought will do."

Zelda tried to kick me, but missed. "Magdalena, don't be rude."

"I most certainly am not being rude. Mennonites always offer their guests something to eat. Clifford knows that, even though only his mother was of the faith."

Clifford cleared his throat, his eyes on the kitchen door. "Actually, ladies, I have to be in Bedford in twenty minutes."

"Instant cocoa will do, then."

"I'm not sure I have any, and I really do need to leave. My bowling league begins a tournament tonight, and I have to practice."

"Bowling?" I asked incredulously. "Don't folks smoke, drink, and cuss in bowling alleys?" There's just no telling what kind of behavior a half Mennonite will engage in.

"It's smoke free, and I don't drink. Frankly, I don't know about the cussing. Reverend Schrock used to bowl all the time."

"I beg your pardon! He was an upstanding Christian man."

Clifford turned and smiled. "I like to think I'm one as well."

Zelda nodded vigorously, precipitating a shower of spackle. "You tell her, Cliff. Lots of Christians bowl. Heck, I used to do so myself until I started thinking about the rental shoes. All those germs—"

"But you're a Melvinist," I wailed.

"Yes, but I used to be a Christian."

"Did you ever stop to consider that it might have been the bowling that led you astray?"

"Ladies, please," Clifford begged, "I'm going to be late for practice."

Having lost her argument, Zelda moved toward the door.

"Just a minute, dear," I called after her. "We're not quite through here."

"I am."

"Then go on. It's Clifford I need to speak to anyway."

Of course Zelda stopped dead in her wobbly tracks. "Make it fast, Magdalena. We've kept him long enough."

I got right down to business.

13

I addressed Clifford. "Was Reverend Schrock on your team?"

"No, we're the Rolling Hammers. Our sponsor is Johnson Hardware on High Street over in Bedford. If you stop in and mention my name, they'll give you a free magnet for your refrigerator."

"One can never have too many. But back to the reverend, which team was he on?"

Clifford cleared his throat. He looked at Zelda, who suddenly wasn't in a hurry to leave.

"Uh, I can't say exactly."

"Why is that, dear?"

"I'm sorry. I may have exaggerated a bit."

"How much is a bit?"

"Well, I really did see Reverend Schrock in a bowling alley— once. I just can't say for sure how often he was there."

"I see."

"Magdalena, like I said, I don't drink and—"

"That's all right, Clifford. What you do really isn't my business. But tell me, was Reverend Schrock there alone?"

He shrugged. "Frankly I was so surprised to see him, I can't remember much. Except that I took off and hid in the men's room for about twenty minutes. When I came out he was gone."

"So you were shocked by Schrock. What was his reaction? Did he see you?"

"Yes, he did. I think he was surprised to see me too, and was just as embarrassed."

Zelda snorted. "For all we know he may have been there witnessing to the masses."

"Too bad the Melvinites weren't bowling that night."

"Ladies, may I go now?"

I allowed as how he could, while Zelda said that he *should*. She went on to say that no one deserved to be interrogated—no, make that tortured—by the likes of me. I bit my tongue until Clifford was gone, and then let her have it with the strips of lacerated lingua that remained.

"Zelda, how dare you say those things about me?"

We had abandoned the alley in favor of the sidewalk that bordered Flowerpot Lane, even though it was the long way back to her house. She took her time before answering and, in my opinion, purposefully broke her mother's back whenever the opportunity arose. Fortunately, Mrs. Root has been dead for years.

"Magdalena, haven't you ever heard of 'good cop, bad cop'?"

"Of course I have."

"Well, you're the 'bad cop.' "

"I *am*?" I am ashamed now to confess that I found my new job description somewhat titillating. My sister, Susannah, often says that bad girls have more fun. Perhaps it was the same way with bad cops. Who knew what plethora of pleasures lay in store for proficient pretend policewomen.

"Yeah, but remember, Magdalena, I call all the shots. You have to follow my lead."

"Whatever you say, dear." That wasn't exactly a lie, given how open my words were to interpretation.

"So, Magdalena, who would you say was the reverend's best friend?"

I stepped on Mama's back a couple of times while contemplating the question. It had never occurred to me that ministers would have personal friends, just like everyone else—well, except for yours truly. No, I take that back. Just because I am my own best friend, and most of my other friends are relatives, does not mean I'm friendless. Now, where was I? Oh yes, surely Reverend Schrock had friends; he would need them with a wife like Lodema. But who were they? Maybe his neighbors? I suggested this to Zelda.

"Hmm. Why don't you pay the neighbors a visit, while I trace the plates of the car that almost got us admittance through the diamondiferous gates of the great beyond?"

"They're pearly gates!"

"Not to we Melvinites."

I took my earliest possible leave of the heretic. Great-grandpa Yoder was killed by lightning while roofing a barn. I was in no hurry to join him.

The Mennonite parsonage occupies a corner at a four-way stop, so that technically speaking, the Schrocks have six sets of neighbors. I picked the neighbor who had a pot of orange mums still blooming on the front porch. Perhaps I should have begun by putting the squeeze on the reverend's sister for more information, but I already knew that the best Catherine could come up with was instant cocoa.

A middle-aged woman with a pleasant face opened the door. She was a newcomer to town—having arrived only a dozen or so years ago—and a Methodist, so we weren't on a first-name basis.

"Mrs. Dalton?"

"Yes. And you're Miss Yoder, right?"

"As big as life and twice as ugly."

"Excuse me?"

"That was intended to be humorous. Unfortunately, I don't have a funny bone in my body. Do you mind if I ask you a few questions?"

A faint line appeared on her forehead. "Is this about Arnold Schrock? I know you sometimes help our Chief of Police."

"Guilty on both accounts—oops, that's not quite what I mean."

She smiled and the line disappeared. "Would you like to come in? I just made a pot of hot chocolate, and there are gingerbread men in the oven right now."

"Instant cocoa?"

"Gracious, no. I use baking chocolate, and real cream. It's more like liquid fudge than a beverage."

"Say no more!"

I followed her into a house that must have been featured in some magazine, sometime, somewhere. While I settled into a comfortable, but very attractive, sofa, she poured the ebony ambrosia and took the cookies from the oven. Both delectables were piping hot upon delivery.

"Sorry I didn't have time to ice the gingerbread men. I'm afraid they don't have faces, or buttons running down their middles."

"Not to worry," I said, and bit off my man's head. Although it was an action I instantly regretted, I chose to burn my tongue rather than embarrass myself.

"Tell me, how can I be of help?"

"Some ice water would be lovely, dear." I may have lisped a bit while making my request.

She practically bolted into the kitchen, and returned seconds later with a sparkling glass of cold water. Believe me, Hernia's H_2O had never tasted so good.

"Now, then, where were we?"

I set the treats on an end table to cool. "How well did you know Reverend Schrock?"

"Very, I'd say. My husband, George, and Arnold have been best friends for years. Almost since the day we moved in."

"You don't say!" What were the odds of striking pay dirt with my first shovel load?

"Yes, George and Arnold did everything together: camping, fishing, hunting—you name it."

"Bowling?"

"Yes, that too. But then, about five years ago Arnold started making excuses. The guys suddenly started seeing a lot less of each other, and I don't mind telling you, George was rather hurt by it." She leaned forward conspiratorially. "Frankly, I was relieved."

"You didn't approve of their friendship?"

"Oh, I had no problem with that. But you see, we had to do a lot of things as a foursome and Lodema is—how shall I put this?"

"A pain in the neck?"

She settled back in her chintz-covered chair. "Exactly. Heaven only knows how hard I tried to be friends with that woman. I tell you, Miss Yoder, it wouldn't surprise me a bit to learn that Arnold committed suicide."

"Suicide!"

"That's not what happened, was it? I heard something about chili and peanut butter. . . ."

"You heard correctly. You did know that he was extremely allergic to peanuts, didn't you?"

She nodded and stared misty-eyed out the window.

I took a sip of my cocoa, which by then was just at the perfect temperature. Scalding hot, without actually scalding. What an interesting prospect Mrs. Dalton had raised. Could someone possibly be so desperate to end his life that he chose to asphyxiate himself, and in public no less? What would be the point of inflicting this gruesome scene on the congregation, unless it was to exact revenge? But the Reverend Schrock I knew wasn't remotely like that. He was the kindest, gentlest man I'd ever known, the Babester included. No, it had to be either an accident or murder.

It was up to me to break the silence. "Mrs. Dalton, can you think of anyone who might have wished the reverend dead?"

She jerked to look at me. "How did you know?"

"Know what?"

"Please don't play games with me, Miss Yoder. Arnold's death has been very hard on me. Yes, it's been five years since we broke it off, but one can never recover from losing a soul mate. Trust me."

I gasped so hard I got cocoa up my nose. "You had an affair with my pastor?"

"An *affaire de coeur.*"

"A what?"

"An affair of the heart. As I said, we were soul mates. We connected on a level that he and Lodema never could. And my own husband—let's just say George isn't big on emotions."

"So you never actually did the mattress mambo?"

"I'm afraid it's my turn to not understand."

"The horizontal hootchy-kootchy. The Sealy Posturepedic polka.

The between-the-covers two-step. The sin almost as bad as dancing."

She smiled. "No, we never did that."

"You know, dear, some women consider an emotional affair—
that's the term I've heard them called—to be an offense more serious than physical intimacy."

Her smile faded. "I know what I did was wrong. Arnold did too.
But try as we might, we couldn't help ourselves. We just happened
to fall in love."

"*Haufta mischt.*"

"Excuse me?"

"Horse manure. You don't just fall in love without noticing it.
And when you notice you're falling in love with a married man,
you're supposed to back away. That's called decency."

I may as well have slapped her. "Really, Miss Yoder, I prefer not
to be judged. And from what I hear, you have no business throwing stones."

"Well, I never!" I jumped to my feet and grabbed a second gingerbread man from the platter on the coffee table.

"You see how it feels?"

"Apples and oranges, dear. I had no idea my pooky bear was
married. If I had, I would have dropped him like a pair of panties
without elastic. You, on the other hand, knew full well what you
were dealing with, and even though you didn't do the bedroom
boogie, you still trod on the sanctity of marriage."

"My gracious. For someone who is so dead set against dancing,
you sure know a lot of different varieties."

Just for that, I grabbed a third cookie before skedaddling.

Woman does not live by hot chocolate alone. Life is more than
one's vocation, even more than one's *a*vocation. It was time I hustled my bustle back to the inn and checked on Alison and Freni.

Let me tell you, home never looked so good. I found Alison at
the kitchen table doing her math homework, with a befuddled
Freni at her side. Neither of them had ever looked happier to see
me.

"How goes it, dears?"

"Hey, Mom. Do *you* know anything about algebra?"

"Try me." The truth is, I knew very little about that subject. But although it was one of my worst in school, I was bound to know more than Freni. The Amish stop their education with the eighth grade, or age sixteen, whichever comes first. Too much knowledge, it is believed, will lead one astray from God's truths, and out into the world, where temptation lurks behind every bush.

Alison shoved her book at me. "I gotta do number thirty-eight through forty-six, and I don't know how to do any of them. Man, this ain't fair."

I stared at a combination of digits and squiggles that made less sense to me than chicken tracks. "Alison, dear, I just saw Dr. Rosen's car in his driveway. Why don't you skip on over there and ask him."

"If they ask, can I stay for dinner?"

"Ach!" Freni squawked. "What is wrong with my food?"

"Nothing, Auntie Freni, but Grandma Ida knows how to make Jewish food, *and* she cuts your meat if ya want her to."

"She isn't your grandmother yet, dear," I said. "And besides, I don't know if Mrs. Rosen is even home this evening."

"She is, Mom. I saw her and Gabe getting out of the car about an hour ago, thanks to you."

"Thanks to *me*?"

"Yeah, I heard about it at school, how you let Grandma Ida and Doc Shafor have it at the Sausage Barn."

"I didn't exactly let them have it—did you say you heard this at *school*?"

"Yeah. Some of the kids think ya should mind your own business, but I think it's kinda cool. I mean, if we kids ain't allowed to hook up like that, why should them old people?"

"Well—"

"So can I stay over there for dinner, Mom? Can I?"

Know when to pick your battles, especially when it comes to parenting. "Yes, you can stay. But remember to mind your manners."

"Can I invite Jason to join us?"

"They haven't even invited you yet. But if they do, the answer is no. You may *not* invite Jason. He's seventeen years old, for crying out loud."

"So what? I'm thirteen. He's only four years older." At least she got that math right.

"Four years is a huge difference at your age. Trust me."

"No fair! Every other girl I know dates guys four years older— even older than that."

"First of all, you're not even allowed to date, and you won't be until you're fifteen. And that's just for group dates."

"But this would be a group date—Gabe and Grandma Ida will be there."

"Alison, dear, read my lips. *N-O.*"

She stamped a foot. "I hate ya, Mom. I hate ya, hate ya, hate ya."

I sucked back a wisp of escaped steam. "You're really pushing it, dear. Keep it up and you won't be allowed to go over there at all."

"Ya mean I can still go?"

"As of this second."

Alison slammed the algebra book shut, gave me a peck on the cheek, and fled from the room.

"Kids," I said. "You can't live with them, and they can't live without you."

"Yah," Freni said, "they are the gift from God that keeps on taking."

It was a rare moment of mutual understanding. Now that I am in my late forties, I shall forever remain as barren as the Gobi Desert, but in no way am I diminished as a mother. And as mothers, Freni and I share a bond of sisterhood. Separately, and sometimes together, we have experienced the joys of motherhood, as well as the frustrations. It was good that we could joke about the latter.

I would have preferred to revel in my reverie longer, but somebody with a good deal of persistence was knocking on the kitchen door. Perhaps a wee bit annoyed, I lumbered over to see who it was.

"Freni," I said, after peering past my reflection in the glass, "your gift that keeps on taking is going to take some more."

"Jonathan?"

"Guess again, dear."

14

Barbara Hostetler tops six feet in her heavy wool stockings. Her black brogans add at least another inch. My description stops there, because who am I to judge someone else's looks? When the Good Lord made me, he slapped a saddle on my back and hollered giddyap.

I opened the door, but not before the look on Freni's face had faded. Barbara, a real sweetheart, and eager to please her mother-in-law, despite the gentle, Amish-style abuse heaped upon her large head, smiled broadly. Her sin, by the way, is the fact that she married Freni's only son.

"Hello, Magdalena."

"Come in, dear. Freni was just saying how much she was missing you while she stays here to look after things for me."

"Ach!"

Barbara may be big, and from Iowa, but she isn't stupid. "Magdalena, I came to see you. We can talk, yah?"

"Step right this way," I said, and flung open the doors to the dining room. We have fixed mealtimes at the PennDutch, and it was too early for guests, but Freni's eavesdropping knows no schedule. I closed the doors behind us, but not before warning Freni that the Devil himself has been known to enter people holding water glasses to their ears.

To be on the safe side, I directed Barbara to the far corner of the dining room, where I keep the quilt frame. Incidentally, when the quilts are completed, I schlep them to a lady over in Lancaster—where anything "Amish" is a business—who sells them for a pretty penny. Of course they aren't authentic Amish quilts, but they are vaguely Mennonite, which obviously counts for something.

"Have a seat, dear," I said, "and feel free to keep those fingers busy."

Barbara picked up a needle. "Magdalena, can *she* hear me?"

"I'm pretty sure she can't. But let's see. Freni Hostetler," I said, raising my voice slightly, "is the world's worst cook."

Silence reigned.

It never hurts to confirm things. "And Jonathan Hostetler loves his wife more than he loves his mother."

When, after a few minutes, nothing extraordinary had happened—like a fierce Freni flying into the room—we both breathed sighs of relief. "So tell me, dear," I said, "what's on your mind?"

"I have been thinking, Magdalena."

"That's always a dangerous activity."

"Yah, that is so. But I have been thinking about our talk in Yoder's Market. You are right, Magdalena. It is time for Jonathan and I to move into a house of our own."

"That was your idea, not mine!"

"Ach, no, I remember that you said—"

"Never mind that. I haven't had a chance to tell you, but I had a pleasant little chat with you-know-who." I gestured toward the kitchen. "She agreed to back off. She's even going to let you cook—for your family. She may want to keep cooking for herself and Mose."

"Yah?"

"Yah—I mean, yes."

Barbara looked down at the quilt, her gaze suddenly intent. "It is not just the cooking, Magdalena. The house is too small."

I knew exactly what she meant. The younger generation of Hostetlers were living in the Grossdawdy house, an addition meant for grandparents. If they had followed tradition, Mose and Freni would have moved into the Grossdawdy house following

Jonathan and Barbara's marriage. But Freni had balked at letting a woman she didn't like take over her domain, so it was the younger Hostetlers who moved into the cottage. This might not have turned into a problem had not the inconsiderate Barbara given birth to yet another generation of Hostetlers. Triplets, in fact.

"I'll keep working on her, Barbara."

"Magdalena, it is not just the cooking that I mind. The Grossdawdy house is so crowded that Jonathan and I cannot even—well, we cannot have privacy."

"You mean do the headboard hula, don't you?"

"I do not understand."

"The deed that produced Cain and Abel."

She nodded gravely. "Yah, the headstone hula. Is that slang?"

"It is now. Look, dear, you're just going to have make Jonathan be firm with his parents. Either they switch residences, or the five of you are out of there."

"I do not think my Jonathan can be this brave."

"Then give him an ultimatum. Tell him that there will be no headboard hula—or even head*stone* hula—as long as conditions remain the way they are."

She smiled slyly. "Perhaps now I do not want them to change their minds."

"Is it that bad?"

"What can I say? It is boring. Sometimes I fall asleep."

"Try planning your menus for the day. Those three minutes will pass in a jiffy."

"Yah?"

"Trust me." I tapped her fingers. "Keep them moving, dear. You make such neat little stitches."

She worked diligently, and in silence, for the length of several hulas. Too bad I couldn't send the quilt home with her.

"Magdalena," she said casually, "what will become of Reverend Schrock's daughter?"

"I beg your pardon?"

"She is such a sweet little girl. But I hear that the mother is not so nice."

"You must be mistaken, dear. The Schrocks never had children."

"I am not mistaken, Magdalena. She called your preacher 'Papa.' "

I grabbed her fingers and held them still. "When? Where?"

"It was in Bedford last summer. There was a cloth sale at the Material Girl. We left the triplets with Mose, and Jonathan took me to town in the buggy. Sometimes a couple needs to be alone—without the headstone hula, yah?"

"Get on with your story, dear."

"Well, I bought thirteen yards of blue cloth at half price, and twenty yards of black cloth at sixty percent off. Jonathan said I made out like a robber."

"The term is 'bandit,' not that I'm quibbling. Can you just skip to the part about the reverend having a daughter?"

"I will try, but you know, Magdalena, sometimes it is very lonely with just the children to talk with. 'Little Magdalena,' I will say, 'please help your mama—' "

"*Tempus fugit*," I said reluctantly. Under normal circumstances I love to hear tales about my namesake.

"Is this more slang?"

"It means 'Time flies,' and if you don't hurry this tale along, it's going to fly out the window altogether."

She glanced at the nearest window and, not spotting an airborne hourglass, shrugged. "So it is after I buy the cloth that my Jonathan says we should have store-bought ice cream at the Tastee-Freez. We go inside—just like the English—and that is when I saw your preacher with his little girl. He was holding her in his arms, and she was licking the cone, yah? So I say hello, but he pretends not to see me. Then the little girl says, 'Papa, that funny lady is talking to you.' But he does not want me to see him, so he turns and walks very fast from the Tastee-Freez. Of course I must tell this to Jonathan, but by then the reverend has gone."

I let go of her fingers. "Are you sure it was him? I mean, don't we English all look alike?"

"This is a joke, yah? Magdalena, your nose—"

"I get the picture. But how can you be sure it was him? It's not like you've seen the man a lot."

She shook her head. "I have seen him many times. When one of our people gets sick, many times it is he who takes this person to the doctor. If there is need, he is always there to help—but now I must say '*was*,' yah?"

"You don't say!"

"Your preacher was a very kind man, Magdalena."

"I knew that—I just didn't know the scope of his kindness."

"And do not forget that I was at your wedding to the pigamist. It was Reverend Schrock who made the marriage that was not a true marriage."

"No need to go there, dear." I pointed to the quilt. "You have just about enough time to finish that row before the folks start filing in for dinner."

Expert that she was, she finished two rows.

Doc met me at the corner of his driveway. His bloodhound, Blue, was at his side.

"Let me guess," I said. "She let you know I was coming."

"Just in time for me to make a pot roast with potatoes and carrots, an Asian slaw salad, and an apple pie. But I didn't have time to make a lattice top, so you'll have to settle for regular."

I knew that Doc ate like this even when he was alone, but I'm sure he would rather shared his meal with Ida.

"Did I spoil things, dear?"

"We're grown-ups, Magdalena. We do what we want to do. She obviously thought it was important to go home to be with her son. At least for tonight."

"So you're not mad at me?"

"Heck, yes, I'm mad—no, make that furious. But you're my friend, and I'm a lonely old man. I'll still have time to be mad after you've eaten supper with me."

I followed him into the kitchen, where there was already a place setting for me—well, maybe for Ida. At any rate, there were three place settings altogether, as Doc still sets the table so as to include Belinda, his deceased wife.

Doc's pot roast was fork tender, and as juicy as a summer peach. We talked between bites.

"How well did you know the reverend?" I asked.

"We hunted together a couple of times. Fished together too. He was a smart man and could carry on a decent conversation. I miss that since my Belinda died."

"So you were close friends?"

"I wouldn't say that. Arnold was a very private man. Seems like he became even more private the last couple of years."

"Like he had a secret?"

Doc shrugged. Although he's been thinned by age, his shoulders are still broad.

"Maybe. But some men are just like that. They build an emotional wall around themselves so that no one can see if they're feeling weak."

"You're not like that, Doc."

"I consider myself blessed on that account. But I have to say, a lot of women seem to prefer the strong silent type. Although that doesn't stop them from complaining that their husbands don't open up to them. Go figure."

"Do you think Reverend Schrock had it in him to cheat on his wife?"

Doc's fork clanked on his plate. "Now, that's a silly question to ask."

"But Lodema is such a difficult woman. And frankly, she's not all that pretty."

Doc laughed. "I'm not arguing with that. It's a silly question because virtually every man has it in him to cheat."

"Not my Babester!"

"I didn't say he *would*, just that he has the potential. He's biologically programmed to spread his seed around as much as he can. Procreation is our number one task."

"That's if you believe in evolution—which, of course, I don't. Our number one task is to convert others to the Lord. Although sometimes I wonder why the Good Lord doesn't just stop creating new, unconverted people. It would make things so much easier."

"Again, I'm not going to argue. Not as long as you tell me what made you ask that question to begin with."

"It's Barbara Hostetler—Freni's daughter-in-law. She said she saw him at the Tastee-Freez with a little girl who called him Papa."

Doc shook his head. "Arnold took his responsibilities seriously. He wouldn't have used his key on anyone else's roller skates, if you know what I mean. Clearly Barbara was mistaken."

"But what if the key fit—never mind, forget that analogy. Just tell me how I can be sure there isn't a little Schrock in a frock running around somewhere in Bedford."

"You could ask the person who knew Arnold best."

I told Doc about Lodema's wedding dress episode, and that she was now under the care of Nurse Dudley and the dud of a doctor who ran Hernia Hospital. He listened intently. When I was through he patted at the corners of his mouth with the tip of his starched white napkin before responding.

"Somehow that doesn't surprise me. The woman has always been on the edge—well, ever since I've known her. A traumatic event, like losing a spouse suddenly, can push a stable person to lose their balance. At least temporarily. Believe me, I know."

"But you didn't go bonkers when Belinda died. Did you?"

"Do you think it's normal for a man to set the table for his dead wife? Especially when he's dating again?"

"Normal, shmormal. At least you don't think she's still alive—do you?"

Doc laid a hand over mine and squeezed it. His hand was so covered with age spots that at a distance it appeared deeply tanned.

"No, I don't think Belinda is alive. But I'd give anything if she were."

"She was a very special woman, Doc. And no offense, but Ida Rosen isn't worthy of touching the hem of Belinda's garment. If Belinda were still alive, that is. You know what I mean."

Doc withdrew his hand. "Indeed I do. And that's exactly what I wanted to talk about after we ate."

Thank the Good Lord we still had our apple pie to devour. Except that now I was going to nibble, rather than gulp. If I nibbled slowly enough, Doc, an octogenarian, was bound to fall asleep before the last crumb disappeared. And I was willing to eat the entire pie by myself, if need be.

"Sure, Doc, we can talk until the wee hours if that's what you want. But first the pie. And if you don't mind, a cup of decaf would be lovely. If you don't have any on hand, I'd be happy to dash home to get some."

"Oh no, you don't, Magdalena. Forget the pie. We're having ourselves that conversation right now."

"But you promised we'd eat first."

"And so we have. The pie can come later—if you're still hungry."

"Of course I'll still be hungry. Why shouldn't I be?"

"I can think of several reasons."

"Spill it," I cried. "The suspenders are killing me."

"Don't try and cute your way out of this one, Magdalena. Like I said, I'm really steamed."

I hung my head. "Sorry."

"As well you should be. My relationship with Ida Rosen is none of your business. Just what in tarnation gives you the right to judge what we do?"

I hung my head even lower, which made my dress gape at the neckline. My Playtex Living bra once starved to death, and its replacement is chronically malnourished. As a result I was able to contemplate my navel while pretending to be penitent. My belly button is definitely an innie, and quite attractive, if I do say so myself.

"Magdalena, that wasn't a rhetorical question."

"What?"

"You heard me. I want an answer."

"Well—uh—I don't have a right to judge what you two do. But just the same, you're making fools out of yourselves, and setting a bad example for the community."

"I'd like you to leave now."

"*What?*" I couldn't believe my ears. Ida Rosen had been in town for only a couple of months, yet somehow she'd managed to insinuate herself between two people who had been friends for decades.

"You might not be sorry, Magdalena, but I definitely am. I'm sorry it had to end this way."

"But it doesn't have to end! Can't we still be friends who agree to disagree?"

"Ida's a part of my life now. Either you accept that, or you and I are through."

A gal has to be practical, doesn't she? "If we're through, do I still get pie?"

Doc pushed the pie out of my reach and turned away from me.

Because the so-called Hernia Hospital is privately owned, Dr. Mean and Nurse Meaner can open and close its doors as the mood suits them. Usually that has to do with their patient load. But several times, particularly during good golfing weather, they have shooed patients out of the waiting room and locked the doors behind them. Therefore, it did not surprise me to find the building as dark and deserted as Aaron Miller's heart.

I stopped long enough to shine a flashlight in each window, and wear the skin off the knuckles of my right hand. But once I decided my quest to speak to Lodema at the hospital was a lost cause, I headed directly for Nurse Meaner's house. It was a five-minute drive.

It's a matter of public record that Amelia Hortense Dudley lives at 234 Mockingbird Lane. There are three ancient maples in her front yard, just begging to be TPed. And since the streetlight is completely blocked on the north side of the house, the windows on that wall are screaming to be soaped. Incidentally, Yoder's Corner Market, just two blocks away, sells everything one would need for a night of fun.

Having never been invited to Nurse Dudley's house, I felt a surge of excitement as I parallel parked beside it. Of course I felt dread as well. To be on the safe side, in case I needed to make a fast getaway, I left my car doors unlocked.

The house has both a doorbell and a pair of humongous knockers in the shape of lions' heads, one on each panel of a wide double door. I decided that whacking the kitties' brass rings was more fun than pushing a bell. But alas, I got to whack only a dozen or so times before the door flew open.

"I could have you arrested for disturbing the peace."

"It's not that late, dear. Besides, it's your knockers that made the noise. Mind if I come in?"

"Yes, I mind. The hospital will be open tomorrow at nine."

She started to slam the huge door, but I slipped a size eleven in just in time. I had to wait until the stars cleared before I could speak.

"I'm here on police business."

"You're not a policewoman."

"Quite true. Would you prefer that I send for Chief Stoltzfus, or Officer Root?"

"You mean Chief Nut and Officer Nuttier?"

That hiked my hackles. No one is allowed to make fun of the mantis, except for *moi*. And Susannah, of course. And maybe Freni and Alison, because they're both family. Possibly even the Babester, because he's practically family. But certainly Nurse Meaner had no right.

"I wouldn't be calling the kettle names, dear. So who will it be, me or the daffy duo?"

"You can come in—but only for a minute." She eased the door open, as if it suddenly weighed a ton, which it probably did.

I stared at the spectacle before me, too spellbound to move my feet at first. The living room was a wonderland of teddy bears. There must have been a thousand of the toys, dressed in every costume imaginable, many of them arranged in charming vignettes.

There was a teddy bear fireman in the process of climbing a ladder to rescue a lady bear from the upper floor of a dollhouse that had faux flames on the roof. There was a teddy bear grocer selling jars of honey to teddy bear shoppers pushing miniature carts loaded with plastic berries and nuts. There was even a doctor's-office scene, in which a grinning teddy bear nurse was giving an injection to a tiny, tearful teddy. The nurse teddy looked remarkably like Nurse Dudley.

"So I collect bears," the real nurse growled. "So what? Lots of people collect things."

"Quite true," I said agreeably. "Dorcas Schwartzentruber collects fungi shaped like famous people. She has a dried truffle that's a dead ringer for Harry Truman, a pickled portobello that portrays Pavarotti, and a shiitake shaped like—"

"I've seen them. They aren't nearly as impressive as Veronica

Saylor's bunion with the face of Elvis. You know it was me who assisted Dr. Luther on that surgery. I even had my picture in the *Pittsburgh Post-Gazette*. It was the best photo ever taken of me." She sighed wistfully. "But you didn't come here to discuss collectibles, did you?"

"Most certainly not. I want to know what you did with Lodema."

Her sigh this time was anything but wistful. "She's upstairs. First bedroom on the left. But I have to warn you, that woman's a real head case. Dr. Luther thinks that if she gets any worse, she'll need to be committed to a state hospital."

"Worse?"

"She's regressed rapidly since you brought her in this morning. Last time I looked in on her she was a teenager getting ready for the prom."

"Can she still answer questions?"

"Like a teenager. Yoder, you do realize, don't you, that in order to have her committed we'll need permission from her next of kin?"

"That would have to be one of her relatives in Missouri. I think I can get a name from her sister-in-law."

"You do that. Dr. Luther and I will not be stuck holding your bag."

"*My* bag?"

She glanced at her watch and then pointed to the stairs. "You have exactly five minutes with the patient. *Jeopardy!* comes on in ten minutes, and I want to be all settled in with my snack."

"What type of snack?"

"Apple pie—not that it's any of your business."

Apple pie! Talk about coincidences. And I'd be happy to watch her show with her. Except for reruns of *Green Acres,* I had no experience with television. Frankly, I was rather curious, and now with my pastor dead, there was no one to squeal to. Besides, someone at church had once said *Jeopardy!* was a show suitable for Christians—just as long as they didn't believe all the answers that dealt with science.

"Make some hot chocolate and I'll be glad to join you, dear."

She hesitated, while I hoped.

"Please. Pretty please with sugar on top."

How stupid of me to push; Nurse Dudley came to her senses with a vengeance. "Four minutes now!" she barked.

I hustled my bustle upstairs before she changed her mind. I wished I hadn't been so quick when I opened the door and saw Lodema.

15

Chilies-and-Dried-Beef Dip

Source: ICS Admin
Submitted by: www.chilicookoff.com

Ingredients:

3 tablespoons butter
4-ounce can green chilies, chopped
4-ounce jar dried beef, diced
1 medium-size onion, minced

1 clove garlic, minced
8 ounces cream cheese, creamed
2 tablespoons milk
4 drops Tabasco sauce

Instructions:

Melt butter in heavy skillet and add green chilies, dried beef, onion, and garlic; sauté until onion is tender. In a mixing bowl, combine cream cheese and milk; blend until smooth. Add Tabasco and blend again. Chill 2 hours or until firm. Serve with crackers or chips.

Servings: 2½ cups

16

My pastor's widow was sitting cross-legged on the floor, in a pale pink nightgown, sucking her thumb. Her prayer cap was missing, and her long hair had been divided into matching ponytails. She was surrounded by teddy bears and play tea things. I knocked gently on the doorjamb with my sore knuckles.

"Yeth?" she said.

"It's me, Magdalena Yoder."

She removed her thumb with a *pop*. "Are you my friend?"

"Would you like me to be?"

"My name's Lodema, and I'm having a tea party with my friends. Mr. Bear said you can join us, if you're my friend."

"Then we're very good friends."

"But you have to sit down and cross your legs like this. Then you have to say the magic words if you want tea."

I had to struggle to achieve her position. I may be bony, but I am anything but supple. If the Good Lord had wanted us to assume pretzel shapes, He would have created us out of dough, not clay.

"Now say the magic words," she commanded.

"Abracadabra."

"No! Them's not the right words. Say the right ones, or you don't get any tea."

We Mennonites avoid magic like the plague. Anything hocus-pocus is bound to have the Devil in it somewhere. Better to cut out my tongue than to babble up Beelzebub.

"Ou're-yay uts-nay," I said.

Lodema beamed. "Now you can have your tea." She handed me a miniature cup and saucer, then proceeded to pour the imaginary beverage.

"Thanks."

"Do you want to play dress-up next?"

"Well—sure. But first I have some questions to ask you."

"What kinda questions? 'Cause if they're grown-up questions, I'm not allowed to answer them."

"Says who?"

"Mr. Bear. He makes all the rules."

I turned to the nearest stuffed teddy. "Mr. Bear, would you please let Lodema answer my grown-up questions?"

Lodema's laugh sounded like marbles rattling in a jar. "That's not Mr. Bear, silly. That's Baby Bear. He don't talk at all."

I willed my fuse to stay unlit. "Then which one is Mr. Bear?"

"That one." She pointed to an identical teddy across from me.

"So Mr. Bear," I growled, "how about it?"

Lodema grabbed the bear in question by its head, forcing it to bob up and down. "He said 'Okay.' "

"Good. In that case, Lodema, I'll get straight to the point. Did your husband—I mean, Reverend Schrock—ever have any children? Specifically, a little girl?"

The marbles got another workout. "Of course, silly, *I'm* his little girl. But you know my daddy's up in heaven now, don't you? Soon he's gonna get his wings and be an angel. Then he's going to fly back down here and make me safe."

"That isn't the way it works—oh, never mind. Are you your daddy's only little girl?"

Lodema stuck her tongue out at me. "I don't like that question. Mr. Bear says you're being mean."

"I'm sorry, dear. I'll think of a better one."

But it was too late. Lodema's thumb was back in her mouth, and try as I might, I couldn't get her attention again.

*   *   *

"It was only three minutes," I shouted to Nurse Dudley as I thundered down the stairs.

She shouted something in return, but I slammed the door on her words. I had a lot to think about. Could the little girl in the Tastee-Freez possibly have been my minister's wife? After all, Barbara's head brushed the heavens, while Lodema Schrock was shorter than most stump posts. But Barbara claimed she'd seen the child in the reverend's arms, and believe me, no Mennonite clergyman would be caught dead holding his spouse in his arms, especially in a public place like Tastee-Freez.

On the other hand, it was quite possible the Amish giantess had superimposed one memory over another. This happens to me all the time. For instance, I remember a very passionate night with David Bowie that probably never happened. But the man who shares his name with a hunting knife did stay at my inn one night, as a paying guest, and I did exhibit passion once during my faux marriage to the Miller with no heart. The fact that I sometimes confuse the two events is of no importance to anyone. But whether or not Barbara saw a child in the reverend's arms, when it was really his wife, made a huge difference to my investigation.

Lacking televisions, and even radios, most Amish I know go to bed with the cows—well, not literally (one notable exception is Lantz Yutzy, who was eventually excommunicated). Given the postdinner hour, Barbara was undoubtedly sawing wood, possibly even cords of it, so I didn't feel it was right to disturb her. The only other person in the area who might have a clue about the existence of a mini-Schrock was Catherine, the reverend's sister. Funny, but I didn't even know if her last name was Schrock.

I gave the horses under the hood of my Crown Victoria their heads, and arrived at the parsonage before I left Nurse Dudley's house. One of the benefits of driving this particular model of car is that most folks, the police included, assume I am a policewoman. Since purchasing this beauty I have not received a single speeding ticket. Of course in Hernia I'm not likely to get ticketed anyway. Who's going to stop me? Certainly not Melvin or Zelda.

Catherine opened the door before I had a chance to ring the bell.

"I've been to the market since we last talked. There's a pot of home-made cocoa warming on the stove right now."

"How did you know I'd be back?"

"I didn't. But you put the idea into my head, and homemade hot chocolate sounded good."

"Any pie?"

"As a matter of fact, yes. Peanut butter pie. I made it myself."

"Excuse me?"

"Oh, there wasn't any peanut butter in the house. Picked that up in the market too. I hope you don't mind me saying so, but that man's prices are outrageous."

"Unfathomable," I muttered.

What kind of sister would make a pie using the same ingredient that had killed her brother, and only a day after the tragic event? And in his house yet! I put the question to her.

She blushed. "Oh, my, it never occurred to me. It's just that I love peanut butter pie—that was really very thoughtless of me. You must think I'm really awful."

But I didn't. The truth is I liked her even more. Not many people would be so quick to acknowledge their mistakes.

"I'll pass on the pie, dear, but that cocoa sounds lovely."

She served it with a cascade of partially melted marshmallows, and an extra napkin. "To what do I owe the honor of this visit, Magdalena?"

"I wish I could say it was purely social, but I'm afraid it has to do with your late brother again."

"Oh? What about him?"

"This may sound really strange, but—uh—did he have any children?"

She appeared startled by my question. "Pardon me?"

"Children. One of the people I interviewed today said she thought she saw your brother with a child who called him 'Papa.' "

"I'm afraid that's impossible. I thought everyone knew Arnold and Lodema were incapable of having children—it was Lodema's fault, I can assure you. Something to do with her eggs being prematurely old. Anyway, I guess this rumor about the little girl is to be expected, given that my brother was one of your town's most prominent citizens."

"Indeed he was. But I didn't say the child was a girl."

"You didn't? Funny, but that's what I heard. I guess that's because I always wanted to have a little girl. Someone I could dress up, and for whom I could buy frilly things. But Jack and I have three boys. It looks like I'm going to have to make do with a granddaughter someday."

Aha! So she was most probably married and was no longer named Schrock—although you couldn't be too sure these days. At any rate, she didn't sound the least bit guilty of keeping a secret of this magnitude. I decided to give her the age test just to be sure that she was incapable of lying.

"How old are you, dear?"

"Pardon me?"

"What year were you born?"

"I really don't think that's your business."

The fact that she'd answered immediately meant that she hadn't taken the time to consider how many years to shave off her age, and was therefore an honest person. If a woman pauses, and then mentions a figure, you can be sure it's not accurate. And by the way, most women foolishly subtract years from their chronological age. This makes no sense at all. If one is going to lie about her age, it is always more flattering to *add* years. A fifty-year-old woman who pretends to be forty is going to draw sympathetic looks. A forty-year-old woman who claims to be sixty is an inspiration for us all.

"You're right—it isn't any of my business. But just for the record, I'm sixty-eight," I said, adding two decades.

"My mother is sixty-eight. I think you two would really hit it off."

"But I'm really only forty-eight," I wailed.

She smiled. "Still, I think you'd like her."

I drained the last of my marshmallow-cocoa residue. "In case you need anything, do you know where to find me?"

"The PennDutch Inn on Hertzler Road, right?"

"Right as rain," I said, and then hauled my heinie out of there before I broke down and asked for a piece of peanut butter pie.

*   *   *

I had to make one more stop before I could call it a day and pull my covers up over my head. Catherine was right; Sam Yoder's prices are outrageous, but he is the only game in town. It wouldn't be so bad if he sold quality goods, but there are cans on his shelves that predate perestroika. Everyday staples like SpaghettiOs and SPAM move fast enough, but I once bought a can of pâté de foie gras as a gift for Gabe. When opened, this supposed delicacy emitted an aroma worse than Alison's gym socks and crumbled when it was touched. Only then did I bother to check the expiration date. That particular goose had been cooked the year Richard Nixon resigned from the presidency.

Sam Yoder is a cousin of mine, who fancies himself kissing kin. I constantly have to remind him that he is married to Dorothy and, in fact, left the Mennonite Church in order to marry her. It wasn't a Mennonite law that required him to switch faiths, but his future father-in-law. Ernest Sprague offered a grocery store to the man willing to marry his less-than-attractive daughter, provided the groom also joined the Methodist Church. My cousin was the first to jump in line.

Sam was bent over a ledger when I walked in, but he slammed it shut and grinned. "You're just in time. I was about to close."

"Don't let me stop you. We can talk in my car."

"The backseat?"

"On second thought, in here will do nicely. And leave the Open sign on the door."

"Spoilsport."

"How's Dorothy doing? I've been meaning to give her a call."

"Okay, I'll quit with the flirting. But just so you know, Magdalena, if I ever leave my Dorothy, and you dump that New Yorker of yours, you and I could make sweet Yoder music together."

I made a hand puppet. "Eew."

"You wouldn't have to change your last name."

"True. But a lobotomy is a great deal more trouble."

"You see, Magdalena? We make a great pair."

"Can you make me a great cup of hot chocolate?"

"Say what?"

"You have a hot plate in the storeroom."

"It's broken. But I can get you some chocolate milk. Whole or two percent?"

"Fat's where it's at!" I waited patiently while he fetched the libation. I even resisted the temptation to peek in his ledger, although I confess to reading the notations on his calendar. Alas, there was nothing on it his mother shouldn't see.

"Two nineteen," Sam said when he returned with my treat.

"Excuse me?"

"Two nineteen. That's with the tax. Have to charge that, you know."

"I thought this was on the house."

"But we agreed not to flirt, remember?"

I took the bottle nonetheless and turned it slowly. "This expired two weeks ago."

He didn't have the decency to blush. "They're always generous with the dates. So, Magdalena, to what do I owe the honor of your visit?"

I set the milk on the counter. "Just so you know, I'm not paying for this. Anyway, wouldn't you agree that you're the most informed man in all of Hernia?"

"Well, I do read the *Pittsburgh Post-Gazette* on Sundays. And not just the sports pages either. Sometimes I get through the whole first section."

"That's nice, dear, but when I said 'informed,' I meant 'plugged in.' You hear all the gossip there is behind that counter of yours."

"Yes, I suppose I do. Just the other day I overhead Maybell Diller tell Amanda Augsberger that she was going to Cleveland to get her toes shortened."

"What?"

"Apparently, it's all the rage now. Ladies get their little toes removed altogether, and then second littlest toes cut back to the joint, all so that they can wear these really pointed shoes. Roach killers, I call them—the shoes, not the ladies—on account the ladies who wear them can chase bugs into corners and crush them with the points of their shoes."

"You're making this up."

"I'm not—Scout's honor. Amanda asked how much it cost, and Maybell said seven thousand for one foot, but only ten for two. Said her Roy pitched a fit when she told him she intended to have the procedure done. Roy swore he wasn't going to pay a dime to have his wife's feet mutilated, but then Maybell threatened to let everyone know that he wears a rug. Seems he pays three grand a year to maintain that toupee."

Sam was regarding me with a look of expectancy. I gathered I was supposed to be shocked to hear that Roy Diller's hair was not his own. Well, not hardly. I took one look at Roy about eight years ago when he first moved to town, and deduced that either he was wearing a toupee, or he had recently hit a muskrat with his car, and the roadkill had somehow landed atop his head. What did surprise me was the fact that one could pay to have the toes on just *one* foot altered. Who on earth would do that? Someone who really did have a roach problem?

"That's all very interesting, Sam, but I was wondering if you had any dirt on Reverend Schrock—may he rest in peace."

"Why, Magdalena, I'm surprised. I thought you worshipped the water he walked on."

"That would be 'ground,' dear. Only the Lord walked on water—and of course the Eskimos, but since that's frozen, it doesn't count."

"I believe we're to call them Inuit now."

"Whatever. Back to the reverend. Was there ever any scuttlebutt on him?"

Sam grinned happily. "You better believe it. You want to sit first?" He pulled a wooden stool around from behind the counter.

I decided to give my tootsies a rest and plopped my patooty on the stool. You can be sure I'm never going to alter my toes. Yes, they are extremely long, but should something ever happen to my hands, I'll have a backup pair. Of course I'll have to shave them.

"Spill it, Sam."

17

Sam took a deep breath. "Well, as you may have guessed, theirs was not a perfect marriage."

"With Lodema in the picture, how could it be?"

"Oh, but that's where you're wrong. It was the reverend who caused most of the trouble in that marriage."

"I beg your pardon? Says who?"

"Says just about everyone who comes in here. The guy was never home, and when he was, the sparks flew."

"He was never home because his wife has a tongue like a box razor. You can't blame for him staying away."

"Well, from what I hear, it wasn't his wife who kept him away. It was the dogs."

"What?"

"There was always talk about him slipping down into West Virginia every chance he got to bet on the dog races. And Sadie Gingerich claims she once ran into him in Atlantic City, at one of them big casinos. Yes sir, by all accounts your pastor had a gambling problem."

"I can't believe that. Gambling is a sin—Reverend Schrock knew that. He even preached a sermon on that once."

"That may be, but gambling is also a disease. It can get a grip on you that's almost impossible to escape—at least that's what I've heard."

In my agitation I was toying with the bottle of chocolate milk. Somehow I accidentally ripped off the foil seal. If the Devil could duplicate the odor that escaped, Hell had a new perfume.

"Generous with the expiration date, my eye."

Sam grabbed the bottle and set it on the far end of the counter. "Magdalena, if you really must know, for years now I've heard stories of how he would come home with only half of his paycheck. Lodema tried to get him into counseling, but he refused. Considering the fact that he would have lost his job if she'd gone public with this, you have to admire her silence. She could have been really mean about it."

I felt like my face had been slapped. "It sounds like it was public knowledge. Why didn't I know? Why weren't the church deacons informed?"

"You really don't want to look under that rug, Magdalena. Trust me."

"What rug? Roy Diller's toupee?"

Sam hooted rudely. "Now, that's a good one."

"I wasn't joking, Sam."

"I know. That's what I like about you. You present yourself as tough and worldly, but you're really as innocent and naive as they come."

"I most certainly am not! Thanks to the PennDutch Inn, I've seen just about everything there is to see."

"That Hollywood crowd doesn't count. Everyone knows they're the Devil's cronies. I'm talking about regular everyday people, and the evil they commit."

"Like killing Reverend Schrock. That wasn't Hollywood, Sam. The killer was one of us."

Sam smirked. "You still don't know if it was even murder, now, do you? I thought not. No, I'm referring to people like Peter Esch, who hits his wife on a regular basis."

"Peter Esch who sings bass in the choir at *my* church? Beechy Grove Mennonite?"

"That's him, all right."

"But that's nonsense. Everyone knows that Elizabeth is just clumsy."

"No, she has a bad sense of direction. She keeps running into her husband's fists."

To be honest, I don't know what infuriated me more: the fact that I was clearly out of the loop, or the knowledge that Elizabeth Esch's constant bruises were caused by a brutish lout who passed himself off as a pillar of the church. Well, I couldn't solve Elizabeth's problem there and then, but for a second I considered getting my foot altered to fit a pair of roach killers, and then proceeding to change Peter Esch from a bass to a soprano with a few well-placed kicks. Of course thinking like that was a sin, which didn't make me any better than Peter. I prayed silently, asking for forgiveness. And since I already had the Good Lord's attention, I tacked a few petitions on as well.

"Magdalena, are you okay?" Sam's voice was surprisingly gentle.

"Fine as frog's hair," I said, coming back down to earth.

"Frogs don't have hair."

"Yes, they do, but it's so fine you can't see it."

"The idea of Reverend Schrock leading a double life really bothers you, doesn't it?"

"It makes me sad."

"And you don't like being a chump either. Am I right?"

"Who does? Sam, do you really think those gambling stories about Reverend Schrock are true?"

"Well, you know what they say: Where there's smoke, there's fire."

"Maybe," I said. And maybe all the gossipmongers were wrong.

Because I'd graciously invited Freni and her husband, Mose, to use my quarters that week, I was forced to bunk with Alison. Fortunately her room has twin beds. My foster daughter thrashes in her sleep like a colt wearing plaster casts, and snores so loudly that guests routinely ask to have their room assignments changed.

I crammed foam stoppers in my ears, put a pillow over my head, and pretended I was in a Pullman car of a diesel-engine train. After about an hour of willing the sandman to visit, I found myself drifting into peaceful oblivion. I was awake, but only barely, when the train jerked to a stop, and someone started pounding furiously on the door to my compartment.

"If you're the porter," I mumbled, "leave the hot chocolate outside. I'll get it in a minute. But if you're Russell Crowe, the silk bathrobe is hanging behind the door."

"What was that?" a woman demanded. "Did you say Russell Crowe was in there with you?"

I sat up and switched on a bedside lamp. Except for the sound of Alison sawing wood, the inn was silent. Apparently too much hot chocolate can produce weird dreams.

"I don't care if Russell Crowe's in there. If you don't come out, Magdalena, I'm going to have to force my way in. I've got the warrant for your arrest right here in my hand."

"Zelda?" I sprang out of bed and threw open the door. I was still in a befuddled state, and if by some chance it *was* Russell Crowe in the hallway, then he was going to be treated to a sight of me in my flannel nightgown with the pink flamingo appliqués. If that was too much for him to handle, so be it.

Alas, it was only the policewoman. " 'You have the right to remain silent—' "

"I beg your pardon?"

"I said I had a warrant for your arrest, Magdalena. I wasn't kidding. Now where was I?"

"Arrest for what?"

Zelda waved the paper, which, of course, made it impossible to read. "For the murder of Catherine Grabinski."

"This is ridiculous! I don't even know a Catherine Grabinski."

"Reverend Schrock's sister."

"She's *dead*? How did it happen? When?"

"You should know, Magdalena. Mrs. Dalton, the neighbor across the street, said she saw you leave the reverend's house tonight in a hurry."

I felt light-headed. I had genuinely liked the reverend's sister. And as I'd been too tired to brush my teeth, the taste of her cocoa was still on my tongue. Sometimes the events that mark the turning points of our lives come at us at dizzying speeds. This was one of them.

"I don't feel so well, Zelda."

"I've often wondered, Magdalena, if killing someone is a tiring experience. You know, like, if it drains energy from your body as well as your soul. Thank you for answering my question."

"I didn't kill anyone! I had no motive."

"But you had opportunity."

"Did I have the means?" My voice dripped enough sarcasm to make the hardwood floor under my bare tootsies as slippery as a greased skillet. Of course I didn't have the means—I didn't even know what it was.

"Absolutely. Mrs. Grabinski was shot with the reverend's shotgun. It was laying right there in the living room, near her body."

"Think about it, Zelda. Would I leave the gun there to be discovered? You know I'm too smart for that."

"You're smart, all right. Smart enough to make it look like you're stupid. And smart enough to distract me with all this talk. Magdalena, you have to let me finish reading the Carmen Miranda rights."

I sighed. There was no point in arguing with someone who, in all seriousness, calls herself a Melvinite.

"I don't think Carmen had much to do with them, but read away!" My blasé attitude was the by-product of innocence. The arrest warrant made no sense. Perhaps I was still dreaming. At the very worst, all I had to do was call my lawyer and the entire mess would simply disappear, like snow in April.

"Now I'm going to have to start over. 'You have the right to remain silent—' "

"Where's Melvin? Shouldn't he be making the arrest? For all you know, I might resist. I may be tall and skinny, not to mention a pacifist, but I'm sure I could pack a pretty mean punch if I wanted. And if I had my feet surgically altered like Maybell Diller plans to, and was wearing roach killers, I could deliver a debilitating blow where the sun doesn't shine."

"Magdalena, you're weird, you know that?"

"You're calling the kettle black, dear."

"For your information, Melvin's waiting downstairs. He didn't want to see you naked."

"Fat chance. Just because he sleeps in the buff—" I shuddered. Susannah made sure I was privy to far more information than I ever wanted to know. Who cared that he named *his* bunny slippers Thumper and Bugs, and that he still carried a piece of his original "blankie" around with him in his wallet?

"Thou shalt not take the name of Melvin Stoltzfus in vain." Zelda's eyes were glazed like those of a crazed zealot.

"My Miranda rights," I said gently.

"Uh—darn it, Magdalena, you made me forget the words."

"I have a right to remain silent. Anything I say can be used against me. I have the right to have an attorney present. . . ."

Hernia has only one attorney, Elias Sand. I would sooner become a Melvinite than swim with that shark. Instead, I use a female lawyer in Bedford—although one shouldn't be under the impression I require her services very often.

Evelyn Wilkerson also happens to be the young mother of three, and it was her babysitter who answered the phone. "They're, like, out," she said, and hung up.

I punched REDIAL before Melvin or Zelda could stop me. "Stay on the line, dear, or I'll tell Mrs. Wilkerson to dock your pay."

"Who is this? Are you like some kind of crank caller?"

"I'm a client. And what on earth are the Wilkersons doing out so late?"

"They're in Pittsburgh. Seeing some kind of play or something. They're going to spend the night there."

"Do you have Mrs. Wilkerson's cell phone number?" Hope springs eternal, even in the smallest of breasts.

"Yeah, I got it, but I ain't allowed to give it to nobody."

"To anyone, dear."

"That's what I said. Look, I gotta go. My show's about to start."

"I'll give you fifty bucks if you give me that cell phone number."

She hesitated for just a second too long. "Nah, Mrs. Wilkerson would kill me if I did."

"Make that a hundred, dear."

A minute later I was on the phone to Pittsburgh, not that it did me a fat lot of good. The Wilkersons had already gone to bed, and Mr. Wilkerson informed me, in not the nicest of tones, that his wife had taken a prescription sleeping pill, and that he would relay my message to her in the morning. My goose was cooked.

18

The Hernia hoosegow has only two cells, one of which I had the displeasure of seeing from the inside several years ago. Mercifully, I seem to have blocked out most of the details of that visit. This time around, Melvin stood idly by, grinning like a Cheshire cat on steroids, while Zelda bustled around changing the sheets on a metal cot and whistling somber Melvinite hymns.

"Are you going to place a chocolate on my pillow, dear?"

"No. But I am going to bring you breakfast in the morning. What would you like?"

"Two eggs poached, medium hard; four strips of bacon fried crisp, but not so that they shatter; half a grapefruit, broiled with brown sugar on top—come to think of it, bring that first; and two slices of raisin cinnamon toast with unsalted butter. Oh, and a cup of cocoa—the kind made with milk. And of course, lots of marsh-mallows."

"You get your choice of Cheerios or Cap'n Crunch. And I think there's a bag of green tea around somewhere."

"I used it yesterday," Melvin said. "But it's still in the mug, in case you want to give it another try."

"Thanks, but no thanks. A cup of your regular jailhouse coffee will do just fine."

Zelda hung her spiky head in shame. "I accidentally broke the

Mr. Coffee last winter. That's why we've been using tea bags—when we remember to bring some in."

I graciously thanked the ditzy duo for their hospitality, such as it was. "Just one more thing before you go, dears. You seem to have forgotten my striped pajamas."

"Sorry, Magdalena, but those striped prison clothes are only in the movies."

"Or the comic books," Melvin added.

"But I look good in stripes! Horizontal ones, of course. The vertical ones make me look like a row of telephone poles."

"Enough chatting, Yoder."

Melvin turned off all the lights except for a bare bulb hanging in the corridor. The light switches, however, were located on the wall just to the left of my cell. I counted to a hundred after hearing the front door to the police station close and two cars drive away. Then I slipped a slim, but shapely, hand through the bars and turned on all the lights. After all, as Hernia's biggest taxpayer, I'm the one who paid for all that juice.

Of course my cell looked better in the dark, and I would have flipped the lights back off again had not some graffiti caught my eye. Having nothing else to read, and no longer at all sleepy, I browsed the walls. Given the fact that Hernia is a God-fearing town, the scribbles were predominantly religious in nature. A few of them, I am ashamed to say, even made me chuckle.

I will lift mine eyes up unto Barbara Hostetler, whose cups runneth over.
For a good time, call the prayer hotline.
Jesus saves, but Moses invests.
Melvin Stoltzfus rocks.
Joy cometh in the morning.
Magdalena Yoder is a big chunk of asphalt.

Now, that was going too far! I scrutinized the handwriting carefully, in hopes of identifying its author. A goodly proportion of Hernia's citizenry have passed through my fifth-grade Sunday school class. A disproportionate number of those children have mysteriously ended up on the wrong side of the law. Go figure.

Unfortunately this delinquent was easy to identify. *"Et tu, Su-sannah?"* I wailed.

In the old days, in the first few years following our parents' deaths, my sister became a tramp. I mean this in more than one sense of the word. Not only did she leave home to see the world, but—well, you get the rest of the picture. She drank a lot too. I was forever having to bail her out of jail, and in fact, it was because of her frequent visits to the pokey that she and Melvin became friendly. At any rate, if I'd known she was going to write mean things about me on jailhouse walls with her waterproof mascara, I wouldn't have been so quick to raise bail.

You can be sure I did my Christian best to rub out the worst of the scribbles, and replace them with inspirational quotes of my own, using a pencil stub I found under my mattress. It may surprise you to learn that I am never without anything to say. Anyway, I was working hard at this noble task when a voice from above interrupted me.

"Psst!"

"Just a minute, Lord. This is a good one—you're going to like it."

"Mom?"

I dropped the pencil and looked up. Near the ceiling there was a small window, smaller even than my noggin. It had been forced open, not that it mattered, because a row of closely spaced iron bars was embedded in the wall. Behind the bars I could see most of Alison's head. Her eyes shone like those of a raccoon caught in the headlights of my car.

"What on earth are you doing up there?"

"I followed you, Mom."

"You did? But you were fast asleep when I was arrested."

"Oh, Mom, don't be so silly. I was only pretendin'. Ya don't think I'd sleep through anything as cool as that, do ya?"

"Being arrested for murder is hardly cool, dear. It breaks my heart that you have to even know about this."

"Of course it's cool, Mom. How many other kids do ya know whose moms get arrested for murder?"

"Which I didn't do!"

"Yeah, I know that, but the kids at school won't. I don't have to tell them, do I? I mean, not until they try to hang you or something."

I stroked my neck. Not bad for my age, if I do say so myself. But I can't even stand to wear turtlenecks. A noose was simply out of the question.

"Whoa! That's putting the cart way before the horse. They're not going to hang me, because I didn't do it. Tomorrow morning when my lawyer gets back into town—but never mind that; how did you get here? It's five miles back to the inn, for crying out loud."

"Promise me ya won't get mad?"

Those six words are the penultimate red flag for parents, a signal for them to gear up and ready themselves for action. But when one is behind bars, there is little one can do but play along.

"I'll try not to get mad. Spill it, dear."

"No way. Ya gotta promise first. Because, like, I know ya don't lie, Mom."

"Really?" This guilt trip was worth enough frequent-flier miles to see me around the globe.

"Yeah. You're always saying how important the truth is, and like, I kinda trust ya, so if the truth is that important to ya, ya ain't gonna lie."

"I ain't? I mean, wow. You really do listen." I crossed my fingers behind my back. "In that case, I promise."

"Okay, here goes." My foster daughter took a deep breath and held it for several seconds, each an eternity. "Ya know your car?"

"I think I do." It was my turn to hold my breath.

"Well, like, I kinda drove it."

"You *what*?"

"Mom! You promised not to be mad."

"I'm not mad, dear. I'm merely extremely agitated. How on earth did you manage to drive it?"

"Uh—like, I've been kinda practicing."

"*What*?"

"Ya know, like driving it around a little bit at night sometimes. I gotta be ready when it's time to get my license."

"But you're only thirteen!"

"Yeah, but ain't ya the one who's always yapping about practice makes perfect, or something like that?"

"When do you do this—the practicing?"

"At night when you're asleep. Ain't nobody out on the road then, except other teenagers, so it's, like, totally safe."

I might have pulled my hair out had I not learned from past experience that it hurts. "Alison Miller, you are—are—well, you're forbidden to ever drive again until you have a learner's permit. And then only when there's an adult in the car. Is that clear?"

"Yeah. I guess I should be glad that I ain't grounded, right?"

"Right as rain. Now drop the keys through those bars."

"Aw, Mom."

"*Now.*"

"How am I supposed to get home?"

"My cell phone is in the car. Call your auntie Susannah, and ask her to come pick you up. She'll need to have her friend Brenda next door drive her over here so she can drive my car home and then get a ride back."

"Can I stay over at her house if she asks?"

That was exactly what I had hoped she'd say. If I couldn't keep the kid under my roof all night, how on earth would Freni and Mose manage? My sister, however, was an expert on sneaking out. If I solicited Susannah's cooperation, Alison wasn't going any farther than her dreams could take her. Not that I was about to let Alison know that.

"I don't think that's such a good idea, dear."

"Please? Pretty please, with sugar on top?"

"Oh, all right."

"You're the best, Mom. Ya know that?"

"Yes, I know. Drop the keys."

She did.

"Now tell me, dear, just what did you hope to gain by coming here?"

"Nuttin'. I just wanted to bring ya some things, that's all."

"Things? What sort of things?"

"Well, I've been here to visit Uncle Melvin, see, so I knew this place is kind of yucky. So like, I brought you some sheets from home, and your pillow, and your jammies and bathrobe, and some instant coffee on account he don't drink nothing but that yucky green tea. And of course ya gotta have some of Freni's coffee cake with that. And some hard-boiled eggs, and some fruit. And some chocolate, on account you like that so much. Oh, and I brought ya some books, and a flashlight—that's in case he makes ya turn the lights out—and some clothes for tomorrow, and your deodorant—ain't nothing worse than a stinky old lady—and your toothbrush and stuff like that."

How could Aaron Miller and his wife have come to the conclusion that the child was incorrigible? If she was, it was only because she was incorrigibly thoughtful. Even my own mama wouldn't have thought to bring all that stuff. Never mind that my mama wouldn't have had the opportunity, because she would have died of a stroke upon hearing about my incarceration.

The tears streamed down my face, so I turned my head. No one has ever seen me bawl like a baby, and no one is ever going to.

"Thank you, dear. I'll tell you what. Why don't we keep this little midnight ride of yours just between us. No point in both of us being in trouble with the law."

"Thanks, Mom."

"Now, as much as I appreciate your thoughtfulness, I don't think it's possible to pass some of that stuff through those bars. They're pretty close together."

Alison giggled. "I don't have to pass it through no bars. I got me a key to the front door, and another key for the cell door. Plus, I know the security code."

"Excuse me?"

"Oops, I think maybe ya gotta promise again about not getting mad."

"Mad? Is that what you think?" I wiped my face with an already sodden sleeve. "Get yourself on down here and let me give you a big hug."

"Don't be getting all gross on me, Mom," she said, and then disappeared.

*   *   *

When Zelda opened the front door to the station in the morning, she nearly fainted. Well, at least to hear her tell it. I was sitting on my bed, which had been made with hospital corners, sipping a cup of java and reading a mystery by a writer named Carolyn Hart. I'd already dressed, and combed, braided, and coiled my mousy brown hair, and was wearing a fresh, crisply starched prayer cap. The eggs, fruit, and coffee cake had long since been consumed.

After Zelda had caught both her breath and her balance—the nonregulation heels she wears are widower-makers to be sure—she gave me the third degree. There was nothing I was willing to tell her. Susannah had answered Alison's midnight call, and had been only too happy to keep knowledge of our high jinks from her somnolent husband.

"Please," Zelda begged. "If you tell me how you got all this stuff, I'll tell you what I keep in the holy box under my altar to Melvin."

I brushed cake crumbs from my bosom. "No, thanks. I don't want to know."

"Okay, Magdalena, if you want to play rough, I'm game. Unless you tell, I'm going to force you to hear what I keep in that little box."

"Force away, dear." I clapped my hands over my ears. "La-la-la-la-la-la."

Zelda thought she could pull a fast one by exaggeratedly mouthing the words, but I simply closed my eyes. When I put my mind to it, I can represent two of those three monkeys one sees in novelty shops. Unfortunately "Speak no evil" is still beyond my capabilities.

Finally, Hernia's second finest gave up. I could tell she'd switched topics, by the change in her tone, muffled as it was, but I let her say a few more things before I uncovered my ears.

"Would you mind repeating that, dear?"

"I said, it doesn't matter anyway because you're free to go."

"You're kidding!"

"I don't know why we didn't catch it, but the coroner saw it right away."

"And what would that be?"

"Mrs. Grabinski was killed with her brother's shotgun, right?"

"That's what you and Melvin said."

"You see, one of the pellets from the shotgun hit her watch and stopped it, pinpointing the time of death. I did some checking and learned that it happened while you were at Yoder's Corner Market talking to Sam. Since you obviously can't be in two places at the same time—well, that means you didn't kill her."

"Which is what I said last night. Repeatedly. Hmm, I wonder if I could sue for false arrest."

"Don't push your luck, Magdalena. I'm sure you broke a law by getting in all this stuff. And if you didn't break a law, then the person who helped you did. Breaking and entering at the least. Do you want me to pursue that?"

"Let's call it a draw, dear."

"Okay, but you got to clear this stuff out before Melvin gets here. He's not going to like it one bit."

I started stripping the bed. "I can keep a secret if you can, dear."

Zelda, who'd been watching anxiously, suddenly looked away. "Can you really, Magdalena? Because if you can, I've got something really big I just have to share with someone."

19

"For the last time, I don't want to know what's in that stupid box!"

"This has nothing to do with the box." Zelda paused and bit her painted lips. And either she was fighting back tears, or the bats were being amorous again.

"Spit it out, dear."

"I'm pregnant."

I jiggled pinkies in both ears to make sure they weren't blocked. "Would you mind repeating that? There seems to be some distortion."

"You heard correctly the first time. I'm with child."

Automatically I glanced around. We were the only two in the jail wing. Perhaps the urchin was hiding behind the door. Unless Zelda meant the child was inside her—

"Oh, my stars! I think I get it now. You're in the family way—am I right? Of course you're not married, which does make this a mite confusing, because although you dress like a hussy, you had a proper upbringing, so I don't think you'd do the tatami tarantella without the benefit of wedlock. On the other hand, Susannah had a good Christian upbringing, and she did the bedspring boogie-woogie at the drop of a hat. The only option would be a repeat of the virgin birth—Zelda, please tell me you're not going to give your kooky religion credit for this."

"For your information, Magdalena, not that this is any business of yours, I haven't been a virgin since high school. And I'm going to ask you for the last time not to make offensive remarks about my faith. I don't mock your beliefs, do I?"

"That's because I believe the right way." I gasped when the rest of what she'd just said permeated my thick skull. "Did your parents know you were doing the four-poster fox-trot in high school?"

"Magdalena, don't make this any tougher on me than it already is. I thought I could turn to you for help."

"But you can! It's just taking me a minute to get used to the idea." It would, however, take longer than that to get over my feeling of envy. Why was zany Zelda to be blessed with a bundle of joy when I, who was as stable as Gibraltar, will forever remain as barren as the Gobi Desert? Where is the justice in that? I know, we are not to question the ways of the Lord—well, at least not in this life. But you can be sure that when I get to Heaven I'm going to have a list of questions a mile long. And I will expect to get answers.

"Well, have you gotten used to it?"

I sighed. "I guess as used to it as I'll ever be. So, how can I help?"

"You can use your influence to help me keep my job."

"My what?"

"You're the most powerful and influential woman in Hernia, aren't you?"

"Flattery will get you just about anywhere with me—as long as it doesn't involve dancing. But please, dear, be more specific."

"As you know, I can't be fired just because I'm pregnant. But people around here are so conservative—you know what I mean. I'm afraid, once they find out, they'll no longer see me as an authority figure. And a policewoman without authority is like a prophet without disciples. Magdalena, I need you to—well—do some public relations work for me."

"I think you're barking up the wrong tree, dear."

"You mean you won't help me?"

"I mean the bad publicity is more likely to involve that bizarre religion of yours. Most Hernians have soft hearts, so no one is going to take it out on the baby, that's for sure. And as for your marital status, offhand I can think of at least six Hernians who are in no position to throw stones. And that's not even counting the Amish. Outsiders think Amish girls must be pure as the driven snow, and mostly that's true, but there are also those who go too far during their *rumschpringe*. Do you think Deborah Troyer's parents were in favor of her marrying at age sixteen? Anyway, like I said, I'd worry more about blasphemy than babies. As you know, folks around here take their religion very seriously."

Zelda had recoiled at my outburst and was rocking back and forth on her strumpet's heels. "Well, I'm not going to recant my faith, that's for sure. I'll die a martyr if I must. But they'll have to wait on the stoning until after my baby is born. You will at least help me find a good home for her, won't you?"

Of course I would. I might even consider taking her in myself, unless, of course, the father objected. The *father*? A terrifying thought popped into my head.

"Is Melvin the daddy? Does Susannah know? Zelda, how could you sleep with my sister's husband?"

"I didn't."

"Then who's the father?"

"Frankly, I don't know."

"For shame, for shame, for shame. Even for you, this is a new low."

She smiled inappropriately. "I didn't sleep with anybody. It was in vitro fertilization."

"What?" I gasped. "You did the samba with a syringe?"

"Magdalena, you're strange, you know that? And it was more like a turkey baster than a syringe."

I will admit to feeling a flood of jealousy. And it wasn't just the baby I envied her, but the fact that she felt free enough to do such an outrageous thing. Having a baby out of wedlock, not knowing the father, starting a new religion—whether I liked it or not, this all took moxie. Maybe one of these days I'd find the strength to rebel and pin a bit of lace to my starched organza prayer cap. White lace, of course.

"Don't worry, dear," I heard myself say. "If anyone gives you any trouble, they'll have me to contend with." It was easy to be generous. After all, Zelda's pregnancy meant the end of her crush on my brother-in-law. Surely she no longer held out any hope that he would abandon my sister and cleave unto her. Not when the bun in her oven was put there by an anonymous baker.

"I knew I could count on you, Magdalena. Just think, seven months from now me, Melvin, and little Melvin Junior will be one happy family."

"In your dreams! The mantis isn't going to want anything to do with you when he finds out you're carrying another man's baby."

Zelda had the temerity to give me a spackle-cracking smile. "But you see, men can't resist pregnant women. They're drawn to them like flies to a pie. As soon as I start showing, Melvin's going to leave that skinny sister of yours and come home to fertile mama."

I am no longer easily shocked, but that doesn't stop me from being dismayed. "You're bringing another human being into this world just to lure my brother-in-law away from his wife?"

"Don't be ridiculous, Magdalena. Finally snagging Melvin is just a side benefit. I'm having a baby because my biological clock was about to run down. I don't want to be left old and childless like some."

"I have Alison!"

"But you'll never have a mini-Magdalena." She patted her belly, which was still every bit as flat as my chest. "This baby is going to look just like me."

"Or its father. Have you given any thought to that? You know I'm not a racist, Zelda, but what if it turns out to be African-American?"

"Oh, it won't be that. I checked blue eyes, blond hair, six feet six, likes long walks on the beach, lively personality. Oh, and that he shouldn't be too intelligent. I don't want a child who's smarter than I am."

"A vivacious vacuous Viking! Just want Hernia needs."

Someone, other than Zelda, tapped me on the back. "Holy guacamole," I cried, and literally jumped out of one of my shoes. Thank heavens Alison had thought to bring me a fresh pair of woolen stockings.

The interloper was none other than Little Samson. "Didn't mean to scare you, Magdalena. Sorry about that."

"No need to apologize, dear. I was just doing my exercises."

Little Samson glanced at Zelda. "Is Magdalena free to go?"

Zelda nodded reluctantly.

"How did you know I was here?" I asked the farrier.

"Magdalena, this is Hernia. Everyone knew you were arrested within the hour. In fact, we held a prayer meeting for you at the church at three in the morning."

I gasped. "You did? What did you pray for?"

"We prayed that God would send an angel to deliver you from prison, just like He did for Peter."

"Alison," I muttered.

"Aha!" Zelda said. "So that's who brought you all the stuff. Well, tell me this, Magdalena. How did she get here?"

"She took a chariot, dear." I gathered up my bedding and the rest of my belongings. "Can you give me a ride home, Little Samson?"

"Sure thing."

We headed for the door, Zelda clomping after us on her life-threatening heels. "Don't forget—it's a secret," she hollered.

"I've already forgotten, dear."

"About my being with child!" she yelled.

So much for her wanting to keep the impending blessed event private. Men are even bigger gossips than women, and Amish men are the biggest gossips of all. The minute Little Samson returned to work, word would start spreading like nits in a kindergarten.

Little Samson told me that what he had to say would take longer than the drive back to the PennDutch Inn, so I suggested we drive up to Stucky Ridge. This mountain (at least by Hernian standards) overlooks the town and is crowned by both a picnic area and a historic cemetery. Just for the record, we parked in the picnic area.

"Keep the engine running, dear," I directed. "It's a mite on the cold side."

Little Samson agreed. "I saw on TV that there's a snowstorm moving this way. Six to eight inches, the weatherman said."

I bit my tongue while I counted to three. "Do you really watch television?"

The blacksmith's face colored. "Reverend Schrock said it was okay to watch the news and some of the educational shows."

"He did?" I sat in stunned silence for a few minutes. Who really was this pastor who'd passed away? When had the world stopped making sense? Were we all headed to you-know-where in a hand-basket? If so, it better be pretty darn large.

"Don't you watch television?" Samson asked, putting an end to my reverie.

"I used to watch *Green Acres*," I whispered shamefully. "But then I felt so guilty about it, I gave the TV away."

Little Samson nodded. "I once watched a show called *Everybody Loves Raymond*. It made me laugh. In fact, I enjoyed it too much. I watched another comedy, and then another. Soon I was watching TV every evening. Finally I had to force myself not to watch these shows because I knew I would get addicted. As you know, Magdalena, straddling the fence between the world and the Kingdom of God can be very difficult. I think the reverend especially would have agreed with me."

"What do you mean?"

"This is what I need to tell you." He stared off across the valley. The bare trees along the ridge clawed at dark clouds like the feet of inverted ravens.

"Spit it out, dear, before those clouds spit snow. It would be embarrassing to get stranded up here with you."

"Magdalena, this is very difficult for me. It's—well, it's about money."

"Which is *not* the root of all evil. It's the love of money which can trip us up."

"It certainly caused our pastor to stumble."

"I beg your pardon? Reverend Schrock lived a modest life. I know that for a fact, because I approved his salary."

"That's what I kept telling myself when I first saw the discrepancy. But I'm afraid there's no other way to explain it."

"Explain what?" Pulling the story out of Little Samson was getting to be every bit as hard as pulling horses' teeth—not that I've done much of that, mind you.

"You know the building fund? For the new Sunday school wing?"

"You mean the one I donated twenty-five thousand dollars to last year?" I'm sure that sarcasm is a sin, but at least it's not one of the big ten.

"Anyway, that had always been Reverend Schrock's pet project. As treasurer I tallied what was in the offering plates, handled the general donations, made the necessary deposits and withdrawals, paid the reverend's salary, but I never even saw the books for the building fund."

I squeezed the armrest on the door. "I don't think I like where this is going."

"After you spoke to me yesterday, I went over the books. The general operating fund is in tip-top shape. In fact, we have a surplus this year of almost eighty thousand dollars. But the building fund—well, I had to rummage through the reverend's desk to find the key to that green filing cabinet in the corner—Magdalena, you're going to need to sit for this."

Ever the cooperative gal, I hoisted my patooty off the seat and repositioned it again. "Fire away!"

"The building fund is depleted."

"What?"

"Well, there's ninety-some dollars left. And change."

"That can't be! I've given at least ten thousand to it every year for the past decade. Yes, I know we had to replace the roof a couple of years ago, but—"

Samson touched my left hand with fingers that felt like loofah sponges. "There is supposed to be half a million dollars in there."

"Really?"

"At least. The building fund bank statement once came to me by mistake. This was several years ago, but even then there was close to that amount in it. I'm sure the roof expenses have long since been canceled out by new contributions. Magdalena, this can only mean that Reverend Schrock had been embezzling."

"But he was a Mennonite, for crying out loud!"

"Even Mennonites aren't perfect. We should have had a system of checks and balances in place."

"We did. It's called God."

"Yes, but God could use a human helping hand from time to time."

I rolled my window down despite the cold. I was feeling the need to "blow chunks," as Alison puts it. Little Samson's car wasn't the cleanest I've seen, but there was no call to dirty it further. For the moment, however, the brisk air seemed to do the trick.

"Magdalena, are you all right?"

"I've just had my faith shaken to its foundation. How do you think I am?"

"I understand. Me too. What do you think the reverend did with all that money?"

"Sam Yoder said there were rumors that he gambled. Have you heard that?"

Little Sam seemed genuinely surprised. "Then he was a lousy gambler. And no, I haven't heard that."

"But your blacksmith shop is the font of all gossip."

"Be careful, Magdalena—you'll make me proud. You're right, though—I hear a lot of gossip. Maybe the men are reluctant to talk about him because they all know I'm a Mennonite."

"Maybe. But if he didn't gamble it away, then where is it?"

He shrugged. "Is it conceivable that—no, I'm sure it couldn't be that."

"Are you thinking he might have had a drug problem?"

"Maybe. What do you think?"

"Well, he did break his leg playing softball with the youth group. Maybe he spent it illegally acquiring prescription drugs."

"Whatever he did, we're going to have to report this to the police. The official police—no offense."

"None taken, dear." I rolled my window up. My nausea had passed, and it had begun to snow—not the lazy drifting flakes of Christmas cards, but dry, stinging granules that mean serious business.

20

Chorizo with Eggs and Chili

Source: ICS Admin
Submitted by: www.chilicookoff.com

Ingredients:

2 chorizos (Spanish sausages)
1 tablespoon chopped onion

2 eggs, lightly beaten
¼ cup green chili sauce

Instructions:

Mash and heat chorizos in a well-greased heavy skillet. Add onion and mix. Turn heat low and add lightly beaten eggs and chili sauce. Stir eggs from bottom of skillet as they become firm. Cook to desired firmness. Serve at once with toast.

Servings: 1

21

By the time we reached the PennDutch the snow was blowing horizontally. Shifting sheets of powder all but obscured the highway, forcing Little Samson to drive at a buggy's pace.

"Come on in and I'll have Freni fix you a nice cup of hot chocolate. Who knows, there might even be a Bundt cake cooling on the kitchen table."

"Sounds good, but no, thanks. There'll be a line of people waiting for me when I get back to the smithy. A horse can't afford to throw a shoe in this kind of weather."

I thanked him profusely for the ride, but reluctantly for the information. We both promised to do more digging and then get back in touch. I left him with the impression I was going to call Melvin right away and report the missing funds.

Freni was standing at the kitchen sink, her back turned to me, when I burst through the kitchen door along with a blast of snow. She didn't bother to turn her head.

"Ach, your mama would roll over in her grave if she knew about the jail."

It warmed both the cockles of my heart and the corns on my feet to know that she didn't, for a second, consider me guilty of Catherine Grabinski's death. A mere five hundred years of inbred aloofness prevented me from spinning her around and hugging her ample frame.

"Where is everyone?"

"The guests all went to Bedford to look for antiques. Tell me, Magdalena, why do the English like old things so much, but the old people, they do not like so much?"

That was a good question, but one for which I didn't have an answer. "I'm sure I don't know. Where's Alison?"

"Mose took her over to that woman's house to play with the triplets."

"*That* woman is your daughter-in-law, and the house is still yours. And why isn't Alison in school?"

"Because the school called and said it was a snow day. So many excuses to close the school, yah? We Amish, I think, are not such woosies."

"The word is 'wusses,' dear. At least that's what Alison says." I cut a thick slice of the warm cake and, not willing to wait for Freni to whip up fresh cream, slathered my portion with the stuff from a can.

Freni wiped her hands on her apron and turned to face me. "Ach, this cake was for the English, for their lunch. Now what will I do? Make another? Magdalena, you forget that I am an old woman."

"Sorry about that."

Her pug nose sniffed the aroma of warm, moist chocolate cake. "What's done is done. So now I will make them stewed prunes instead. Cut me a piece, yah?"

We had two slices each, and were in the process of mashing the last crumbs into our fork tines when the door flew open and in tumbled Melvin Stoltzfus. He was accompanied by a cloud of snow.

"*Ach du leiber!*"

"It's the abominable policeman," I said.

Melvin blinked snow from his walleyes as he brushed it from his clothes. Fortunately the white stuff was too dry to stick.

"Yoder, I need you—is that chocolate Bundt cake?"

"Only a dollar a slice, dear."

"Is there milk?"

"That's a buck fifty a glass."

"Make it a twelve-ounce, then, and fill it to the top."

He pulled a chair away from the table and made himself comfortable while I fixed his snack. A thin slice of cake, no whipped cream, and a ten-ounce glass three-quarters full was what he was getting, like it or not. He didn't seem to notice.

"Yoder, I've been at the Schrock house since dawn, going over it with a fine-tooth comb. Guess what I found?"

"A bunch of loose hair?"

"Warm, but not hot."

"My guess, or the cake?"

"I found a plastic photo insert from a wallet halfway under the couch." He waited expectantly.

"So?" I asked pleasantly.

"What's usually found in photo inserts?"

"Little green men from Mars?"

"Exactly. So I figure—very funny, Yoder." He turned to Freni, who, incidentally, carries neither purse nor wallet. "Photographs is what you find. Usually photographs of loved ones. Susannah carries a picture of me and one of Shnookums. Even one of you."

"And not me?" I wailed. I was serious of course.

"Back to business, Yoder. So anyway, Mrs. Grabinski's wallet was still in her purse, and still contained her driver's license and a handful of credit cards. But there weren't any photographs in it—zilch, nada. That isn't normal, Yoder."

"I'm sure there are a lot of normal people who don't carry photographs around with them," I said in defense of myself.

"Oh yeah? Who?"

"Back to your brilliant hypothesis, dear."

"Well, like I was about to say before you so rudely interrupted me, I figure that whoever shot the reverend's sister stole the insert from her wallet, pocketed the photos, and then tossed the empty holder aside."

"Why would he do that?"

"What makes you think it was a *he*, Yoder?"

"Because most murderers are. But go on, Melvin. Answer my question. Why would anyone steal photographs from someone's purse?"

Melvin snorted and the milk I'd served him appeared from places where lactose was never intended. "Because, you idiot, one of the pictures was of the perpetrator."

Freni and I exchanged glances. Melvin's mother, Elvina Stoltz-fus, is Freni's best friend, but there is no denying the fact that somewhere a village had lost its idiot. Ever since Melvin was kicked in the head by a bull, one he was trying to milk, my sister's husband has not been the brightest bulb in the chandelier. Once he even sent a gallon of ice cream to his favorite aunt in Scranton. By UPS.

"What is it you need me to do?" I asked calmly. After all, there was still some milk and quite a bit of cake to sell.

"Find the missing photographs, of course. That will solve everything. Sometimes, Yoder, I don't think you have a brain in your head."

I rapped my noggin with my knuckles—gently of course. It did sound fairly empty.

"I'll do my best," I said. "Care for another slice of cake?"

"Hmm." One eye surveyed the dessert: the other studied the falling snow through the kitchen window. "How much will you charge if I take the whole thing with me?"

"Five dollars."

"That's highway robbery, Yoder. I can buy an entire cake at Pat's I.G.A. over in Bedford for that amount."

"Okay then, I'll mark this one up to twenty. Then I'll reduce the price to ten dollars, which is fifty percent off. The marked-down cakes at the I.G.A. are a day old, but this one was baked this morning."

"Deal," Melvin said, and slapped a ten-dollar bill on the table.

For the record, I was taking advantage of my brother-in-law because it was my money he was spending to begin with.

I always think best on the throne, not that it's anyone's business. But I had no need to reign just then, even for a short while, so I elected to do my brainstorming in Big Bertha. She's my one vice, now that I have given up sitting on my Kenmore. Big Bertha—that's her catalog name—is a 125-gallon, 30-jet-spray, whirlpool bathtub. She's located in my private bathroom, of course, where I'd ensconced Mose and Freni, but my cook gave me permission to invade her temporary quarters.

I know—a lot of people prefer showers, and 125 gallons is a lot to waste on a single bath, but I think the Good Lord wouldn't have allowed such a luxury to exist if He didn't approve of it. After all, this particular tub is practically deep enough for one to be baptized in—although we Mennonites prefer the more sedate method of "pouring."

Gardenia-scented bubbles and near-scalding water are tools the Good Lord provided us with to boost our brainpower. Come Christmas our Chief of Police was going to find a jar of bath salts among his presents.

There are some people who should never sing in public, and I must confess to being one of them. It is my firm belief that the Almighty gifted me with this condition as a safeguard against the sin of pride. Just why He added humongous feet, a flat chest, and a nose deserving of its own zip code is one of the mysteries I hope to have answered when I get to Heaven. At any rate, my not-so-dulcet tones have been known to start hound dogs braying a mile away.

Because I was alone with Freni in the inn, I felt free to let loose some of my favorite hymns, or at least some approximation thereof. As I belted out "Bringing In the Sheaves," I contemplated the matter of the empty photo holder.

Perhaps it didn't come from Catherine Grabinski's wallet. The inserts I've seen are unisex. They also tend to rip and fall apart with use. This particular one might well have belonged to the reverend, or to Lodema, either of whom may have purchased a new insert and casually tossed the old one aside. For all anyone knew it might have been lying on the floor for weeks. It was common knowledge that Lodema wasn't the world's best housekeeper. One Hernia wag is quoted as saying our pastor's wife even named her dust bunnies.

But just for the sake of argument, if it had belonged to the reverend's sister, whose photos might it once have contained? Her children's, her husband's, perhaps even her pets'—although personally I think it's silly to carry around photographs of animals when one can just as easily carry the real thing around in one's bra.

To be fair, however, Catherine had been a large-busted woman, and even a medium-size dog, like a cocker spaniel, would be a tight fit.

Since I'm not the sentimental type, the only pictures I carry are those of dead presidents. But if I *were* to schlep photos around, they would most certainly include ones of Susannah, Freni, and the Babester. And, of course, Alison. Not only is she my foster child, but photographs of children are de rigueur for wallet inserts. Should Susannah and the mantis ever produce offspring, I would feel compelled to include a photograph of their chrysalis in my portable collection.

What if the reverend really had a child stashed somewhere, and Catherine not only knew about its existence, but carried proof in her purse? Could it be that my pastor had been blackmailed, perhaps even by his own sister? Maybe he had been on the verge of taking his predicament to the police when she stopped him with a bite of lethal chili. True, she hadn't been at the church that fateful night, but she had shown up afterward with remarkable speed. For all I knew, she was already in town when the fratricide occurred— assuming that's what it was. Still, that would explain only his death, not hers. One thing was for sure. I wasn't going to come up with any new theories if I let my bathwater turn cold.

I added a sprinkling of fragrant salts to the tub and a smidgen more of scalding water, then settled back amid the refreshed froth. There have been times when solutions to my problems have popped into my head before the first bubbles burst, but on other occasions I have been forced to emerge from my soapy sanctuary as puckered as a California smoker. It was beginning to look like I was headed for Wrinkle City, when a bolt of lightning shook the house. A few seconds later I heard the muffled sound of a trumpet. Three short toots, and one long blast.

I could barely believe my ears. Only once before in my life have I witnessed lightning during a snowstorm, and that was in the spring when two weather fronts collided. It had certainly not been this cold that day. Perhaps I was mistaken; perhaps it wasn't lightning. Albeit quite rarely, Hernia has experienced minor earthquakes. Then again, the tremors I had experienced previously lasted for several seconds, and weren't nearly as loud as what I'd just heard. And in neither case had I heard trumpets. But if it wasn't lightning, and it wasn't an earthquake—I jerked to a standing position and did some quaking of my own.

Could it be? Could this possibly be the moment I'd dreamed about my entire life? Was this the rapture? *The* rapture?

My heart pounded with excitement, but it wasn't a pure emotion by any means. You see, I'd always pictured myself rising up to greet my Lord dressed in my Sunday best, not covered in a vanishing coat of gardenia-scented bubbles. And in my finest fantasies I was driving on the Pennsylvania Turnpike when the big event happened, and thus had a bird's-eye view of all the nonbelievers crashing into the cars vacated by those of us who had been born again. Yes, I know—one shouldn't take pleasure from the misfortune of others, but those folks who'd been left behind had been given their chance, had they not? It was their fault, not mine, that they'd gotten themselves into such a pickle.

Even so, I was about to ask the Good Lord to forgive my gloating when I realized that I wasn't rising at all; the bathwater still came up to my knees, and my head wasn't any closer to the ceiling. Needless to say, I was horrified. What could I possibly have done wrong? I believed in the message of salvation with all my heart— well, I was pretty sure I did. But maybe it was possible to believe harder, and I just hadn't gotten the hang of it.

If anybody was capable of stronger belief, that person had to be Freni. Ironically, most Amish don't claim to be assured of salvation, a claim they equate with arrogance. Nonetheless, my kinswoman was the most resolute Christian I knew. If she was still in the inn, the rapture had yet to happen.

Throwing a thick Egyptian cotton towel around me, I climbed out of the tub and sloshed downstairs. "Freni, dear, are you still here?"

Alas, there was no answer. Spurred on by mounting panic, I dashed from room to room, but found no one. Calling Gabe flitted through my mind, but of course that was silly, since as an unconverted Jew he would not be among the redeemed—at least according to the Gospel of John, 14:6. This stringent criterion eliminated

Doc Shafor as well, because although he is a very kind man, the octogenarian is an agnostic. Even Susannah, the lapsed Presbyterian, was not a reliable indicator of the Second Coming. Calling *someone*, however, was a good idea.

With trembling fingers I dialed Priscilla Neumeyer, the leader of Beechy Grove Mennonite Women's Bible Study. Not only is she a devout Christian, but the woman is deeply involved in outreach, and often puts the needs of our community before her own. *She* would have made a perfect wife for our deceased reverend. At any rate, I called her on her cell phone, in hopes that she had taken it with her to the Great Beyond.

"Hello?"

"Priscilla, is that you?"

"Magdalena, if you don't mind, I'm pretty busy right now, as you can imagine."

I gasped. "So it really happened, didn't it?"

"I can hardly believe it. I'm in Heaven, that's what. Isn't it glorious?"

"I'm afraid I'll have to take your word for that. It appears as if I've been left behind. All this time I thought I was on the right track, but apparently I got it wrong. Now I'm damned for all eternity."

"Nonsense. I'm sure you'll catch up in no time."

"Do you think that's possible?"

"Certainly. Well, if I may be absolutely frank—uh—are you willing to double the donation you gave last year? Because that's what it's going to take."

"You mean I have to *pay* to get in?"

"We prefer the word 'donation,' of course, but yes, that's how it works. You know the score."

"It says that in the Bible?"

"Excuse me?"

"Tell me where in the Bible it says we have to pay to get into Heaven. You can't, because nowhere in the Bible does it say that, not even in the fancy-schmancy versions that come out these days. Besides, it doesn't make any sense. I mean, the streets of Heaven are paved with gold, right? Why would God need any money?"

"Maybe God doesn't need money, Magdalena, but the homeless shelter does."

"I beg your pardon?"

"Look, like I said, we're pretty busy right now, what with the snowstorm. But if you want to match the donation we just received from Elijah Yutzy, so you can attend the Top Five Givers' luncheon next month, just make sure your check is postmarked by the fifth. You can send it to me here at the shelter, or to my home address."

"Uh, you mean you're *not* in Heaven?"

There was a moment of silence, as the earthbound signal from my phone struggled to find its way out of our universe and to her cell phone. "I'm on cloud nine," she finally said.

"So you're still on the way?"

"Magdalena, I don't mean to be rude, but is there some medication you've forgotten to take?"

"Apparently." In the background I could hear the distinctive sound of a snowplow and the irritating notes of pre-Thanksgiving Christmas carols. Needless to say, my relief at not being left behind was immense, but so was the level of my embarrassment.

"Oh, I get it now! You thought the rapture had occurred, didn't you?"

"That's just silly—what makes you say that?"

"Been there, done it myself. But then I got right with the Lord, and ever since, I have no doubt that when the time comes I'll be swept up with the saints of God."

How dare that woman say her faith was greater than mine, even if it was true! It was time to change the subject. Pronto.

"I'll triple Elijah Yutzy's contribution," I heard myself say.

"That's wonderful! This is turning out to be a red-letter week for the shelter."

"I just might end up in the red myself."

"What was that?"

"Nothing."

"In that case, I've really got to go. A family just walked in, all covered with snow. Oh, one more thing—make sure you check your choice of entrée on the entry form. We always seem to run out of beef."

"Will do," I said, and hung up.

Just for the record, I didn't terminate my call to Priscilla Neumeyer because I was so embarrassed I needed to find a hole into which to crawl. Neither did I hang up because she made clear she had an important, altruistic task to perform. I plunked the receiver into the cradle because I had a brainstorm that made braving the snowstorm a no-brainer.

22

But I also admit that I felt incredibly stupid when I opened the back door and saw two sets of rapidly fading footprints in the snow, and one set of tire tracks. The thunder I'd heard had been the kitchen door slamming, and the blare of trumpets nothing more than a car horn. Well, at least Priscilla Neumeyer had a reputation for being circumspect.

As you can imagine, it took me a while to regain my composure, time I spent seated at the kitchen table sipping a cup of homemade cocoa and pondering my existence. A true Christian, aside from the Amish, should not live in terror of being left behind come Judgment Day. It was obvious that my spiritual life was going to need a good deal of overhauling. And while I was as sane as the next person, it was possible that my personality could use a bit of fine-tuning. On the other hand, a kinder, gentler Magdalena would deprive Hernia of its spice, and leave the community a bland stew, devoid of distinction. No, the Good Lord intended me to be pepper, just as long as I didn't get carried away and assault anyone.

Feeling better about myself, I poured a thermos of cocoa to go, slipped several of Freni's homemade cinnamon rolls into a plastic bag, and donned my warmest winter coat, a bright, sinfully red wool affair with both a cape and a built-in hood. And no, I wasn't off to see Grandma who lived in a wolf-infested woods; I was headed to visit the little old lady who lived in the shoe.

The Livengoods don't really live in a shoe, but it is true that Little Samson and his wife, Sarah, have so many children they don't know what to do. And certainly there are shoe closets somewhere—Imelda Marcos's comes to mind—that are bigger than the Livengood house. I was pleased, therefore, to see that an addition was in progress, and that Sarah Livengood didn't have a bun in her oven. At least none that was obvious.

She did, however, greet me with a toddler on one hip and an infant on the other. "Why, Magdalena, to what do we owe this honor?"

Fortunately I was ready with a little white lie. "Well, I knew school was canceled. I thought you might like some help entertaining the children."

Her laugh was mercifully brief. "Come in out of the cold. Help with the children—now, that's a good one!"

"I have a foster child now. I'm no longer totally inexperienced."

"Your girl is in her teens, right? My children are all seven and under."

My teeth found their familiar grooves along the top side of my tongue. It wasn't my place to inform her that there were several options readily available to help prevent pregnancy, like little rubber hats and things. They even came in sizes, but curiously there was no small. No condom minimums. At any rate, I'd even seen them offered for sale at Pat's I.G.A. in Bedford.

"In that case, do you mind if we just chat?"

She motioned for me to sit on an ancient dinette chair that was missing part of its stuffing. Setting the toddler on the floor, she sat on another chair that was in even worse shape. The displaced little boy regarded me balefully, all the while smearing jam around his cheeks with plump hands.

"What do you want to chat about?" Sarah asked. There was no mention of refreshments, which made me wonder if she'd been adopted into the faith as a child. If so, I'd forgotten.

"Well, we could talk about the weather. It's certainly comment-worthy today."

"Or we could discuss the rapture."

"*What?*"

"I heard it happened this morning." She said this without a hint of a smile.

So much for Priscilla Neumeyer's circumspection. And while I was dismayed, I certainly wasn't surprised. "Mennonite telegraph" is the fastest means of communication in the world. Even our cousins the Amish, who lack electricity, are capable of spreading gossip at breathtaking speed.

"It obviously didn't happen," I said calmly, "seeing as how we're both still here."

"Thank you. I'll take that as a compliment. By the way, do you mind if I feed the baby?"

"Feed away!"

Without further ado she whipped out a set of mammary glands worthy of a Holstein and shoved one to the baby's mouth. Needless to say, I was properly horrified. If the Good Lord wanted us to expose this part of our anatomy, He wouldn't have sewn animal-skin clothes for Eve in the Garden of Eden.

Sarah Livengood read my face just as easy as if I'd had a text message stamped on it in large print. "You don't approve, do you?"

"There are children about," I whispered. Forsooth, none of the urchins were paying the slightest bit of attention except for the one receiving nourishment.

"Breasts were intended to feed babies, Magdalena."

"But in private."

"This is in private—this is my home. But I admit that I do it in public too. Discreetly of course, with a blanket over my chest. Nursing is a natural function."

"Yes, but I can think of several natural functions that should remain private. *Totally* private."

"You need to lighten up, Magdalena. Feeding a baby is a beautiful thing; there's nothing tawdry about it. Funny, but we live in a society where the tops of breasts—euphemistically referred to as cleavage—can be flaunted on the street in a sexual manner, but the mere knowledge that one is feeding a baby, and behind a blanket, is scandalous."

"I certainly don't display cleavage," I said. The truth is, had I any to display, I would possibly even convert to Presbyterianism for the right to do so.

Sarah Livengood is every bit as bright as her husband, and less willing to tolerate fools. "Enough with the small talk, Magdalena. Now out with it. What's plaguing your overactive mind today?"

"Overactive? Why, I never!"

She regarded me with steel gray eyes that were capable of pinning me to the wall, like a butterfly on a mounting board.

"Okay, okay. I'll get to the point. Where were you the night of the chili cook-off?"

"Right where I am now, nursing Hannah. And, of course, taking care of the rest of my brood."

"So you weren't at your mother's over in Somerset?"

The piercing peepers flickered. "Is that the story my husband told you?"

"Yes. He was lying, wasn't he?"

"That doesn't make him guilty of murder. But if you must know, he was here at home, puking his guts out. Hugging the toilet as if it was his best friend."

"I'm so sorry to hear that. Was it the flu?"

"The bottle."

"I beg your pardon?"

"My husband, Little Samson, as you call him, pillar of the community, school board member, church treasurer, father of seven, is a drunk."

"Daddy drunk," the toddler said, and began licking what jam remained on his fingers.

"You mean an alcoholic?"

"Sounds classier than drunk, doesn't it?"

"Well—uh—I mean—"

She stood, the infant still sealed to her breast. "Look. That's all the time I have. Johnny's taking a nap, but the other four are at a neighbor's. I promised to pick them up in a few minutes."

I stood as well, but the sticky dinette chair didn't release itself from my bottom until I was halfway up. When it hit the floor it toppled backward with a crash, causing the two-year-old to wail like a banshee on steroids. It wasn't the first time I thanked God for a barren womb.

The snowstorm did not appear to impact Little Samson's business. If anything, there were more Amish than usual waiting patiently in line to have their horses shod. The men glanced at me from under the snow-covered brims of their felt hats and clucked among themselves in Pennsylvania Dutch. No doubt I was the subject of their conversation.

"*Gut marriye*," I said, drawing from my years of experience as an innkeeper. Believe me, forced cheer is a skill that can be honed into an art form. I was accomplished enough to shame the men into silence, but it lasted only a minute or two.

"What that woman needs," one of them said to my back in perfectly unaccented English, "is a good husband."

"Make that two husbands," a compatriot said. Mercifully their laughter was muted somewhat by the snow.

Inside the farrier's shed the temperature jumped fifty degrees, but I elected to keep my coat on, lest I need to make a quick getaway. Little Samson was pounding the last nail into a buggy horse's hoof, too busy to look up. After finishing the job, he offered the animal a sugar cube, then another, and another, whispering softly to it all the while. Both man and beast glistened in the firelight, like subjects of a Currier and Ives greeting card. I found it impossible to picture the man embracing a commode.

"Ahem," I said, intentionally interrupting the sugar-forged bond before the horse became diabetic.

"So my wife told you," Little Samson said, still avoiding eye contact.

"She said you stayed home the night of the chili cook-off."

The next few minutes were anything but silent. Inside the fire crackled loudly, outside the Amish men cackled softly, and the stupid horse made a variety of sounds, not all of which emanated from its mouth.

"I'm not really an alcoholic," Little Samson finally said. "Sometimes I just have more than I can handle."

"She called you a drunk." It wasn't my intention to be unkind, merely to break through his denial.

"Do you think I wanted to be a blacksmith?"

"Your father was one."

"Exactly—and I didn't want to be anything like him. You may or may not remember, but I was bound for college when Sarah came along. She talked me into marrying her first, so she could get away from her parents. Then our Amos was born, and before I knew it, going to college was a distant dream. Shoeing horses was the only way I knew how to provide for my family. I haven't had an easy life, Magdalena. The Lord knows."

"Who has?" Did I ask to be born looking like something Little Samson would try to shoe? Did I choose to have my parents squished flatter than a crepe? Did I volunteer to raise a sister, a girl with the morals of an alley cat, only to have her marry an arthropodan maniac who is my nemesis? I think not. You don't see me asking for special consideration, do you? No-sirree-bob! I, Magdalena Portulaca Yoder, pulled myself up by my brogan laces, and I don't think it's too much to expect others to do the same.

"You don't understand, Magdalena. My father had one heck of a temper. Even my mother was afraid of him. He never hit my mother that I know of, but still it was like walking on eggshells in our home. I grew up thinking I was missing out on something. Now I know what it was—love. But I'll never find that with Sarah."

"Find it with your children."

"I'm not a drunk. You have to believe that."

"There's nothing wrong with getting help. I'm sure there's an Alcoholics Anonymous—"

He grabbed the horse's bridle and gave it a yank. As the animal lurched forward it slapped me in the face with its tail.

I spit out a mouthful of coarse, rank hair. "Does that mean our conversation is over, dear?"

"Mind your own business, Magdalena," he said, and kept walking.

Laziness is a heathen virtue, but I will concede that there are times when it seems to make sense. For instance, by the time I emerged from the blacksmith shop, my car was covered with snow. But it was the dry sort of snow that blows away as soon as the vehicle picks up speed, and anyway I had a good set of wipers with newly replaced blades. Thus it was that I felt justified to enter my car without first brushing it clear.

As I turned the key in the ignition I hummed a calming tune. "Trust and Obey." When things feel hopeless what a relief it can be to turn our troubles over to the Lord. And I'm sure there are those who would benefit by trusting *me* more—and most certainly by obeying me.

The Crown Vic engine sputtered twice, but caught the third time and purred like a puma—which, by the way, is the largest cat species capable of purring. I stopped singing just long enough to grunt with satisfaction; then I burst into a lung-wrenching version of "Joyful, Joyful, We Adore Thee." But my joy was cut short when I felt a gun barrel pressed against my neck.

"Thank heavens you've stopped that awful racket," someone in the backseat said.

"Edwina?"

"Face it, Magdalena—you can't hit two consecutive notes on key."

"How rude! Didn't your mother teach you to tell white lies?"

The barrel dug deeper into the soft spot behind my ear. "I'm not here to talk about your abysmal lack of talent. I want to know when you plan to drop this shenanigan."

"Excuse me?"

"This cops-and-robbers game. Don't you think your time would be better spent ripping tourists off than sticking your big nose in where it doesn't belong?"

That hiked my hackles, always a dangerous thing when one is seated. "At least I've never killed anyone."

"Neither have I."

"You know, you could get twenty years in the pokey, just for poking that thing in my neck."

"Ha, that's what you think! This 'thing,' as you called it, is my mascara wand."

"I beg your pardon?"

"Oh, that's right; you don't use makeup—although it would do wonders for you. Those skimpy, wheat-colored eyebrows of yours could really be improved with a warm brown pencil, and do you have eyelashes, Magdalena, or just lizard lids?"

"Lizard lids?"

"Your lips—or rather your lack of them—contribute to that reptilian look for which you are so famous."

"I am? I mean, I always thought I look horsey."

"Don't flatter yourself."

Risking death by mascara wand, I slowly turned my head. It was indeed Edwina Bishop in the backseat. Her body was facing forward, but her face was in profile. Not that it mattered. In the dim light of the snow-covered car, I could barely make out my assailant's features.

I pushed her weapon-wielding arm aside. To my surprise, she offered no resistance.

"What is it you want, Edwina?"

"I told you. Quit meddling."

"Does this mean you are guilty of killing Reverend Schrock?"

"It most certainly does not."

"Than why are *you* meddling?"

She took her sweet time answering. During the ensuing silence, I considered bolting from the car and calling for help. The element of surprise would be on my side, and what was the worst she could do to me? Tackle me? Hit me up the side of my head with a handbag full of cosmetics?

But as long as she posed no immediate physical harm, I had nothing to gain by attempting a getaway. And quite possibly I had a lot to lose. After all, even someone as unstable as Edwina Bishop would not brave the elements on a day like this just to tell me to mind my own business. Not when that could be accomplished by a phone call, or even a nasty letter.

"Magdalena," she finally said, "do you remember the time the carnival came to town?"

"How could I not? That was the first and last time it happened. Everyone was scandalized by the games of chance, the sideshows, and the fortune-teller. Especially the fortune-teller. Sodom and Gomorrah, my mama called it. But she went to see the fortune-teller anyway. Can you believe that? The fortune-teller told her that she and my papa were going to die. . . ." I shook my head. After all these years I still wonder how a faux gypsy, staring into a globe light fixture from McCrorys five-and-ten store, could foresee my parents' grizzly death in the Allegheny Tunnel. She'd gotten only one detail wrong: Mama and Papa were not squished to death by a *gas* tanker and a semitrailer carrying state-of-the-art running shoes. It was a milk tanker.

Edwina Bishop surprised me by maintaining a respectful minute of silence before speaking again. "Do you remember the two-headed man?"

"Do I ever! I took Susannah to see him. She'd begged relentlessly. We had to wait in line almost an hour, but when we finally got in there, Susannah got mad because it was so obviously fake. She demanded that we get our money back, even though I was the one who paid for both of us."

"It wasn't fake."

"I beg your pardon?"

23

"The smaller head was made up a little—a tiny toupee, glue-on eyebrows—and it didn't need those glasses (couldn't see at all, in fact), but it was definitely real."

"How do you know?"

"Because I slept with that man."

"Get out of town," I said, borrowing one of Susannah's expressions. "Wait—you must have been only a teenager then."

"I had just turned eighteen. It was my very first time. In retrospect, I did it to rebel against my parents, and not because I was in love. That came later."

"You're serious, aren't you?"

"As serious as a Mennonite having sex."

"I resemble that remark. But go on, dear."

"Magdalena, are you sure you don't already know this?"

"*Me*? Why would I know this?"

"Because you're obviously investigating me. If you're any good, you were bound to come across this little incident sooner or later."

I highly doubted that. Not the part about me being good—because, in all humility, I am—but the part about me eventually unearthing her teenage indiscretion. The type of questions I ask don't normally lead to this kind of disclosure.

"Edwina, is this why you waylaid me in my car and assaulted me with your eyeliner?"

"It was mascara, not eyeliner. You really should become familiar with both of them. Just don't go too dark with the eyeliner. With your pallid complexion you might end up looking like a raccoon. And definitely stay away from blue."

"You didn't answer my question."

"I thought the answer was obvious. Magdalena, you're not going to tell anyone about this, are you?"

"No one would believe me. Besides, you've hardly told me anything."

She took my hint. "Jim and I saw each other every day the carnival was in town, although we didn't actually hook up until the very last day. He was only twenty-three, so it wasn't like there was a huge age difference. After the carnival left town we wrote each other almost every day. Sometimes the little head wrote too. He had a different name, you know. Oh, and he couldn't speak, because he didn't have a proper mouth, but he could bob up and down, so that's what they called him. Bob. When he wanted to write, he used Jim's arms. Anyway, it was hard to keep in touch because the carnival moved around so much. I honestly think I might have married Jim Bob—that was their names put together—if either of them had worked at a regular job. Of course Reverend Schrock would probably have disapproved of that too. I'm sure there's someplace in the Bible that forbids you from marrying a man with two heads."

I made a mental note to look it up in my Bible's concordance. "Well, if that's it—if that's everything you have to tell—I've got to get going. And just so you know, you can count on me to keep your secret."

She opened the car door, inviting a flurry of powder to enter. "There is one more thing. Jim Bob got me to pick the pockets and purses of the people who came to see him. But that's it. And remember, I was just barely eighteen. I know better than to ask a Mennonite to swear, Magdalena, but if you ever tell anyone, I swear I'll make you sorry."

"I will not be threatened, dear." My words were as crisp as the outside air.

Edwina Bishop hopped out and slammed the door behind her, causing miniavalanches on both the front and rear windshields. I locked the doors behind her, but I didn't drive off right away, preferring to stay put in the powder to ponder. What was the woman's real purpose in ambushing me? Did she really think that a teenage tryst with a two-headed huckster was newsworthy in this day and age? Or was this merely a ploy, meant to get me to close my casebook on one of my prime suspects? Edwina comes clean about the carny; ergo, she must be telling the truth about everything else. As for filching a few bucks from gawking bumpkins, unless she had been arrested and had a record, who would care anymore?

Jim Bob indeed! The more I thought about it, the more I thought that Susannah had been right. That wasn't a real second head on the man's shoulder. A rutabaga quite possibly, but not an authentic noggin. Edwina Bishop had been yanking my chain. Well, she wasn't going to get away with it. Until I found out what she was really up to, I was going to glom on to her like a leech on bare skin. Of course I'd keep my word and not tell anyone, but only because I wasn't about to embarrass myself by repeating such a ridiculous story.

I hadn't driven more than three blocks when I saw Edwina's car pulled up alongside one of Hernia's three public mailboxes. Believe it or not, the woman had gotten out of her vehicle and was brushing the snow off the cold blue fixture. I pulled over and watched between the strokes of my wipers. When she resumed driving I followed her until she turned left on Route 96, headed toward Bedford.

At that point a good Magdalena would have driven straight back to the inn, climbed into bed with her thermos of cocoa and bag of cinnamon rolls, and waited out the storm. A bad Magdalena would have swung by Babester's house first and added him to the list of her warm, sweet goodies. But I had a job to do, come rain, sleet, or snow, so I made a beeline for Edwina Bishop's house.

Most folks in Hernia still don't lock their doors unless they plan to be away for an extended amount of time, like a vacation. Even when they do lock their doors, they invariably hide the keys under the front mat, above the lintel, or, if they consider themselves really hip, in a hokey-looking rock beside the steps. Edwina was a lintel lady.

The downstairs of her house consisted of a formal dining room, a formal living room, a small den, a half bath, and of course a kitchen. I was after something of a personal nature—although just what, I didn't have the foggiest—and it seemed unlikely that I would find it in this practically sterile setting. Although I am a mature woman, I do not claim to be perfect, so it was not entirely outside the bounds of my character to subtly rearrange an armchair, tug the tablecloth down on one corner, and leave the kitchen faucet dripping.

But you can imagine my surprise, as I rounded the stair landing, to discover that the second floor was a pigsty that spilled out of the rooms and into the hallway. At the very least, Edwina Bishop was guilty of committing an immaculate misconception.

I had never seen such a mess. Even on its worst days, Alison's room was neat by comparison. My inclination was to return another day with hip boots, a shovel, and a box of large garbage bags. Clearly the woman was as unstable as a piece of California realty.

Wading through the detritus was time-consuming, but fortunately the first room I came to appeared to be a home office. I might have found something incriminating among the stacks of papers and magazines that covered the floor, but being a traditionalist, I made my way to the desk. That's where I keep all my secret documents—in the second drawer from the top, on the left. Edwina Bishop might have had secrets scattered everywhere, but I discovered she definitely had some interesting things in *that* drawer.

I made myself comfortable in a fancy leather chair, possibly even one from Office Depot, and poured over the contents of that treasure trove. There were numerous photographs of my suspect as a young woman—pre-face-lift—with a variety of men, many of whom I knew. Husband number two was even more handsome than I remembered, but Husband number four had a little potbelly going that I'd somehow missed. Husband number one had bad posture, but otherwise—wait just one Mennonite minute! Here was a picture of Edwina Bishop with the two-headed man, a close-up even, and he did have two heads! If that was a rutabaga, I'd eat that pillbox hat stashed away in my freezer. Well, what do you know? The two-faced woman was telling the truth!

The ring of her desk phone had me jump so high in my seat that my behind nearly missed connecting with it on the way down. What to do, what to do? I stared, shaking, at the phone through three more rings. It stopped only because the machine picked up.

"Edwina, are you there?" a vaguely familiar voice asked. "Pick up if you are. Edwina, you're not going to get away with this. I'm going to the police as soon as I hang up. You can't blackmail me, Edwina. You hear that, you witch? You can't." Actually she said a word much worse than "witch," a word no Christian should say unless speaking to, or about, a female dog.

I am not good at impersonations, or I might have picked up and responded. Instead, I waited until the caller was through, and then resumed my investigation. The second time the phone rang, my buttocks barely achieved liftoff. Again I had no choice but to listen to the message.

"Look, you witch, I know you're there. This is your last chance. You hear that? If you don't pick up by the time I count to three, I really *am* going to the police. One, two—"

I couldn't help myself. "Yes?"

"Aha! I knew it. You're a coward and you're evil. I meant what I said, Edwina. Either you back off and swear you'll never say a word, or I'm turning you in. I've seen enough TV and movies to know that once I start paying you, you're just going to keep asking for more. Yeah, I know—if I go to the police it's all going to come out anyway, but I'm prepared to deal with that. The question is, are you? Blackmailing is a crime, Edwina. How do you think you're going to like prison?"

"Will I have to wear stripes? If I do, they better be horizontal. Yes, I know—most people think horizontal stripes make them look fat, but I'm built like a carpenter's dream. A nice, wide horizontal stripe—"

"Who is this?"

"I might ask the same thing of you."

"I'm Clarisse—hey, I asked you first. You're not Edwina Bishop, are you?"

"Not the last time I checked, dear. If you hang on a minute, I'd be glad to check again."

She hung up.

Clarisse. Both her name and her voice sounded familiar. It wasn't a Mennonite name, so she probably wasn't a Hernian. In fact, the only Clarisse I could remember ever meeting had been the masseuse at Happy Backs Massage Parlor over in Bedford. That was it! What a small world. Edwina Bishop not only knew Clarisse Thompson; she was blackmailing her.

But why? A dozen possibilities ran through my mind, which, unlike my womb, is as fertile as the Nile Delta. Well, there was only one way to find out, and that was to put the screws to Clarisse Thompson.

I gave the piles of papers and ledgers on the floor a perfunctory glance and then made a beeline down the stairs and out the front door. But I got only halfway to my car when I stopped, turned, and dashed back inside. Just to shake things up a bit, I neatened her office and the portion of the hallway that led to it. It took only about ten minutes, because all I really did was straighten slanting stacks and push things against the walls. The visual impact, however, was well worth the time and effort. Edwina Bishop was in for a surprise.

Much to my surprise the sun came out from behind the clouds just as I was leaving town. Route 96, while snow-covered, was certainly passable, although it was evident that only a very few foolish motorists like myself, and Edwina Bishop, dared venture out. It was the Amish buggies one had to be careful about. I, with my lead foot, had to constantly reign in my Crown Vic's team of horses to avoid hitting the real horses that seemed to clog the road.

It took almost an hour to make a trip that usually takes me twenty minutes. By the time I pulled into the almost empty parking lot in front of Happy Backs Massage Parlor, I was exhausted from exercising patience. To be sure, I was in no mood for obstructive behavior.

Alas, Anti-Barbies 1 and 2 never even bothered to look up when I entered. "Do you think they'll deliver today?" Anti-Barbie 2 asked her coworker. "Because if they will, I'm going to order 'Da Bomb.' "

Anti-Barbie 1 stopped fingering through files. "What's that?"

"It's that new sandwich Gutbusters has been advertising. It's got seven kinds of meat and eight different cheeses. And it comes with a tub of cheese fries and a gallon of whatever drink you want."

"*Are* there seven kinds of meat?" I asked pleasantly.

That got their attention. "It's you," they said in unison.

"As big as life and twice as ugly, dears. Frankly, if you ask me, it's called the Bomb because you'll explode if you eat the entire thing."

"We didn't ask you," Anti-Barbie 2 said. "And that's 'da,' not 'the.' "

"Duh. Silly me. I should have known better."

They stared at me.

"That was a joke, ladies. The two of you look like you're posing for license photos. I thought you could use a laugh."

"What do you want this time?" Anti-Barbie 1 snapped. She was definitely the crabbier of the two.

"I came here to see Clarisse Thompson. Is she in?"

"You don't have an appointment."

"You haven't even looked."

"I don't need to. Miss Thompson no longer works here."

"She doesn't? Why not?"

"Maybe you should tell us," Anti-Barbie 2 said.

"*Me?*"

"You're the one who made her quit."

"I beg your pardon?"

"She left in a hurry the last time you were here, and never came back."

"You probably scared her away with your hairy legs," Anti-Barbie 1 said.

"They're not hairy anymore," I wailed. "You should know."

"Serves you right," she said, not the least bit contrite. "Now if you'll excuse us, we were about to order lunch."

"Order away! But first do me a big favor and give me Clarisse Thompson's address."

"I'm not allowed to give out the addresses of our employees."

"But she's no longer employed here. You just said so yourself."

She glared at me, as did her buddy.

It was clear they could use a little cheering up, so I slipped them a portrait of Ulysses S. Grant. I'm sure it helped that said picture was on the back of a fifty-dollar bill. At any rate, Anti-Barbie 2 tapped a few keys on the computer.

"She lives at 429 Amherst Lane. Apartment 4C."

I thanked the woman for her help, even though she'd already buried her nose in a menu and was, no doubt, beyond hearing.

The Amherst Lane apartments are where folks go to live when Hell is temporarily full. Those are not my words, by the way, but Susannah's. She once dated a man at this address, and judging by his behavior, I'd have to say she was right.

I was fortunate to find a clear parking spot two blocks away and, after checking twice to make sure my car doors were locked, ventured forth with a folded umbrella as a weapon of self-defense. Nonviolence is the Mennonite way, but the founding fathers of my faith had never been to the Amherst apartments. Besides, it could resume snowing at any minute.

Clarisse Thompson's unit was located at the far end of a curry-scented hallway. To get to it I followed a runner of burgundy carpet that was peppered with cigarette burns. Virtually every step sent cockroaches scurrying. Those that didn't immediately disappear into the wide cracks along the baseboards regarded me curiously, their antennae twitching.

There was a child's crayon drawing taped to the outside of the door of Clarisse's apartment. I think the animal pictured was supposed to be a cat, but it had six legs. Perhaps it was a cockroach with yellow stripes.

The doorbell was apparently out of order (I certainly couldn't hear it ring), so I rapped briskly with my trusty knuckles. Immediately I heard a child's voice, but it stopped abruptly seconds later. I rapped again, and although I could hear the footsteps of one or more persons through the door, it did not open.

I peered into the peephole, but of course saw nothing except a distorted version of myself. "Ms. Thompson, I know you're in there. It's very important that I speak with you."

"Please go away."

"Aha, so you are there. Look, it's about Edwina Bishop trying to blackmail you."

I heard the rattle of a chain, the thunk of a bolt jerked back. The door opened slowly as two pairs of eyes studied me. One pair was considerably lower than the other, and as my eyes adjusted to the dimness of the room behind them, I realized it belonged to a small child.

"Come in," Clarisse Thompson said. It was an order, not an invitation.

I stepped in and she slammed the door behind me. The chain and bolt were returned to their locked position.

24

"Who are you?" the child demanded.

"I'm Miss Yoder. Who are you?" It would surprise most folks to learn that I have a way with children.

"Romaine."

"What did you say?"

"I said my name was Romaine. Can't you hear so good?"

"My hearing is just fine, dear. But Romaine is a type of lettuce. You're not part of a salad, are you?"

"You're silly, Miss Odor. I don't like you."

"Her name really is Romaine," Clarisse said. "She's my daughter."

"Oh, my. Well, to each his own, dear. There's a cashier at Pat's I.G.A. named LaTrina—"

"Miss Yoder, you said this was about Edwina Bishop."

"Yes." I waggled my scant eyebrows at the child. "Perhaps we should speak in private."

"This is Romaine's home too. She stays."

I sighed so hard curtains fluttered on the far side of the room. Too many people these days treat their children as if they are miniature adults. They are subjected to violent movies and TV shows that are guaranteed to give a grown man nightmares, and they witness sexual shenanigans that would make the Whore of

Babylon blush. Children aren't miniature adults, with all the rights of grown-ups. If they are, we should send them into the workforce, possibly as chimney sweeps, and have them earn their keep, just like we adults must.

"Very well, but when I touch on mature subjects, I elect to speak in Ig-pay Atin-lay."

"She means pig Latin," Romaine said.

I scowled at the urchin, and then for good measure I scowled at her mother. "It's your call, dear. But when she grows up to be a sociopath, it will be my tax dollars that support her in prison."

"My daughter was right; you are silly." She pointed to an armchair with a concave cushion. "Can you get to the point, Miss Yoder? There are things I need to do."

"Like make a run for it before Edwina Bishop gets here?"

"What?" She sat on a side chair with a wobbly leg. Romaine hoisted her tiny patooty atop a barstool covered in genuine imitation leather. It is not my intention to be mean when I say that the apartment was decorated in Early Attic style.

"I saw her headed for Bedford about an hour ago. You might think I'm silly, Ms. Thompson, but that woman's nuttier than a PayDay. She accosted me with her mascara tube."

"Did you whack her back with your lipstick?"

"My brand of Mennonites don't wear makeup, dear. We're satisfied with what the Good Lord gave us—although frankly, I wouldn't be adverse to a little rhinoplasty."

"Yes, I can see why you might want that procedure."

"Why, I never!"

"That's obvious as well. Tell me, what makes you think she was headed this way?"

"Your phone call, of course. About you being blackmailed."

"How did you find out about that?"

"Clarisse, I hate to be rude, but some hot chocolate would really hit the spot."

"Sugar's not good for you," the pip-squeak piped up.

"Then sugar-free would be fine."

"You're not supposed to snack between meals."

"And you should mind your own business, dear."

"Mommy, this lady's being mean."

"*Moi?* If you were my little girl—"

"Which she isn't. Miss Yoder, I'm afraid if you don't get to the point, I'm going to have to ask you to leave."

I knew she wasn't going to give me the old heave-ho, not until she'd gotten the lowdown. Knowledge is power. Of course the reverse isn't necessarily true. I know of a lot of politicians—mostly men—who are powerful, but appear to be bereft of knowledge. Then again, of what use is knowledge, if it isn't implemented? . . . .

"Miss Yoder, are you even listening?"

"I was lost in thought," I wailed. "It's unfamiliar territory."

"How do you know about the phone call I made to Edwina Bishop? Do you have her phone tapped?"

"Gracious, no. That would be illegal, wouldn't it? *How* is not important. I want to know why she's blackmailing you. And just so you know, I'm asking these questions on behalf of the Hernia Police Department."

Clarisse's eyes flickered from me to her child, and back again. "Are you saying that you're a policewoman?"

"Not officially. I do legwork for Chief Stoltzfus. If you want to check, I'll give you his office and his cell phone numbers."

"Does he know you're speaking with me now?"

I thought about my answer. Seeing as how I was in her home, she had a lot more to conk me with than a mascara tube.

"Absolutely," I said, after crossing my toes in the privacy of my brogans. It helps to wear loose shoes.

She sighed but, lacking my experience, was unable to budge the curtains. "I may as well confide in you. I mean, it's probably all going to come out sooner or later."

"Confide away!"

"Miss Yoder, I can do without your smart-alecky attitude."

I pretended to lock my lips and throw away the key.

She glared at me before continuing. "You see, Edwina Bishop knows—or thinks she knows—something about my daughter."

"What, Mommy?"

"About your daddy, hon."

"What about Daddy?" The child turned to me. "My daddy's in Heaven. He was going to take me with him, but Mommy said he had to leave in a big hurry. Isn't that right, Mommy?"

"Romaine, baby, would you like to go upstairs and watch Mommy's TV?"

"No, I want to stay here."

"Please, baby."

"No! I don't want to."

I found the imaginary key. "I'll give you five dollars if you do what your mother says. Think of all the candy that will buy."

"Candy's bad for you." She snatched the money from my hand, but she took her sweet time about climbing the stairs. Every few steps she would stop, tilt her chin, and give me a look of smug defiance. Her mother watched placidly, like a cow observing a tractor plowing in an adjacent field.

"Kids these days," I said, and clucked like a hen who had just laid an egg.

"There's nothing wrong with kids these days. Do you have children, Miss Yoder?"

"A thirteen-year-old." Alison's foster status was none of her business.

"Well, in that case you must be from the old school. Most of us do things different these days."

"Respect never goes out of style, dear. But please, go on, tell me what Edwina Bishop thinks she knows about your child's father."

"Arnold Schrock—I guess that would be Reverend Schrock to you—was Romaine's father."

She paused and looked at me meaningfully, while I struggled with the meaning of her words. I wasn't shocked, because the rumors had prepared me, but I was almost overwhelmingly disappointed to learn that what I had half expected was true. The man I had looked to for moral and spiritual guidance for so many years was a sinner. Just like me. Yes, I know—we are *all* sinners, but we hold people of the cloth, with the exception of some televangelists, to higher standards. To put it bluntly, Reverend Schrock's sin should not have involved sex.

"When did you two do the bedstead ballet?" I finally asked.

"Excuse me?"

"The satin-sheet shimmy?"

"You're not making any sense, Miss Yoder."

"You know, *it*."

"Ah! Well, that's none of your business. But just so you know, it wasn't like we were having an affair. Arnold was my husband."

"Come again?"

"Arnold and I were married on Thanksgiving weekend, five years ago. Would you like to see our marriage certificate?"

Now I was shocked. I sat in stupefied silence while she regarded me with disdain. That's what I thought at first. But then I saw the tears puddle in her eyes, and her chin quivered.

"Yes," I said softly, "I would like to see the certificate."

She took the stairs three steps at a time. For a minute or so I heard her muffled voice and that of Romaine, before Clarisse descended, a document in her hand. She thrust it at me.

"It's all there."

I scanned the paper. "Las Vegas?"

"We stayed at the Riviera. It's a bit out of the way, but it was the best we could afford. But we saw Siegfried and Roy. Of course that was way before the tiger bit Roy. Still, I was glad we were in the cheap seats. Big cats scare me."

I returned the paper. "But Reverend Schrock is—was—married to Lodema."

"In name only. He tried to get a divorce years ago, but she wouldn't hear of it. I think he would have pushed harder, but he was afraid she would make things difficult for him. You know, because he was a priest and all."

"A pastor, dear, not a priest. And his career as a Mennonite minister would most certainly have been over if he'd divorced Lodema to marry you."

"We were very happy."

"Do you know," I said gently, "that your marriage wasn't legal?"

"Yes. I'm not a fool. We did it because it meant something to us. A great deal. I kept my maiden name, of course, and didn't change my religion—I'm a Methodist, by the way. Arnold said he didn't want to remake me; he loved me for who I was. We were very different, you see. I think initially that's what brought us together."

"How did you meet? Where?"

"Happy Backs. He came in for a massage. It was all that stress Lodema was putting on him. It started out innocent enough—I'm a professional, after all—but it didn't take long for us to discover that we really needed each other. We were the other's missing half. We stayed friends, nothing more, for a year, and then—well, we took our relationship to the next level. And just so you don't think I'm some kind of slut or something, it was a mutual decision. Plus, Lodema hadn't been acting like a wife for years. Arnold called her the Iceberg. He said she'd been frigid from the very beginning, but refused to get help."

"You don't say!"

"Miss Yoder, you're not going to put this in your report, are you?"

"About Lodema being an iceberg?" Why is it that the juiciest gossip is always something I wouldn't dream of passing along?

"Any of this. I know you have no reason to care about me, or my daughter. You probably even hate me. But Arnold cared deeply about his flock. Think what it would do to them. Think about what it would do to his reputation. His memory."

Frankly, I was amazed that Clarisse Thompson had not brought up the subject of my bogus marriage to Aaron Miller—Alison's father. That wasn't my fault, of course; I hadn't known about Aaron's existing marriage. It was possible that Clarisse, not being a Mennonite, and not being from Hernia, hadn't heard about my inadvertent adultery. At any rate, she had a point about shielding the members of Beechy Grove Mennonite Church from the truth. I knew of a few folks whose faith would be shaken to the foundations. I knew of others who would find solace in their pastor's sin, even validation for their own shortcomings. But the majority of us would be brokenhearted by this revelation.

"His flock," she said, pushing me. "Think of his flock."

"Keep the flock out of this," I shrieked. "Schrock's flock is not my main concern at the moment. I'm trying to solve the riddle of his death."

"And I'll help you with that. I'll tell you everything I know. But you have to promise you're not going to make our relationship public."

"I won't put it in my report—for now. But Edwina Bishop knows. She's trying to blackmail you, for pity's sake."

"Yes, she knows. But I don't have to worry about her anymore."

"What do you mean?"

25

Bottom-of-the-Barrel Gang Ram Tough Chili World Champion 1984

Source: Dusty Hudspeth
Submitted by: www.chilicookoff.com

Ingredients:

2 pounds beef, chili grind
1 tablespoon Wesson oil
1 8-ounce can Hunt's tomato
   sauce
1 onion finely chopped
1 teaspoon garlic powder
¼ cup Gebhardt Chili Powder

1 teaspoon oregano
1½ teaspoons salt
2 teaspoons ground cumin
¼ teaspoon Tabasco sauce
½ teaspoon cayenne pepper
½ can beer

Instructions:

Sear meat in covered 2-quart pan with Wesson oil. Add tomato sauce, onion, and garlic powder. Cover and simmer for 30 minutes, stirring occasionally. Add remaining ingredients and stir; simmer for 1 hour. Add water if necessary. Serve with side dishes of pinto beans, chopped onions, and grated cheddar cheese for garnishes. ENJOY!

Servings: 6–8

26

"She was just here. Minutes before you arrived. She won't be coming back."

"How's that? What happened?"

"It started a couple of weeks ago. Arnold and I were in Pittsburgh, enjoying ourselves at a mall. Romaine was with us. It was a family occasion. Anyway, Edwina Bishop was at the mall as well, only we didn't see her. The day we got back she started blackmailing Arnold. Well, he wouldn't have budged if it hadn't been for his congregation, and the heartache this knowledge would have caused them. He asked for more time while he got some funds together. When—"

"The building fund for our new church!"

"Arnold was going to pay it back—somehow. You know, when you came to the spa and told me what happened—that was how I learned Arnold died. I was still in shock, trying to process everything, when Edwina called me here to say that just because Arnold was dead, she wasn't letting me off the hook."

"Do you mean Reverend Schrock had yet to hand over the money when he died?"

"Right. But the thing is, I searched through his things—the ones he kept here—and I couldn't find the money. I told that to Edwina, but she said that was my business, not hers. If I wanted to preserve

Arnold's reputation, I had better come up with the two hundred thousand dollars. Well, Miss Yoder, I thought about it, and I came to the conclusion that I'd had enough. There was just too much on my plate—for your information, I was fired that day when I left work early."

"That wasn't my fault! I had no idea you and Reverend Schrock were doing the bedspread bossa nova."

"Hmm. Now where was I?"

"Your plate was full."

"Yes. Well, I called Edwina to tell her that I didn't care anymore. That I was going to take this matter to the police, when lo and behold, just minutes later she shows up here. Boy, was I in for the surprise of my life."

"You mean the fact that she virtually has two faces?"

"No, I'd seen her before. I just hadn't realized it was the same person. You see, before I worked at Happy Backs, I worked as a masseuse for a chiropractor—Dr. Scapulano over on Pitt Street. One day we get this patient in complaining of whiplash. Carries on something awful, neck in a brace, the whole works. Supposed to have gotten hurt in a car accident that was someone else's fault. Pretty soon Dr. Scapulano gets summoned to court to testify on this woman's behalf, and guess what? She wins. No big surprise. By the way, this kind of thing happened all the time. Dr. Scapulano sort of had a reputation for taking on these kinds of cases—draw your own conclusions. But I remember Edwina Bishop because I had to use the restroom one day, and she was in it, but had forgotten to lock the door. She'd taken the brace off and was stretching her neck out like a giraffe, looking at her face in the mirror, first one side, and then the other. I was so surprised that I just stood there and watched for a minute. When she saw me she slapped the brace back on and hunched over, like she was in pain."

"Then what?"

"There is no 'then what.' I'd signed a confidentiality agreement. I couldn't talk about the patients."

"When Edwina Bishop saw you at the mall with Reverend Schrock, acting like one happy family, didn't she recognize you?"

"Apparently not. I didn't work on whiplash patients at Dr.

Scapulano's. I just saw them in the hallway, or in this case the bathroom. She wouldn't have had any reason to remember me. But I couldn't forget that face."

"Let me guess. When she came by, just a little while ago, you told her that you recognized her as that whiplash patient, and that you'd report her to the insurance company if she persisted in her blackmail scheme."

"That's exactly what I did. I called her bluff. I picked up the phone and told her to call someone from your church—anyone— and tell them what Arnold had done. When she saw that I meant it, she took off like a bat out of Hell. Pardon me, Miss Yoder."

"Apology accepted."

We sat silently, across the room from each other, worlds apart. I could see that the woman was grieving, but even if I hadn't been genetically predisposed to physical restraint, I couldn't have brought myself to hug her. The woman had assisted my pastor in betraying not only his wife but the entire congregation. And while I could understand, but not condone, Reverend Schrock's need to seek solace in the arms of a woman other than Lodema, what was Clarisse Thompson's excuse? People don't just fall in love like they fall off a cliff. There are indicators along the path of romance, posted signs that warn you deep emotions are about to be encountered.

Although somewhat ordinary, Clarisse Thompson was not unattractive. She was definitely intelligent—perhaps too smart to be a masseuse, which is not intended as a put-down of that occupation, I assure you, but rather is meant to suggest that she had talents that lay beyond her fingertips. Oops. I'm sure she had a high IQ as well.

"I know you have this thing against sugar," I finally said, "but are you sure a nice cup of hot cocoa is out of the picture?"

"I'm sorry, but I don't keep chocolate of any kind in the house." She glanced at the stairs. "It's not because I don't want Romaine to have it; it's because I'd eat it. I'm a chocoholic, you might say. But I can offer you a hot toddy. In fact, that sounds kind of good right now."

I'd never heard of this cocoa substitute, but let it not be said that

Magdalena Portulaca Yoder is a fuddy-duddy spoilsport. "Hot toddy it is!"

She excused herself to make the beverage, while I sat in silence made tolerable by her absence. She was already sipping her drink when she entered the room, and seemed to be in a better mood.

"Here. I hope it's not too strong."

Strong? My word, but it was a foul drink. At least it was warm and had a sweet aftertaste. I guessed it to be cider gone bad. In order not to offend the grieving pseudowidow, I gulped mine down until the glass was empty.

"You can get really good cider from Harlan Troyer out on State Route 3010 just before you get to the Somerset County line. He sells it all the way up to the end of November. I know it's a bit of a drive, but folks I send out there always thank me."

"I'm not much of a cider fan, Miss Yoder."

That much was obvious. "Well, I never cared much for rhubarb myself," I said pleasantly.

"Would you like another one?"

"Oh, why not." The spoiled cider was warming me to the bones, just what I needed for the cold drive home.

She refilled my glass in short order, and I drained it in even less time. "I must say," she said, "that you are somewhat of a surprise."

"*Moi?*"

"Arnold often said he counted you as one of his best friends, even though you were one of his most traditional members. 'A bit narrow-minded,' I think were his words."

"Well, if you're too open-minded, your brains will fall out." I laughed heartily at my own joke, seeing as how exceptionally clever it was.

"Touché. But I find you anything but narrow-minded."

"I'll drink to that, dear." I held out my glass.

"Perhaps you've had enough, Miss Yoder."

"Nonsense. Give me one for the toad—I mean, road." By helping her consume the awful cider, I was performing a random act of kindness.

The refill was barely more than half a glass, and they were small glasses to begin with, so it wasn't remarkable that I should down its contents with one swallow. But remark she did.

"Miss Yoder, I had no idea you had a drinking problem. Arnold never said anything about that. Believe me, if I had known, I never would have offered you a hot toddy."

"Drink, schmink, what on earth are you talking about?"

She stared at me for a while, and I stared back. Unlike mine, her mousy brown wasn't even her natural hair color. Perhaps she'd started to gray early, but in that case why not pick a more provocative shade? I would never dye my hair—if the Good Lord wanted it mousy brown, who was I to change it?—but if I did, I'd pick platinum blond. Of course I'd have to stuff my bra with a million tissues. Victoria's Secret indeed! A blond bombshell, that's what I'd be. Va-va-voom—isn't that what they say?

"Could it possibly be that you have no idea?" Her voice sounded like it was coming through a tin can on the end of a string.

"I have lots of ideas. Why, just last night I was thinking about asking Freni to reline the kitchen shelves with new contact paper. Something fresh and racy—you know, with a touch of sinful red in it."

"Miss Yoder, you're drunk."

"I most certainly am snot—I mean, not. I haven't drunk anything like that since that time I inadvertently drank a pitcher of mimosas. Now, those were tasty. Not like these hot teddies."

"Toddies, not teddies."

"Is that a fact? Frankly, dear, I wasn't going to say anything, but this cider's been sitting around too long. Tastes almost like vinegar. You won't catch any flies with this—although why anyone would want to catch flies is beyond me. But if you did want to catch flies, I'd go with shoofly pie, instead of honey. I've never liked how sticky honey is. Doesn't it seem like the stickiness gets on everything? If we can send a man to Mars—although personally I think the Good Lord will never allow that—don't you think we could come up with nonsticky honey? Now where was I going with this? Oh yes, even though this is about the worst cider I've ever tasted, I believe I'd like another glass." I held it out. "Would you be a dear?"

"I will not."

"No need to be rude, dear. I'd be happy to get it myself."

"There isn't any more."

I struggled to my feet; it wasn't an easy chair to get out of. "In that case, I'll just toddle on home and make some toddy of my own." I chuckled pleasantly. "Toddle and toddy—get it?"

That's when Clarisse Thompson did the most unbelievable thing. She lunged for my pocketbook, which was still on the floor by the chair, and rummaging through it, she whipped out my car keys.

"You're not driving anywhere, Miss Yoder."

"Don't be ridiculous. You had no right to go into my purse. Now give me back my keys."

She held them well away from me. "I can drive you home. Or you can call someone. But you're not driving anywhere until the alcohol has worn off."

"That's what you think." I took a step in her direction, but for some odd reason my legs turned to rubber and I found myself un-intentionally sitting on the floor.

"You see?" she said.

I tried to get up, but not only didn't my legs cooperate; I sud-denly felt dizzy. Then the horrible truth dawned on me. Clarisse Thompson had poisoned me.

"You're not going to get away with this, you know."

"Try and stop me."

"Good-bye, cruel world," I said as I succumbed to her diabolical deed.

It's bad enough to think the Second Coming has passed you by, but to die and then discover that you've gone to the "other place" is even worse. Yes, I know, I jumped the gun on the rapture, but this had to be Hades. How else does one explain the presence of a preschooler's jam-covered puss and peanut butter breath just inches from one's face?

"Lady, you snore. You know that?"

An urchin's raspy voice and a pounding headache confirmed my suspicions concerning my whereabouts. I closed my eyes to pray.

"I'm sorry, Lord, for *all* my sins, including that time I told Mary Hooley that our Bible study luncheon was going to be held at two, instead of noon, because she talks too much and says the stupidest things. But nobody else can stand her either, Lord, so it's not like I did something the others wouldn't have done, if they'd had the nerve. Don't I get any points for bravery, Lord? I'm just asking. Now about Esther Gingerich, I didn't really mean it when I drew horns on her picture in the newsletter the time she won first prize for her dahlias. But in all fairness, she sat on my sandwich one day in the fifth grade. She did it on purpose, and it was my birthday and Mama had packed store-bought bread and real bologna—not the headcheese Grandpa used to make. Was it too much to ask for Wonder bread and packaged bologna on your tenth birthday? Because that sandwich was the only present I got—"

"You're silly, lady, but I still don't like you."

I opened my eyes wide and concentrated on my blurry surroundings beyond the child's face. Hell is supposed to have flames and brimstone, whatever that is. It's not supposed to have mismatched furniture and cheap draperies. After all, I'm not an Episcopalian.

Struggling to a sitting position, I scrutinized the little one. "Why, it's you. Your name is Radicchio, right?"

"Nuh-unh. It's Romaine."

"Lettuce, schmettuce. Where's your mother?"

"Mommy," she screamed at earsplitting decibels.

Seconds later the murdering masseuse came into view. "I see you've come around," she said, just as calmly as if she were reading the minutes from our annual church meeting.

"Your poison didn't work," I snarled. "What are you going to do now? Whack me on the head with a blunt object?"

"Miss Yoder, you passed out."

"You're darn tooting I did." Honestly, that's as bad as I can swear. "Your lethal brew may not have killed me, but you're still guilty of attempted murder. And I don't mean to be rude, dear, but you don't have the best figure for stripes. Even vertical ones. But I suppose that's just the price you're going to have to pay."

"You were drunker than a skunk, Miss Yoder, so I let you sleep it off. But now I'm going to have to ask you to leave."

"Drunk, my eye!" Come to think of it, my eye—both eyes felt like they were being poked from behind by an ice pick.

"There was rum in those hot toddies. Lots of rum. You had enough to make a grown man pass out. And you may be tall, Miss Yoder, but you're as skinny as a beanpole split three ways."

"Look here, missy, I can't help—wait a minute. Did you say rum?"

"Myers's Golden Rum, to be exact. It's not cheap, you know."

"That's a kind of alcohol, right?"

"My favorite."

"You made me sin!" I wailed.

"Drinking is not a sin. Jesus drank, you know."

"The Bible has it wrong; that was grape juice, not wine. Hey, wait a minute—did Reverend Schrock drink as well?"

"What do you mean, 'as well'?"

"As well as cheat on his wife. Did he?"

She clamped her man-size mitts over the urchin's ears. "You will not talk that way in front of our daughter. And no, he did not drink."

"I guess I should be grateful for that."

"Miss Yoder," she said, her tone as crisp as iceberg lettuce, "I took the liberty of calling your boyfriend to give you a ride home."

"*Excuse* me?"

"That Jewish doctor. You were stirring a while ago, so I looked in your purse and found his name on your emergency calling card. Arnold mentioned him a couple of times, so I knew who he was."

"Gabe is coming here? He knows I was—uh—imbibing spirits? Inadvertently, of course."

"He knows you were drunker than the Sixth Fleet on their first night of shore leave."

The doorbell rang before I could correct her.

27

"I can't believe you got drunk without me," Gabe said.

"What?"

His eyes were fixed intently on what little remained visible of the road, but the corners of his mouth curved upward into a maddening smile. He had thanked Clarisse Thompson profusely for her supposed kindness to me, but had refused to say a word until we were halfway home.

"You're usually so uptight, hon. I've often thought what it would be like if I—well, you know."

"Not until after we're married!"

"I'm beginning to think I'd be lucky even then. No, I meant what it would be like if I got you drunk. You know, if you were totally relaxed. Totally uninhibited."

"Inhibition is a gift from God," I huffed. "And I don't know why you guys didn't let me drive my own car home."

"Look outside," Gabe said. "It's a virtual whiteout. If I hadn't driven this road a million times, I wouldn't be able to do it either. It's like my car knows the way."

"I've driven it a hundred times more than you."

"True. But Miss Thompson and I weren't sure if you were up to driving just yet."

I switched subjects, which is my prerogative as a woman. "She claims she was married to Reverend Schrock."

His eyes left the road for a second. "Say what?"

"She claims they had a ceremony in Vegas, even though he was still married to Lodema. You know that little girl you saw there?"

"Cute as a button. Kind of what I imagine you looked like when you were that age."

"She's named after lettuce and she's a brat. But besides that, according to Clarisse Thompson, that child's biological father was Reverend Schrock."

Gabe whistled. "Holy moly, you Mennonites are a lot more interesting than I thought."

"We don't all act that way—and besides, she's a Methodist. But can you believe this? He was my pastor, for crying out loud."

"No wonder you hit the sauce."

"Which I thought was cider. Gabe, what am I going to do? How do I tell the congregation? How do I tell Lodema? As much as we've never gotten along, I actually feel sorry for the woman now. His death has sent her completely around the bend."

Gabe was properly shocked, and we drove in silence for the next mile or so. "Hon," he said at last, "do you think there is a connection between the reverend's death and this whole second life of his?"

"Well, Edwina Bishop was trying to blackmail them. She wouldn't quit even after the reverend died, not until Clarisse Thompson fired back with some ammunition of her own. And there's the not-so-little fact that the reverend allegedly embezzled two hundred thousand dollars from the church building fund to support this second life."

"Holy moly guacamole! This just keeps on getting better. I bet the next thing you're going to tell me is that Reverend Schrock was really Jimmy Hoffa."

"I'm pretty sure Zelda is Jimmy Hoffa. But did I mention that Noah Miller claims Reverend Schrock was hooked on something called uppers? Have you heard of those?"

"Unfortunately, yes. But it's no wonder, given that he was living two lives."

"Gabe, I know of at least three people, Noah included, who felt—in fact, still feel—betrayed by the reverend. But is that motive enough to kill?"

"Have you considered suicide?" he asked softly.

"I beg your pardon?"

"Think of the pressure he was under. Never mind that he created it himself. It might have become just too much for him to take."

"Would someone commit suicide in public like that?"

"Suicide is not rational behavior. There are about as many exceptions as there are rules."

We had slowed to a crawl by then. Route 96 was now a one-lane road. Each time we encountered a car coming from the other direction, one of the drivers was forced to pull off into the drifts. Gabriel Rosen, recently from Manhattan, was not inclined to do the yielding. I finally decided that it was better, for both my mental health and our relationship, if I closed my eyes.

I soon found that I could think almost as well with my eyes closed as I could in Big Bertha or on the john. Perhaps that's why I have so much trouble praying in the proper way. The second my peepers close, my mind turns on like a movie screen. Lately I've tried praying with my eyes open, but I feel so guilty. Still, it's easier to pray with my eyes open, especially in church, even though I have to witness women stealing those moments of perceived privacy to hike up their girdles, while the men pick their noses or rearrange their trousers.

That afternoon, with my eyes tightly closed, and my foot working an imaginary brake, I had an epiphany. "Gabe," I practically shouted, "the person who has the most reason to feel betrayed is Lodema."

"Jeepers creepers, hon, you scared the shiitakes out of me."

"Did you hear what I said? It's Lodema!"

"But you said she was so devastated by her husband's death that she went around the bend."

"She could be faking it."

"She'd have to be an awfully good actress in order to fool you."

"Really?" I reveled in Gabe's compliment for a moment, expecting him to expound on my keen powers of observation. Alas, he did not expound. "You were saying, dear," I prompted.

"Saying what?"

"Never mind." But of course I minded. I whistled loudly until Gabe minded as well.

"Okay, hon, out with it."

"You implied that I was a good judge of character. Did you mean it?"

"Absolutely. You're the crème de la crème. Nobody judges character as well as Magdalena Yoder."

"Thank you, dear. Do you think Dr. Mean and Nurse Meaner are good character judges as well?"

"Not as good as you."

"I'm serious."

"So am I. But what do they have to do with this?"

"Lodema is staying with Nurse Meaner—I mean, Nurse Dudley. Surely if Lodema's faking it, Nurse Dudley would know."

"One would hope. Magdalena, I know this case has got you wired, but there's something else we need to discuss."

"I've been thinking about that too, Gabe. It's not going to be easy finding another Mennonite minister to marry us. I know— you've already made it clear that you won't even consider becoming a Christian, but—"

"Now isn't the time, hon."

"But now is the *perfect* time. If we get hit by a school bus coming the other way, and squished flatter than pancakes, would you be prepared to meet your Maker?"

"School was canceled, Magdalena. I want to tell you something about Freni."

"Don't worry about Freni. I know she's been saved."

"She's missing."

"What did you say?"

"No one seems to know where she is. I stopped by the inn before coming to get you. Mose and Alison had just gotten back—the triplets were driving her crazy—and all your guests were there as well. But there was no sign of Freni."

"She was there this morning when I took my bath. I was lollygagging about in Big Bertha—I mean thinking in the tub—when I heard a door slam, and then a car horn toot. At first I thought it was—well, never mind. All that matters is that when I got downstairs Freni was gone."

"Amish are allowed to make telephone calls, aren't they?"

"Yes. They just can't have phones in their homes. Sometimes they keep community phone booths out in a field. Or they can use their English neighbors' phones. Why do you ask?"

"It's just that if she knew her absence was causing worry, she could call, right?"

"Well, she couldn't call home, but she could call me. At the Penn-Dutch. Or my cell phone. Except that I don't normally keep it on."

"Too thrifty to keep it on," Gabe said, which was mild criticism when it came to that subject. Scrooge McYoder is one of his less flattering pet names for me.

"I take it she hasn't called the inn."

"Nor your sister, nor Melvin. What do you say we swing by the Hostetler place on our way back to the inn?"

"You're the driver," I grunted as I pushed my imaginary brake to the floor. Looming ahead of us was one of those awful vehicles that take up more than their fair share of the road. Bummers, I think they're called. I closed my eyes, steeling myself for the impact of an exploding air bag. But the bummer graciously yielded, and the rest of the trip to the Hostetler farm was uneventful.

Both Mose and Freni are related to me in so many ways that figuring out our family tree is like solving a Rubik's Cube puzzle. Suffice it to say we are all descended from the patriarch Jacob Hochstetler, a Swiss Amish immigrant who arrived in Philadelphia aboard the Charming Nancy in 1737. Twenty years later Jacob and several of his children survived an Indian massacre in Berks County, Pennsylvania. Despite hardships, the family thrived, and descendants gradually moved westward, some settling where Hernia stands today. Mose and Freni's farm has been in the family for over two hundred years.

As we crept up the unshoveled, untraveled lane that leads to the main house, I caught a glimpse of an abominable snowman headed for the Grossdawdy house. Yes, I know—such things don't really exist, because if they did, their souls would be problematic. Does a near–human being get into Heaven? I think not! Yet one cannot deny what one's God-given eyes see.

"Do you see what I see?" Gabe gasped.

"I do," I wailed. "It really does exist. I once pretended that I was one of them, but it was just to get some reporters off my back. I didn't do it because I thought they existed. Now everyone's going to call us crazy. We don't have to say anything, you know."

"When did you pretend to be Amish?"

"Well, I've done that on several occasions—why are you bringing that up now?"

"You're the one who brought it up, hon. Just now when you saw Barbara Hostetler. I can't believe that woman is out and about in this storm."

"That was Barbara?"

"Who did you think it was? An abdominal snowman?"

I chuckled pleasantly. "You've always had such a wonderful sense of humor."

"Thanks, hon."

We had to hoof it through three-foot drifts to reach the door. I would have asked Gabe to carry me—I am, after all, as light as a bundle of kindling—but that would have appeared unseemly to the Hostetler family. At any rate, when Barbara answered the door, she was still wearing her outdoor cape.

"Ach, come in! The weather is terrible, yah?"

"Not if you're an abominable snowman," I quipped.

"What is that?"

"Nothing real, dear. We just dropped by to see if Freni was here."

Barbara clucked like a hen looking for a place to lay her egg. In the meantime she hung her cape on a peg beside the door.

"Well, is she?" I prompted.

"No." She glanced around before continuing in a low voice. "I would not waste such precious time milking the cows if she was here."

"So that's what you were doing out in the blizzard? Where's Jonathan?"

As if on cue Jonathan Hostetler appeared in the doorway, a child on each hip, and one clinging to his leg. He looked like a stray dog that had fallen asleep and awakened in a cattery. I'm not partial to any of the triplets, mind you, but I hurried over and snatched the toddler in his left arm, the one named Little Magdalena. The child, that is—Jonathan's arm doesn't have a name, as far as I know.

But no sooner was the urchin in my grasp than she hollered and twisted as if experiencing some horrible physical agony. I handed her back, but not without a tinge of embarrassment.

"Somebody probably needs to nap," I cooed from a safe distance.

"They have had their naps," Jonathan said gently. "But perhaps they are hungry."

"Feed away!" I cried, and then clapped a hand over my mouth. I was pretty sure the children had been weaned. If they hadn't, I didn't want to witness suppertime.

"Yah, I will feed them," Jonathan said, and then, bowing slightly, shuffled from the room.

Jonathan and Barbara do not have the typical Amish marriage. Forget the fact that Barbara towers over her husband, and that he unabashedly adores her in a way that other Amish consider unseemly. What sets them apart is the fact that they feel free to swap gender roles whenever the need, or even just the desire, presents itself. Their loosey-goosey approach to tradition drives Freni up the wall, but she feels justified in placing the blame entirely on Barbara's broad shoulders.

With Jonathan gone, Barbara visibly relaxed. "Today I think this house is like the Grand Central Station."

"What do you mean?"

"First it is the doctor from Hernia, then it is your preacher's wife, and now you. . . ."

"Lodema Schrock?" I shrieked.

"Surely not Dr. Luther?" Gabe said. The two physicians do not get along.

Barbara nodded, her huge Iowa head moving slowly up and down. "Magdalena, what is going on?"

I pointed to a straight-backed bench, one of the few places to park one's keister in the simply furnished room. "May I sit?"

"Yah." But before I could plunk my patooty on the plank, she swiped it with her sleeve, removing most of a glob of red jelly.

"Are you saying that Lodema Schrock, who's been nerts to Mertz the last couple of days, was *here*?"

"What is this 'nerts to Mertz'?"

"I haven't the foggiest. It's something Susannah says."

"Foggiest? Magdalena, sometimes I think you do not speak this English very good."

"Never mind that! Was Lodema here?"

"Yah, she was here just before the milking." She reached down the top of her dress and withdrew a much folded envelope. "It says here that it is for you, and that it is from Lodema Schrock."

"So you didn't see her?"

"No. This was on the door when I went out to milk. I am sorry if it is wet. You know the snow."

I took the note, which was no longer wet, but warm from its nesting place. "Did you read what is inside?"

"Ach, no. It is yours."

"Let me see," Gabe said. Lacking Amish manners, he tried to grab the precious envelope and its contents from my hands.

Long gangly arms are good for something, like keep-away, and presbyopia. I was able to open the envelope and read the note it contained aloud. It was, by the way, typewritten, and in italics, which I find aggravating to read.

Ha-ha! You think you're so smart, Magdalena. But you're not. Now I've got Freni Hostetler as a hostage. If you want her back safe and sound, then you have to fork over a million bucks. I'll let you know when and where. If you so much as tell one person about this, then it's curtains for your cook. Curtains—cook, ha-ha, get it? I guess I'm not so dumb after all. P.S. I never liked you, and I never will.

"What is this curtain?" Barbara asked. She was remarkably calm.

Gabe made a slashing gesture across his neck. "She's threatening to kill her."

The Devil and an angel wrestled in Barbara's heart. It was a brief match and the angel won.

"Ach!" Barbara said appropriately.

"Mags," Gabe said, "I only get the half of it. Why would your preacher's wife kidnap Freni?"

"Because she knows how much Freni means to me."

He shook his head. "This is all so hard to believe. Reverend Schrock seemed like a nice enough man. Yes, I know—Lodema is as mean as they come, but I still have a hard time picturing him treating his wife that way."

Gabe's experience with my pastor was pretty much limited to our premarital counseling sessions. The two had gotten along famously, and there had been talk of a future golf date. But the reverend was forever pushing the golf date into the future, and now it made perfect sense. A man with two families could ill afford the time or money to play such an expensive sport.

"It was revenge," I said for Barbara's benefit. She'd undoubtedly heard of the reverend's death from Mose or Alison, but she wouldn't be aware of the motive. "You see, Reverend Schrock was not the saint I thought he was," I said, not without bitterness. "He had a second family stashed away in Bedford. When Lodema found out about it, she killed her husband."

Barbara gasped. "Ach, the child!"

"She saw him at Tastee-Freez," I explained. "He had his daughter with him."

Gabe shook his head. "And to think New York gets a bad rap. I tell you, hon, if we ever decide to have children of our own, we're moving to the city."

"The Bad Apple," Barbara said, displaying her vast knowledge of the world.

"That's Big Apple, dear. But never mind that—we should be thinking about what to do next. The woman is stark raving mad. It's a wonder she made it all the way here. The last time I saw her she was infantile. Unless she was faking all that, there is no way she could have typed this note. Oh, shoot," I cried. "The note! It says not to tell anyone, and I just read it aloud to the two of you."

Gabe smiled weakly. "Ransom notes always say that. Besides, she doesn't know that you shared this with us."

"What do I do now?"

"Well, you could wait for her to contact you again, like the note says, or—"

"But I don't have a million dollars! At least not to spare."

"Or you could go to the police. And, as luck would have it, this farm is outside the town limits, so it would be Sheriff Watkin's territory, not that doofus Stoltzfus's. Besides, kidnapping is a federal offense, and he'd have to turn it over to them anyway."

"Let us whisper," Barbara said. "It is best that my Jonathan does not learn of this."

"But he has to know," I snapped. "She's his mother."

Gabe placed a hand gently on my shoulder. "Easy does it, hon."

I shrugged loose from his touch. When someone tells me to stop, I see it as my duty to go. Saying "Easy does it" is like waving a red flag in front of my faded blue gray eyes. Fortunately I had recently made a commitment to mature.

"Sit on it," I hissed. "I mean, sit down. I'm sure we'd all be more comfortable that way."

They persisted in standing. "Let's go back to the car," Gabe said. "I'll try my cell phone there, although I doubt I'll get a signal. We might be better off driving straight to Sheriff Watkin's office."

"I still think that's the wrong thing to do."

"Trust me on this one, hon. I've seen a lot more television than you have. The law always gets involved anyway. Invariably there's a big shoot-out, the victim gets wounded, but not fatally—" He stopped and looked at Barbara. "Sorry."

"Don't get your hopes up, dear," I said. "She might come out of this unscathed."

"Ach!"

Gabe grabbed my arm and dragged me to the door.

28

Gabe was right. He was unable to get a call through to the sheriff on his phone. In fact, he couldn't reach anyone, including Melvin and Zelda.

"You've gotta love technology," Gabe said. "Just when you get used to something new, pow, Mother Nature comes along and gives you a big wallop."

"Well, at least we've got the car. Barbara and Jonathan would have to hitch up the horse and sleigh."

"We may need a sleigh. I'm not getting any traction."

I prayed for traction. It was probably a first, which is why the Good Lord paid attention. I know it was the first prayer I'd had answered in ages.

The car slid a little, mostly around corners, but we were making good progress toward Bedford when the most horrible thought imaginable occurred to me. Okay, so maybe it wasn't the most, but it ranked high up there on my list.

"Turn around, sweetie."

It was the first time I'd ever called Gabe a term of endearment, and it startled me as much as it did him. Thank heavens he had a tight grip on the wheel.

"What did you just say?"

"I said, 'Turn around.' "

"No, what did you call me?"

"Not now, dear. I've been barking up the wrong tree."

"There, you just did it again."

"I call everyone 'dear.' If you don't turn around, Gabe, I'm going to do something drastic. Like jump out."

Gabe slowed the car. "Magdalena, what's gotten into you?"

"I figured out who really killed Reverend Schrock, and I can hardly believe it, that's what."

The car slid to a stop in a snowbank. "So it wasn't Lodema?"

"Not by a long shot. I'm shocked, Gabe. I really am."

"You're shaking too, hon." He tried to slide his arm around my shoulder, but I was too agitated to accept comfort.

"You'll never guess who it was."

"Well, it wasn't me."

"It was Melvin."

He stared at me, shocked as well. Then a smile spread slowly across that handsome face. "Always a kidder, hon. I must say you got me this time."

"But I'm *not* kidding. Didn't you hear what the note said? *'I'm not so dumb after all.'* I know it's not Christian of me, but I've always consider the mantis an idiot. That's never been a secret, and he knows that more than anyone. He hates me for it, always has. Even in this note, demanding a million dollars, he couldn't resist letting me know that he'd finally made a smart move. Of course it's not, but—"

"Whoa there. This is your brother-in-law you're talking about. Our town's Chief of Police. You can't possibly think he murdered someone. No offense, hon, but this time you might have missed your mark."

"I wish I had," I moaned. "This is going to kill Susannah."

"But hon, even if the mantis, as you call him, is capable of murder, what's his motive?"

"One of the oldest motives on the books. One that causes half the wars on this planet."

"Religion?"

"The other half: greed."

"But you Mennonites pay your preachers a pittance. You should see what some rabbis make."

Bristling on a cold day is a good way to stay warm, especially if one is hirsute—which I am not, by the way. I tried to speak as calmly as I could.

"Our preachers will get their rewards in Heaven. And anyway, it wasn't the reverend's money he was after, but the building fund."

"Excuse me?"

"Melvin has known for a long time that his days as our police chief were limited. After all, there is only so much incompetence the mayor and town council are willing to put up with. It is not my intent to be cruel here, but there isn't really anything else a man with his temperament and skills can do. When he lost the election to the state legislature, he saw the writing on the wall. I don't know how long he's known about Reverend Schrock's double life, but it's been long enough for him to buy a new car, and for Susannah to buy herself some bling bling. No wonder Clarisse Thompson couldn't find the money she knew her lover had embezzeled. It was already gone."

"What is bling bling?"

"Sparkly stuff. Jewelry. Anyway, Melvin blackmailed Reverend Schrock, who had a whole lot to lose, including his standing in the religious community. Maybe in his mind the reverend thought he was 'borrowing' from the building fund, but the fact is he stole from it."

"You're kidding!"

"I wish I was. Gabe, what are we going to do?"

"Get back on the road—assuming we can—and keep driving until we get to the sheriff's office."

"Darling," I said quite purposefully, "I've known the mantis his entire life. Since he was still in his cocoon. And Freni is his mother's best friend. To kidnap her means he is really desperate. If we get the sheriff or the FBI involved right now, it will push him right over the edge. You don't want Freni's blood on your hands, do you?"

"I don't want your blood on my hands either. Hon, we don't have a choice."

I snatched the keys from the ignition and opened my door. "We really won't have a choice if I chuck these out into the snow. Freni will die, and so will we. And if you think I'm going to share my body heat with you, think again."

Believe it or not, Gabe laughed. "You're a riot, hon."

"Well, what's it going to be? We do something about Melvin ourselves, or we die of hypothermia?"

"You're not thinking straight, hon. Melvin is a wild man and he has a gun. It's part of his uniform. What's wrong with this picture?"

"But we have his mother."

"We do?"

"She lives on Kalbfleisch Road. That's less than a mile from here."

"And then what? What if she refuses to believe us? What if she won't come with us?"

"Then we kidnap her, like Melvin kidnapped Freni."

"And spend the rest of our lives in a federal penitentiary? You may not have noticed, hon, but I'm on the cute side. I really am not looking forward to having a girlfriend named Mike."

"Do you think I want a boyfriend named Michelle? Well, if she was blond and had green eyes—never mind. My point is that I don't want to go to prison any more than you do. And we won't. Trust me. Elvina Stoltzfus has a terrible memory. We'll tell her that she asked to come with us. The FBI will believe us."

"And if they don't?"

I jiggled the keys. "Cooperate or freeze. Those are your choices."

"Give me the keys. I know when I'm beat."

We had to leave the car at the end of Elvina's driveway. It was a good quarter mile from there to the house, and by the time we got there the hem of my skirt was wet, as were my shoes and socks. More importantly, my not-so-tiny tootsies were numb. But there is almost always a bright side to the dark moments of life, and this was not one of the exceptions. If I lost my toes to frostbite, I would be able to buy shoes off the rack for the first time since I was ten. And if I lost just my baby toes and the top halves of their companions, I could wear roach killers.

"Knock harder," I instructed Gabe after we'd spent a good five minutes shivering on the porch. "She hears like a man."

"What is that supposed to mean?"

"It means that if she is zoned out—"

The door was flung open with surprising force. "I already belong to a church. Please go away and do your witnessing someplace else."

I pushed Gabe aside. "It's me, Magdalena Yoder."

"I'm sorry, child, but I am not Magdalena Yoder. She lives over on Hertzler Road. It's a big white farmhouse that's been converted into a full-board inn. But I'd think twice about staying there if I were you. The food is really good—I can vouch for it myself—but Miss Yoder is a bit of a grump."

"I most certainly am not!"

Melvin's mother peered over the tops of her reading specs. "Oh, my. I didn't realize it was you."

"As big as life and twice as ugly."

"Yes, of course. And who is this handsome young man?"

"I'm Dr. Gabriel Rosen, ma'am. I'm Miss Yoder's fiancé."

"Hmm. Haven't we met before?"

"Yes, ma'am. I was here for—"

"Magdalena, what is it you want today?"

"I want you to come with us, in Gabe's car, and talk some sense into your son."

She tried to close the door, but of course she couldn't. Take it from me—numb toes are good for something.

"Go away, Magdalena."

"It's vitally important, Elvina."

"And so is my newspaper. It's yesterday's of course. Thank heavens I didn't have time to do the crossword. I don't know why a little bit of snow like this stops the paper woman from delivering. Why, in my day, we walked three miles to school in knee-high snow. Or was it waist-high? Yes. Knee-highs are those stockings I wear when I don't have the energy to pull on a proper pair of hose." She made eye contact with Gabe, intentionally I'm sure, and blushed. "Oh, my, I forgot there was a man present."

Waist-high? Right! Never mind, there was no time to waste.

"Elvina, your son's taken Freni hostage."

Her eyes reluctantly left Gabe. "I don't believe I heard correctly. Magdalena, you really must work on that mumbling."

There was no time to pray for patience, so I prayed for guidance. "Melvin—uh—outdid himself this time and has kidnapped Freni, your best friend, and is holding her for ransom."

"Nonsense. My Melvin would never do such a thing. Why, that's just absurd."

Did it really matter *how* I got the woman to accompany us? "Elvina, dear, you're right—that was absurd. I just needed to get your full attention. But your son is in trouble. I'm sorry to have to tell you this, but Melvin's done that thing again."

"What thing?"

"You know. The thing that almost got him arrested over in Bedford on his thirtieth birthday."

"He wrote his name in the snow?"

"And a whole lot more. I'm afraid he's had a lot to drink." There is nothing wrong in calling the kettle black, particularly when one has recently been potted herself.

"I'll be right with you. Let me grab my coat."

She didn't invite us in, but neither did she slam the door in our faces. We stamped the snow off our shoes and helped ourselves to the warmth of her foyer. Elvina took her sweet time in getting her coat. She even answered the phone. When she rejoined us, it was minus her spunk.

"That was Melvin on the phone. He said to meet him on Stucky Ridge. No police, though. He made that very clear. Magdalena, what have you done to him now?"

"*Moi?*"

"My boy said that none of this would have happened if you hadn't stuck your big Yoder nose into his business." Well, maybe a little spunk remained.

"My Yoder nose ferreted out the fact that he was blackmailing one of the most beloved pastors this town has ever known."

"He was a sinful man! Melvin said the man was an adulterer. Like you."

"I didn't have a second life with a child—never mind. If you don't stop him, Elvina, he's going to get into a whole lot more trouble than he already is." Of course that was a lie. A murder *and* a kidnapping count—it couldn't get much worse. Those jail doors were going to slam behind him and remain closed for the rest of his unnatural existence. What difference did a second life sentence make?

"Well, I'm riding up front. And don't play that loud music you young people are so fond of. And none of that drag racing either."

Was it any wonder Melvin turned out the way he did? And one mustn't forget his long dead father, Eliphus Stoltzfus, who criticized his son's every move, but never once stood up to his wife— at least to hear Melvin tell it. From the day he was hatched, until the day he married my sister, the mantis never stood a chance.

It was Susannah's all-encompassing, unconditional love that had turned his spaghetti spine into bone. I never would have thought their relationship could work—she with a free spirit, he spirit free—but they glommed together like cold dumplings. As much as I hated to admit it, theirs was a marriage that worked. They would kill for each other. . . .

Oh, my heavens! Oh, my stars! It couldn't possibly be. Violence was not in Susannah's nature. This was a woman who scooped up bugs on a piece of paper and ferried them outside. She spent five years as a vegetarian, for crying out loud. Besides, she'd always been very fond of Reverend Schrock. The man had helped her through a million rough spots—mostly with Melvin (working marriages are not always smooth). *However*, she had been in the church the day I tallied the chili pots. For Susannah, stepping inside a church is bad luck. But no, she couldn't have been involved in the reverend's death. Nevertheless, it was possible that Melvin had confided in her, thus putting her at risk.

"If Susannah's involved in any way," I said to Elvina, "you're going to pay." It was a terrible thing for me to say, and I regret it to this day.

Hernia still has fewer than two thousand people, and it has only one main drag. The logical thing to do would be to hit Main Street, follow it until it crossed Slave Creek, and then make a right turn on the dirt road that winds up Stucky Ridge. However, I badgered

Gabe into making a detour into Foxcroft Estates, the middle-class subdivision where Melvin and Susannah live. Elvina Stoltzfus nearly had kittens.

"Melvin said to meet him on Stucky Ridge!"

"We're going to their house first."

"That's not what Melvin said. Don't forget, Magdalena, he is the Chief of Police."

It was time to trot out the truth. "He murdered the reverend, Elvina."

"You're mumbling again."

"I am not. Listen closely," I said, enunciating each syllable as if I were giving the words at a spelling bee. "Your son killed someone, and that someone was Reverend Schrock."

I could just see the back of her grizzled head, but I got the impression the septuagenarian was about to bolt from the moving car. I cannot be blamed, therefore, for lunging forward and throwing my arms around her wattled neck, causing her to squawk like a captured chicken, none of which should have surprised Gabriel.

Nonetheless, the Babester squealed like an eight-year-old girl and lifted his hands from the wheel just long enough for us to slam into a snowbank. If I hadn't already been leaning forward, I might well have sailed over the headrest and through the windshield. If I hadn't had my gangly arms around Melvin's diminutive mother, who had foolishly undone her seat belt, Elvina would have smashed into the glove compartment.

Gabe's car had only a driver's-side air bag, and it deployed, leaving him stunned and temporarily incommunicado. My mind is notorious for its athletic leaps, and I immediately arrived at the conclusion that his silence was a sign that he had passed from this world. I cannot adequately describe how relieved I was when he began to thrash and flail from beneath the collapsed bag.

"Look what you've done, Magdalena," Elvina said. "Because of you the car's broken. Now how are we going to get to Melvin?"

"What about Freni? She's your best friend. Aren't you afraid for her?"

She pretended not to hear me, which is just as well. I'd let go of her neck, but my fingers were quite willing to grab her by the wattles again and shake some sense into her Stoltzfus head. Surely one cannot be punished for what one's digits do on their own accord.

Fortunately Gabe was not seriously hurt, and after disentangling himself from the deflated air bag, he took control of the situation. That is to say, he gave me a meaningful look, which I chose to take under consideration. He also sized up our situation. Given the fact that he had an air bag draped over the steering wheel, and we were deeply embedded in the snowbank, he declared his car inoperable.

After enduring a good deal of verbal abuse, we managed to get the old lady out through a back window. By the time we joined her, we were sweating from exertion, but it didn't take more than a few minutes for us to get chilled to the bone. Being the boniest by far, I lay claim to having been the most uncomfortable.

We were standing in the middle of Foxmoss Boulevard, a pretentiously named street that serves as the main entrance into Foxcroft Estates. Susannah and Melvin's house was still five blocks away. The snow was ankle-deep and the north wind was howling like a banshee with its tail in a vise. Unless we climbed back into the car, or sought shelter at the nearest house, we would all perish. When the inevitable thaw came, some poor child would find us twisted into grotesque shapes like in that game "statues." Of course if the Babester enfolded me in his arms, and pressed my body close to his, the two of us might be able to survive long enough to be discovered by a nearby homeowner walking his or her dog. However, the murderous Melvin's mother would still end up as a petite Popsicle.

"Group hug," I cried generously.

My two companions stared openmouthed. It took me a second or two to realize they weren't staring at me. Creeping down the street, in our direction, was Hernia's lone police cruiser. Could it be that the maniacal Melvin had lied about waiting for us up atop Stucky Ridge? Why not? Anyone who would kill a preacher in his own church, in front of the congregation, was capable of just about anything. The rogue police chief could be trying to mow us down with the car, or maybe a fusillade of bullets. Or perhaps his anger was now turned inward and he was contemplating insecticide.

"Run for your lives!" I screamed.

29

They ignored me, although Gabe did put a protective arm around Elvina's shoulder. She promptly shrugged it off.

"Hit the decks!" I bellowed, but to no avail.

"Why, I'll be dippity-doodled," Gabe said calmly. "That's Zelda and Susannah."

"It is?" I've always been proud of my eyesight, which until just recently has been twenty-twenty.

"Harlot," I thought I heard Elvina say.

"I beg your pardon, dear?"

"Magdalena, are you losing your hearing as well? I said your sister was a harlot. I told Melvin that no good could come from marrying a divorcée, and a Presbyterian at that. This is all her fault, you know. My baby boy never needed any money when he was living with me. Maybe just a few dollars now and then for his comic books. Then she comes along and snares him with her feminine wilds and he turns into a totally different person from the one I raised."

"That would be 'wiles,' dear."

"What?"

"Never mind. The truth of the matter is that Melvin pursued Susannah, not the other way around. My sister could have had any man she wanted, and in fact she probably did, if you get my drift.

Why she settled down with your son is beyond me. I think she must have suffered a mild stroke that impaired her judgment even more than it already was."

"Ladies, please," Gabe begged.

We watched in agitated silence as the cruiser advanced. When it got close enough that I could peg it with a snowball, I was able to confirm the identity of the occupants. Much to my astonishment it was Susannah behind the wheel, not Zelda. My sister learned to drive wearing six-inch stilettos and a dog in her bra. Stopping on snow was a cinch for her.

"Get in," she ordered.

Now that wasn't the Susannah I knew! She has spent her entire life defying orders, not giving them. I must confess to experiencing a bit of a thrill as I piled into the backseat along with Gabe and Mrs. Stoltzfus. The thrill intensified when the Babester spread his legs in that manly fashion, and I felt his firm calf pressed hard against my bony one. These were, of course, sinful thoughts, but I don't mind sharing, seeing as how I have long since confessed them.

"Your sister's gone over the deep end," Zelda shouted from the front passenger seat.

"I told you," Elvina mumbled.

"Mags," Susannah said through clenched teeth, "my Melkins is in big trouble."

"Do you know the whole story, dear?"

She didn't say anything, but a good sister can tell when her sibling is crying, even if just the back of her head is visible. I wanted to lean forward and pat her lovingly on the shoulder, but I knew that she would hate the gesture. In my family when we hurt, we are like wounded animals that seek solitude in their dens, and if lacking dens, we seek it in silence.

"It's all lies," Zelda said. "It's religious persecution—that's what it is. Melvin is a righteous man. He would never do those things, and even if he did, he had a good reason. A holy reason."

"Zelda, did you ever trace those last three digits of that license plate? You know, the one that nearly put us on an early train bound for Glory?"

"You know I did, Magdalena. I'm a professional."

"And?"

"Like I said, Melvin must have a good reason for what he did. A woman knows in her heart when the man she loves—"

"Shut up, dear," I said, not unkindly.

"Susannah," Gabe said after a few minutes, "do you want me to drive?"

Her response was to accelerate, sending the car into a spin. But my baby sister, a product of Hernia High driver's education, and tutelage by yours truly, managed to remember the counterintuitive advice to steer into the direction of the skid. Our collective sighs of relief temporarily depleted the vehicle of its oxygen and I, for one, was glad that I was wearing an extra-absorbent pair of sturdy Christian underwear.

The steep gradient of the road up to Stucky Ridge can be a stretch for some cars, even when the road is dry. The most common type of weather-related automobile accidents in Hernia involve teenagers who cannot afford good tires. They slide back down the mountain, and sometimes even off it. The cruiser was able to make it to the top that day only because Zelda is zealous about maintaining the vehicle in tip-top condition. She does all the work herself, including changing the tires.

The higher we climbed, the deeper the snow on the road, and the faster it seemed to fall. By the time we reached the summit we couldn't see more than a car length in front of us. Fortunately, Susannah had whiled away many a summer evening "parking" in the picnic area, and could probably have found it blindfolded.

Much to everyone's consternation, however, Melvin's new green car was nowhere to be seen. Neither were there any tire tracks.

"Maybe he's in the cemetery," Elvina said, referring to the opposite side of the ridge. "He's such a respectful young man. Always thinking of his elders. The passed-away ones too. Why, just last week he did the sweetest thing for his father."

"Sent him a gallon of ice cream?" I asked. "By UPS?" I wasn't serious, of course. Melvin's father is either up above us flying around or down below us frying around. Either way, UPS doesn't deliver to his current address.

Gabe put a hand on my knee, but it wasn't meant as a romantic gesture. "Magdalena, sometimes you go a bit too far."

"Most of the time," Zelda said. She grabbed the handheld microphone that hung from the dash and pressed a few buttons. There followed a smattering of static. "Melvin, if you can hear me, they're on your trail. Right now they're—"

I lunged forward for the second time that day and knocked the microphone from her hand. "Don't do anything stupid, dear. You claim to have a bun in the oven; you don't want that oven serving time. And just so you know, Susannah, your sweetiekins is not the father."

"She's right," Gabe said. "You don't want to do anything to screw up the rest of your life."

"But I love Melvin! And he loves me. I would do anything for the man I love."

"Zelda would have made a better wife for my baby boy," Elvina muttered.

If the Good Lord gives you sharp elbows, you can be sure He expects you to do something more with them than crack open eggs. Elvina grunted, but said nothing further on the subject.

"I'm sure he's not up here," Zelda said, her attempt at aiding and abetting foiled. "We better get back down before we get stuck up here. If that happens, then we'll have to start eating each other, like in that movie about the plane crash in the Andes."

Of course I'd never seen that movie, but for once I was truly glad to be nothing more than a bag of skin and bones. So what if my dresses didn't hang right? No one was going to get a steak off me; they'd be lucky to scrape together enough meat to make a bowl of chili.

But things would never get that bad. Stucky Ridge was just not that high. We could slide back down the road in our tire trails, if need be. I, for one, would be happy to use Melvin as a sled. And that would be my prerogative, given that I knew where he was. But of course! He had to be there.

"I know where he is, guys."

"Yeah?" Zelda was undoubtedly afraid of having to conduct a search in a snowstorm. Only the Good Lord knew what would happen to all that putty.

"He's back where the teenagers hit their home runs."

"Don't be silly, Magdalena. There isn't a baseball field up here."

"She means sex," Susannah said, speaking for the first time since we'd left Foxcroft. "They go back in the woods, between the cemetery and the picnic area, and get it on."

Gabe removed his hand from my knee. "Hon, how do you know about this?"

"A case I helped Melvin investigate last year. You go past the cemetery, almost to the edge of the ridge, and make a sharp left turn into the woods. It could be terribly dangerous in this weather. If we hit an icy patch, we'll go sailing out over Hernia."

"We don't have a sail," Elvina murmured. "We could all be killed."

I no longer believed gypsies had dropped Melvin off on her doorstep as an infant. "We could walk from here," I said. "There's a footpath into the woods from this end."

Gabe returned his hand. "If Melvin has a gun and is lying in ambush, then we're as good as dead. Unless—Zelda, give me your gun."

"Darling, what are you going to do? Do you know how to fire a gun?"

"There you go again with the terms of endearment. And no, I don't know anything about guns, but they can't be hard to handle. Most criminals are idiots, aren't they?"

"Melvin's not in the woods," Zelda said. "He's not up here at all. I'm sure of that now."

"How do you know?" I asked.

"I feel it in my soul."

"Then are you calling him a liar? He told his very own mother that we should meet him up here."

"I'm sure he couldn't have made it up here with that new car of his."

"I'm going into the woods," I said.

"I'm not giving you my gun."

"Fine. I wouldn't use it anyway."

Gabe's hand closed like a vise over my knee. "You're not going anywhere, hon."

"Oh yes, I am." I pinched the back of his hand with nails that hadn't been trimmed in several weeks. It's been said that my fingers can squeeze water from a stone. Getting Gabe to let go was child's play for me.

"Ouch!" The vise lost its grip.

At that point it was easy for me to slip over diminutive Elvina's lap and out the door. Gabe jumped out on his side and ran around to intercept me. I dodged, but he turned on a dime and caught me by a coat sleeve.

"Don't be a fool, Magdalena."

"This isn't just a maniac mantis we're talking about, Gabe. Freni's with him. Ever since my parents died, she's been like a mother to me. In fact, she's more of a mother than mine ever was. What would you do for your mother?"

"I hear you. Okay, let's go."

"What about the others?" The others, the three women who loved Melvin the most, were paralyzed, not by fear of bullets, but by the fear of having to face an ugly reality none of them were willing to accept. But *three* women? What was up with that? I wasn't nearly as unlikable as Melvin, but I had only one man fooled. Okay, maybe Doc Shafor would step up to the plate—but only if I offered him a home run.

"I'm going to tell them to stay put and keep the engine running. If we're not back in twenty minutes—no, make that fifteen—I want Susannah to turn around and head right back down to the police station. In fact, I'll have her turn around now, so there's less chance of getting stuck. Correction, I'll do it myself."

While he did that, I stamped my feet and shivered. My winter coat is wool, but only knee-length. Because of the size of my clodhoppers, I have to make an extra effort to find boots that fit over them. Being a bit on the frugal side, I have long since settled for an old pair of Papa's rubber galoshes. The snow atop Stucky Ridge was no respecter of boundaries, and kept falling into my rubbers. If I died of hypothermia, it would be a simple matter to drag me over to the cemetery and plant me between my parents. Assuming the ground wasn't frozen.

"Hon, you're freezing," Gabe said when he returned. "Here,

take my coat. I've got a thick sweater on under it, a long-sleeve shirt under that, and a T-shirt under that."

I was tempted. But only because I wanted a good sniff of the Babester's man smell. However, it was my feet that were freezing, not my upper body. And as for Gabe's shoes, I knew from experience that they were too small.

"No, I'm all right," I said. "Let's go."

But Gabe wasn't through with his preparations. He'd found several bungee cords in the trunk of the cruiser. He fastened one around his waist, made me do the same with another, and hooked us together by a third.

"In case we get separated in a whiteout," he said.

"We can bounce back together?"

"Exactly. Hon, I have never loved anyone—my mother included—more than I love you. I'm not about to lose you to a stupid snowstorm."

That raised my temperature a few blessed degrees. "Off we go, then," I cried. But ever mindful of the male ego, I let the Babester lead the way.

The snow was even deeper when we reached the woods. It was also snowing harder. But being a follower for a change, and not a leader, had definite advantages. For one thing, even though I could barely see past the end of my nose, I could at least see well enough to place my galoshes into Gabe's footprints. Also, my beloved is both taller and broader than I am, and although I would hate to have him hit by a bullet, well—let's just say that he made a good shield.

We'd slogged about fifty yards into the copse, which was almost a third of its length, when Gabe stopped abruptly. I smacked hard into his back, shnoz first.

"I see something," he whispered. "Something green."

"Well, it's not the sky."

"No, I think it's a car. Yes, that's what it is."

"Hold it right there!" It was Melvin's voice, thin and high-pitched. A second later a shot rang out.

"Gabe," I shrieked, "are you hurt?"

"No, hon, are you?"

"I'm f-f-fine as frozen frog's hair," I chattered.

"And quit yapping," Melvin shouted. He fired a second shot, but I could hear it hit a tree well to my left.

Police Chief Melvin Stoltzfus is a nincompoop, but there's nothing wrong with his aim. In his home he proudly displays a shadow box filled with marksmanship medals from the police academy and from his stint in ROTC. Sometimes, like at local festivals, he pins the medals to his scrawny chest and struts around like a bantam rooster. The point is, if Melvin had intended those two bullets to hit us, we'd be dead. Pushing up daisies with Mama and Papa.

"Hold your fire," I hollered, and stepped out from behind Gabe. He tried to push me back, but I gave him a sideways punch on the groin. Yes, generations of Mennonite and Amish ancestors turned over in their graves, but the heat they generated collectively did nothing to ameliorate the intense cold.

"Yoder, I'm warning you," Melvin said.

"Susannah and Zelda are right behind us. You wouldn't want to hit one of them."

"I don't see anyone else."

"That's because your sweet wife has trouble negotiating the snow in her platform espadrilles. But she sent a message on ahead with us. She wants you to give up and turn yourself in. Of course Zelda says the same thing. And you know how fond she is of you. She might not even cuff you."

"I'm not going to jail, Yoder. Do you have that million dollars?"

"Absolutely, dear." I think sometimes the Good Lord expects us to lie; otherwise He wouldn't have given us the brainpower to think so fast on our feet.

"I can't see it. Show me the money."

"You didn't expect us to drive around with that much money in a briefcase, did you? It's sewn into the lining of my coat." You see what I mean?

"Then take off your coat."

"First I want to speak to Freni."

"You can't. She's tied up in the backseat with duct tape across her mouth." He giggled eerily. "Who knew that stuff had so many uses?"

"Take the duct tape off," I barked.

"Not until you open your coat."

I may have said this before, but it bears repeating. The most valuable lesson one can learn from a teenager is that when the going gets tough, change directions.

"Your mother is waiting in the cruiser too, Melvin."

"Mama?"

"She said that it will break her heart if anything happens to Freni. But frankly, I think her heart is already breaking. You know you've always been her pride and joy. Her baby boy. Can you imagine what all this is doing to her? It's not too late to stop the breaking, Melvin."

"Nothing will happen to Freni, you idiot. I wouldn't do that to Mama."

"Then let her go."

"I can't. Not until you give me the money."

"Elvina," I called over my shoulder, "your son has your best friend bound and gagged. He's threatening to kill her."

There was no way the sound could carry back to the car, but Melvin believed that the others were following us. One eye locked me in its gaze, while the other rolled around like a loose marble, trying to locate his mother.

I took advantage of his distress to take several small steps forward. Apparently the eye on me wasn't up to the job, because I was able to advance undetected, even though I almost tripped over a fallen branch.

"You're lying, Yoder. I don't see her."

"She's wearing a white coat." I took another baby step, Mother-May-I style, scooting the fallen branch in front of me.

"Hon, stop," Gabe hissed.

"What was that?" Melvin had sharp hearing. No doubt all that space between his ears made for good acoustics.

"I said 'one stop.' Your mother wanted to make one stop on the way. A pit stop. That's why she's trailing behind us."

Melvin cringed, as any normal red-blooded man might have done at the thought of his mother peeing in the woods. His eyes flickered shut for a second, and that's all the time I needed. I scooped up the stick, along with a handful of snow, and flung it at him. He reeled backward in surprise, and tripped over one of his own feet. The gun went flying, and so did Gabe—directly at Melvin.

The rest, as they say, is history.

30

Sharon Wilkerson's Beef Chili

Ingredients:

2 large onions, chopped
6 garlic cloves, minced
3 tablespoons vegetable oil
⅓ cup chili powder
1 tablespoon ground cumin
½ teaspoon cayenne
½ teaspoon cinnamon
4 pounds boneless beef chuck, cut
    into ½-inch pieces

3 cups water
2 cups beef broth
28-ounce can pureed tomatoes,
    including the juice
1 teaspoon salt
1 jalapeño, seeded and minced
19-ounce can kidney beans, rinsed
    and drained
⅓ cup finely chopped parsley

Instructions:

In a large heavy pot cook the onions and garlic in the vegetable oil over moderate heat, stirring, until the onions are softened. Add the chili powder, cumin, cayenne, and cinnamon; cook for 30 seconds stirring continuously. Add the beef, water, broth, tomato puree, and salt, and simmer, uncovered, adding more water when necessary to keep the beef barely covered, for about 1½ hours. Add the jalapeño and simmer for 30 minutes or until the beef is tender, stirring occasionally. Stir in the beans and simmer for an additional 5 minutes. Stir in the parsley. The chili may be frozen or made 4 days in advance.

Servings: 8–10

31

Susannah coped remarkably well. I mean that literally, however. Her behavior, while generating plenty of remarks, was, in my opinion, not indicative of good mental health. She swaddled herself in fifteen yards of black crepe, and veiled her face with black netting. She went so far as to dye Shnookums, who had always been a suspicious shade of rat gray, an inky shade of black.

"I'm just a poor widder woman," she'd say just about every other sentence, although that was far from the truth. Melvin was alive and well on death row. Unable to rationalize her shnuggy-wuggy's actions, my sister prematurely declared him dead. She even went so far as to install a headstone in the family plot up in Settlers' Cemetery.

I tried to get Susannah to see a therapist, but she would have no part of it. I even organized an intervention, but getting a Yoder to do something against her will has less chance of succeeding than getting Congress to pass a bill without pork. If she wanted to play the part of a "widder woman," so be it. At least I was finally convinced that the pitiful pooch she carries in her bra really is a canine, and not some rodent refugee from the Big Apple.

Freni also did a remarkable job of getting on with her life. To this day she appears totally undamaged by her stint as a hostage. I think the reason for that is simply because Freni never believed Melvin was serious about his threats. She had known him since he was a pupa, knee-high to a mantis, and could not conceive of him as capable of murder. Ask Freni to explain Reverend Schrock's death, and she'll shrug. "Ach, the English. Their cooking is terrible, yah?" Pressing her beyond that is both pointless and cruel.

It is obvious that Elvina mourns for her son, but she refuses to talk about what happened. Perhaps she discusses the situation with Freni. I hope that she does. From what I can see, the two remain friends, and I'm grateful for that. Perhaps I'm just borrowing trouble, but I think Melvin's actions, and subsequent incarceration, will lead his mother into an early grave. If indeed Melvin is executed—well, I don't think Mrs. Stoltzfus will live that long.

At the trial—which was held in adjacent Somerset County—it was revealed that Melvin, unbeknownst to Susannah, who was home watching reality TV, sneaked store-bought chili into the church supper, after first stirring in peanut butter. I will not mention the brand. Since Reverend Schrock was the judge, he was bound to taste it sooner or later. He, of course, tasted it sooner. When the reverend died and Melvin was called to the church, he used the opportunity to remove the evidence.

As for Lodema, the woman really was nerts to Mertz. I visit her weekly at the County Home for the Reality-Challenged over on Church Lane just on the other side of Bedford. Lodema has actually improved some, and the last time I saw her she was purporting to be ten years old. We played jacks and Go Fish, and dressed Barbie dolls properly in sturdy Christian underwear (courtesy of *moi*). I won all the games, and felt no compunctions about doing so. After all, during our play periods Lodema called me names and stuck her tongue out at me numerous times.

I'm doing fine. Our police department has been overhauled, and we have a new chief, an outsider from Pittsburgh. I have tried to patiently explain to her how things are done in Hernia. I don't think she gets it. Her assistant officer is a very handsome young man with smoldering brown eyes and long dark lashes, which he flutters when he speaks. Already he has caused numerous hearts to flutter. Gabe says the man is light in his shoes, and while I will admit that he is on the thin side, I still think it is his lashes that send Hernia women into a tizzy.

Of course I'm too much in love with the Babester to be swayed by smoldering eyes and fluttering lashes. Alas, since the reverend's death, we at Beechy Grove Mennonite Church have been unable to find a new pastor, so my marriage to a man of another faith has been put on hold. My beloved has suggested several times that we elope and get the knot tied by a justice of the peace, but I firmly believe that a knot that doesn't include God is just a mess of tangled rope.

Zelda is one such mess. She was relieved of her duties as a police officer. Beyond that, she was found guilty of obstructing justice and sentenced to five years in the penitentiary. But given her imminent motherhood status, the sentence was commuted and she was placed under house arrest for six months, to be followed by two years of probation. She remains a Melvinite, which remains a mystery to me. I've heard rumors that the sect is actually growing.

Speaking of messes, there was the problem of Clarisse Thompson and her love child to straighten out. It is possible Clarisse may have known that Reverend Schrock was embezzling from the church building fund, but I think it is more likely that she didn't. Despite the fact that he was both a bigamist and a thief, my pastor was basically an honorable man. I honestly don't think he would have involved the mother of his child in such nefarious doings. The subject came up only briefly at Melvin's trial, and he himself said he dealt only with Reverend Schrock. My point is that I saw there was nothing to be gained by pursing a felony conviction for the struggling mother of a young child, even if said urchin was named after a salad ingredient. To ensure that the matter was put to rest as quietly and as soon as possible, I volunteered to replace the money taken from our building fund.

As for the matter of Edwina Bishop's thwarted attempt at extortion, Clarisse and I agreed that there was nothing to be gained by exposing her either. Better to let the scandal die as quickly as possible—not that scandals ever really die. But to ensure that Clarisse's little bundle of endive had the best chance of escaping the fallout from her parents' mistakes, I staked Clarisse with fifty grand and made arrangements for her to move to South Dakota, where she had an aunt living in the Badlands. Lest one call me a saint, I will share that Clarisse never properly thanked me, and her seeming ingratitude still irks me.

On the plus side, I did honor my promise to Noah Miller and write that article for the *Hernia Herald* concerning his innocence. Alas, the editor of that canary cage rag not only rejected the piece, but told me that I had absolutely no talent as a writer. Not even a shred. If I wrote a book, she said, she'd hurl it across the room. Just to show her up, I submitted the same article to the *Pittsburgh Post-Gazette*. They didn't accept it either, but one of their staff writers took an interest in the piece, wrote his own version of it, and won the Pulitzer prize. Story of my life. At any rate, things have improved for Noah Miller, and I'm glad of that.

About the only thing in Hernia that hadn't changed was Doc Shafor's relationship with Gabe's mother. They were still dating and causing grateful tongues to wag again now that the trial was over. You can imagine my surprise, then, when I received a call from Doc inviting me to dinner.

"Doc, I thought you were never going to speak to me again."

"Men are allowed to change their minds too."

"So I'm not evil personified?"

"You are a meddler—there's no getting around that—but despite yourself, Magdalena Portulaca Yoder, I'm mighty fond of you. So what do you say? Six o'clock, my place? I promise you hand-cranked ice cream for dessert."

"Do I have to crank it?"

"You do not."

"Then it's a date—I mean, deal!"

I was even more surprised, and somewhat alarmed, when upon arrival at Doc's house it soon became evident that the two of us were to dine alone.

"Where's the ball and chain?" I asked, chasing my inquiry with a mischievous smile.

"Having dinner with your main squeeze. It's only fitting, don't you think?"

"Doc, is there anything wrong between you and Ida?"

"Things couldn't be better." He bade me sit at the table set for two, but laden with enough food to feed a family of four in Ohio. "In fact, we're getting married."

"I beg your pardon?"

"You heard me. Of course neither of us wants to convert to the other's religion. You see, they have this thing called a bris—a ritual circumcision, as I understand it, but at my age you don't want anyone monkeying around with your whatchamacallit—"

"T.M.I.!"

"At any rate, we've decided we're flying to Hawaii and having a civil ceremony there. We're calling our families from there too. If our relatives choose to disown us, we'll stay in paradise."

"What about your dog, Blue?"

"I'm leaving him with my grandnephew over in Somerset. They adore each other. But this is all top secret, Magdalena. You can't tell anyone until it's a done deal."

"Why are you telling me? And what about your grandnephew in Somerset?"

"He knows I'm going to Hawaii, but he doesn't know with whom, and why. As for you, it's only fair that I tell you—seeing as how you always had this thing for me."

"*Moi?* Doc, dear, it's you with the thing. Ever since Belinda passed, you've been making passes at me."

He grunted and stabbed a stuffed pork chop, which he dropped on my plate. "We're each entitled to his or her own point of view. Anyway, I have another reason for talking with you."

I pretended not to hear, and scooped a slab of sizzling macaroni and cheese onto my plate. It was, of course, the homemade, baked variety; not that stuff with the powdered cheddar. Doc sprinkles extra cheese on top, which forms a nice brown crust.

"Doc, do those greens have bacon in them, or ham hocks?"

"Bacon. Don't you want to know what else I have to say?"

"Talk away, dear." I knew it had to be a slew of compliments: what a fine job I'd done of catching the reverend and his sister's killer. How generous I'd been to replenish the building fund. Yada yada yada, as the kids say these days.

"It's about Zelda."

"Thanks—excuse me?"

"I'm ashamed of you for the way you've been treating her."

I jiggled a pinkie in each of my ears to make sure they were in proper working order. They seemed to be just fine.

"For a moment there, Doc, I thought you said I'd been mistreating Zelda."

"I did."

Suddenly I no longer had an appetite. Box up the chops, mac and cheese, even the beans, and send them to the starving children in India for all I cared. I was in for another of Doc's lectures, and the Good Lord knew I didn't deserve it.

"I most certainly have not been mistreating Zelda. In fact, I hadn't been treating her at all."

"My point exactly."

"You're not making sense, Doc. Maybe you *could* use a nice long Hawaiian vacation."

"Bear with me. Who loved Melvin?"

"Susannah. His mama. I guess Zelda—but believe me, it sure wasn't a healthy kind of love."

"It doesn't matter. That woman's heart was broken. It's still broken. She needs someone to acknowledge her loss."

"Loss, *schmoss*, that's one angry woman. She's walking around with a chip as big as Buffalo Mountain on her shoulder. If you even as much as say 'Hi,' she'll snap your head off. But if you insist, Doc, I'll try to be nice to her. Lord knows, it's not going to be easy. And just for the record, I'm not making any promises."

"Good. Did I tell you I've got a nice cherry cobbler warming in the oven for dessert? We can have homemade ice cream too, just like I promised."

"Sure. But Doc, why are you so interested in how I treat Zelda, anyway?"

"Because she's your sister."

"Save the jokes for after the cobbler, Doc. On second thought, save them for your next dinner guest. Whatever you do, don't give up your day job."

"I'm retired, remember? Besides, I'm not joking."

Suddenly I felt like an elephant was sitting on my scrawny

chest. "Doc, are you trying to say I'm adopted? That Mrs. Root gave me away at birth?"

There was no telling how angry I'd be at my parents for having lied to me all those years, but being adopted would answer a lot of nagging questions. Despite my infamous Yoder nose, I have very little in common with my forebears. They were conservative to the core, whereas I am a fence-sitter, an admittedly uncomfortable position, although it does improve one's view. Susannah is even less like our ancestors, all of whom would roll over in their graves upon learning they had spawned a divorced Presbyterian, and a lapsed one at that.

Doc cleared his throat. "Earth to Magdalena. Come in, Magdalena."

"Very funny, Doc. But please, just tell me who my birth parents are. I promise not to tell Susannah unless she brings the matter up herself."

"You're not adopted, Magdalena."

"That cat's out of the bag, Doc. There's no use trying to stuff it back in."

"I quite agree, but you're not the cat, Magdalena. Zelda is."

"Zelda's adopted?" My head was spinning. "Are you saying that Mama—Miss Perpetual Virgin, Miss Holier-Than-Thou—had a baby out of wedlock, and gave it up for adoption?"

"No. Your father had an affair with Mrs. Root."

"That's impossible! Papa was the salt of the earth. He would never have cheated on Mama."

"He may have been the salt of the earth, but that didn't stop him from putting his pepper—well, you know what I mean."

I stood. As a Christian, and a pacifist, I couldn't very well kill the messenger, but I could refuse his cobbler.

"Doc, you're sick. You need to see a shrink. I can't believe you expected me to fall for this trash. I mean, if it were true, don't you think someone in Hernia would have spilled the beans years ago?"

He regarded me calmly. "No one knew except for Odelphia Root, your papa, and myself."

"Is that so? What about Mr. Root? What about Mama? And how come you know?"

"Angus Root had a farming injury, a bad experience with a hay baler. Had to quit farming and went into sales—although I can't for the life of me remember what he sold. Anyway, the doctors told him he could never father children, but he was in denial. When your father and Odelphia learned that Zelda was on the way, they came to me for help. Do you follow me so far Magdalena?"

I nodded, my tongue cleaving uselessly to the roof of my mouth.

"So, like I said, your papa and Zelda's mama came around asking my help. They figured a veterinarian might be able to do something, but they figured wrong. I can give a horse an abortion, but I wasn't about to try it on a human being. Back then abortion was illegal, and even if it wasn't, if anyone had found out, the stigma of it would have been impossible to live with. At least in a two-bit town like Hernia.

"Of course they were really angry with me—and Odelphia turned the waterworks on something crazy—but that all changed when Angus learned about his wife's condition. He saw it as proof of his virility, and since your papa and Odelphia were on the verge of ending their affair anyway—the stress had gotten to be too much for them—there was no reason for anyone to say anything."

"Holy guacamole!" I swore when I regained use of my tongue. "Zelda Root really is my sister?"

"Yes. So that's why you should cut her a break. She's your flesh and blood, Magdalena."

"But she has such big—"

"Jugs. Little brown jugs of genuine maple syrup, that's what Angus sold. But he had to quit that too when folks started complaining that he was watering down the syrup. Died of shame, some folks said, but at least he died a father. That's more than I'll ever have."

"Doc, you've always been like a father to me—you know that."

"Hmm, I guess I'll have to take that as a compliment."

"As well you should." I started for the door.

"Aren't you going to wait for the cobbler? It's got extra cinnamon in it, just the way you like it."

"Can't. I've got an errand to run."

"What's so all-fired important, if you don't mind me asking?"

"I want to see my sister."

"Susannah?"

"Zelda."